RAINBOW RIDER

Other Five Star Titles
by Wayne D. Overholser:

Nugget City
Riders of the Sundowns
Chumley's Gold: A Western Duo
The Outlaws
Gateway House

RAINBOW RIDER

A Western Trio

Wayne D.
Overholser

Five Star • Waterville, Maine

Five Star First Edition Western Series.

First Edition, Second Printing.

Published in 2001 in conjunction with
Golden West Literary Agency

Cover photograph by Johnny D. Boggs.

Set in 11 pt. Plantin by Minnie B. Raven.

Printed in the United States on permanent paper.

Library of Congress Cataloging-in-Publication Data

Overholser, Wayne D., 1906–
    Rainbow rider : a western trio / by Wayne D. Overholser.
        p.   cm. — (Five Star first edition western series)
    Contents: The leather slapper—The fence—
Rainbow rider.
    ISBN 0-7862-2738-9 (hc : alk. paper)
    1. Western stories.   I. Title.   II. Series.
PS3529.V33 R35 2001
813'.54—dc21   2001040523

TABLE OF CONTENTS

The Leather Slapper

This story first appeared as a four-part serial in *Ranch Romances*, beginning with the Second March Number dated March 17, 1950 and concluding with the Third April Number dated April 28, 1950. Other four-part serials by Wayne D. Overholser published in this magazine, one of the longest-lived of all pulp magazines, were issued in book form, such as "The Nester" that appeared as THE NESTER (Lippincott, 1953) by John S. Daniels or "Steel to the South" that appeared as STEEL TO THE SOUTH (Macmillan, 1951) by Wayne D. Overholser. This was not the case with "The Leather Slapper," and so it appears here for the first time in book form.

I

There is a part of every man in two worlds, one of reality, the other of ideals—the former with its pressures of daily living, its ruthless demands of economic necessity, and the latter that has to do with a man's heart and the fullness of his soul. Some, like Pete Fargo, recognize only the first and build their lives upon the premise that nothing else matters. Others sense the presence of the second, a shadowy world never fully understood, yet subtly influencing every action. It was so with Rick Marvin.

It was late on an August afternoon when Rick and Fargo came over Raton Pass and crossed the state line into Colorado, two men who had been partners for almost a year. In some ways they were much alike —in the way they carried their guns, low and tightly thronged down, in the way they cared for their horses, and their constant, wary watchfulness and quick reaction to danger.

By some standards they made a good team, each supplementing the other. In another way they were not a team at all, for the chasm that lay between them was deep and steadily widening. The issue was seldom discussed, yet it was there, and both felt it. It was as hard to grip as a handful of fog, but as real.

Dusk caught them with the town of Stone Saddle not yet in sight. It was a new country to both, so, not knowing the distance to the settlement, they made camp beside Raton Creek. There was never any dissension about such decisions, and anyone traveling with them would have said they got along with a minimum of friction. Still, the thing that was between them had grown through the past months, while they had worked for the Isham Grant Company.

Dusk thickened until the ridge lines above the creek were lost against a dark sky. They built their fire under a giant pine and cooked supper. Then, with the meal eaten, they lay back and smoked, the shifting light of the flames upon their weather-burned faces. For a time there was no talk, no sound but the creak of the pine and the whisper of the creek. Suddenly lightning made distant forked streaks above the horizon, and thunder boomed along the crest of the range.

Fargo stirred and sat up. He was a tall, chunky man with china-blue eyes and light yellow hair. There was something of the dude about him, and most of his money that didn't go over the poker table went for fancy duds like his pearl-colored Stetson that he wore at a rakish angle, his expensive boots, blue silk shirt, and calfskin vest. He carried a silver-plated Peacemaker; his gun belt and holster had been especially made for him by the best saddle maker in Santa Fé.

"We'll get rain tomorrow," Fargo said.

"Looks like it," Rick agreed.

"Reckon the range needs it. Won't make us no never mind, either way. We'll get a room in Stone Saddle come morning, a steak a foot long, and a drink. Then we'll see how good the local tinhorns are."

Rick said nothing for a time. He was a taller man than Fargo, a little over six feet without his boot heels, and legs so bowed that Fargo swore he could throw a beer keg between them any time Rick stood still. He had the long bones and whipped-down muscles of a man who had spent most of his twenty-seven years in the saddle. His clothes were common range duds, worn and patched, for he had none of Fargo's love for fancy gear. His gun belt and holster were old; his Colt was a walnut-handled .45 he had carried for ten years.

"I don't like it, Pete," Rick burst out at last. "Damned if I do."

Fargo tossed his cigarette stub into the fire. "Then why the hell don't you quit?"

Rick grinned sourly. "Yeah, that's the question."

"You don't need the *dinero*. Not with that chunk you've got in the Santa Fé bank."

"Not enough."

"What are you saving for, a fancy coffin?"

"May turn out to be that."

"Or a purty woman. Well, that ain't the kind of huckleberry I am. Man's days are short and full of sorrow, so I aim to have my fun while I can."

"Trouble is I can't get them Sandovals out of my head," Rick said. "Old Juan standing up there in front of the judge looking like a stepped-on pup."

Fargo laughed derisively. "You mean the pups was strung out across the room. And his wife so fat three of the kids were hiding behind her. Hell, they got four hundred dollars from the Grant for their improvements, didn't they? I call that good."

"I don't. They lived on that place for years. They thought it was theirs."

"That's what they got for listening to Jason Galt. If anybody oughta be run out of the country, it's that chuckleheaded preacher. Stirs the settlers up, and for what? Nothing! Just gets their hopes raised. You can't beat an outfit as big as the Grant. That's why I like working for 'em."

Rick let it go at that, for there was no use arguing. Not with Pete Fargo. That was one of the differences between them. Fargo gave his unqualified loyalty to anyone who employed him. Rick could not. There was a right and a wrong side to every issue, and usually Rick had no trouble distinguishing one from the other.

But this was different. The Sandovals had had a bad deal, and they were only one family of many that had settled on the Grant, believing the land was open to entry. Still, the Grant Company had the law on its side. It was just that Rick knew and liked the Sandovals. He and Fargo had stopped at their place many times. There had always been water and hay for the horses, food on the table for two strangers.

When Rick had tried to pay for their meals, Juan would shake his head, and say: "I would not feel right about it, *señor*."

"Hell, it's Grant money," Rick had argued. "Besides, you're doing us a favor. If we didn't eat here, we wouldn't eat till we got to Springer."

"That's right," Fargo had added. "The rest of these damned settlers would show us the talking end of their scatter-guns. When Wade Verling figgers out that hot lead is the only thing that'll move 'em off the Grant, I'll come back and pay 'em off right."

Wade Verling was the general manager of the Isham Grant, a shrewd, careful man who understood the power of public opinion. He gave Rick and Fargo good wages, because there was value in hiring men with formidable reputations. Often a simple visit by Rick and Fargo was enough to convince an obstinate settler.

"No threats," Verling had said. "No shooting. Just let them see your guns and tell them you're Grant men. If that doesn't scare them out of the country, we'll use the courts."

But mere visits to Juan Sandoval had not been enough. He'd given them a toothy smile, invited them into the house, and stubbornly clung to his home. In the end

Verling had been forced to call in the law to evict him.

The Sandovals' day in court had stirred Rick in a way he had never been stirred before. After the judge was finished, Rick had said: "I'm sorry, Juan. I tried to tell you it would be this way."

María was crying. So were the children who were old enough to understand. Juan had shaken his head, brown face showing his hurt. "The law . . . she is something I do not understand."

Now Rick pictured the Mexican's troubled face, and a sickness crawled into him. Suddenly he was aware that Fargo had risen and was staring down at him Fargo said: "Let's get this straight, friend. Are you going soft?"

Rick came to his feet, a coolness in him now. He scratched his thin nose, gray eyes locking with Fargo's blue ones. He said: "I'll do my own thinking myself, Pete."

"Yeah, you always have," Fargo said in a thin voice, "but that ain't what I asked you. In the past we've worked together pretty well, but tomorrow's another day. Verling figgers there may be trouble up the river, with Jason Galt putting out them circulars of his like he is. I ain't sticking with a *hombre* who's soft. Not when it's a proposition of living or dying. Me,"—he grinned with the corners of his mouth—"I like to live too well."

"Feeling sorry for the Sandovals is one thing," Rick said. "Going soft is something else. When I quit my job, it won't be when the chips are down."

Fargo's grin worked up to his eyes. "Well, now, that's fair enough. I reckon it's your business going around feeling sorry for a Mex family long as it don't slow down your draw."

Later, with Fargo snoring on the other side of the fire, Rick lay with his head on his saddle, eyes on the tall black bulk of the pines. A sour discontent with himself and his way of life had worked into him. This thing that had grown up between him and Pete Fargo had never come into the open before, but now he saw the shape of it, and it was not a pretty sight.

There had been little affection between him and Fargo, and little common ground. They respected each other's cool courage and gun skill, but that was all. Pete Fargo wanted to be a gunman. Moral questions were of no interest to him. Beating another man to the draw was a game to him; he enjoyed the fear that his reputation brought to others. That was, Rick knew, the basic difference between them. The big money was the only reason he had hired out to the Grant in the first place. It was a temporary job, and he'd be glad to be finished with it.

If a man was ever going to put his boots down, he would need a little money to start, and Rick had mentally set five thousand dollars as his goal. He had nothing against the Grant. Verling was not the kind who would ask a man to dry-gulch someone who was in the way. Until the Sandoval case had gone to court, Rick had felt no real doubts about the side he had chosen. Tonight the doubts would not die. When at last weariness brought sleep to him, discontent still lay in him like a smoldering coal.

They were in no hurry to break camp in the morning, for unless necessity demanded it, haste was never a part of their way of life. Black clouds hung low along the Raton crest, and the smell of rain was heavy in the air.

"We'll get wet today," Fargo said. "We'd better slope along."

"Looks like it," Rick agreed.

It was nearly ten miles to Stone Saddle, down the ancient trail that had been followed for centuries after the

Cimarron desert route of the Santa Fé Trail had fallen into disrepute. They left the pines, dropped down from the foothills with their scattered piñons and scrub oak, and in late morning saw Stone Saddle, sprawled without order or pattern on the south side of the Purgatory River. For a long time Rick's eyes were pinned on the stream, a muddy torrent swollen by heavy rains in the mountains. He said softly: "They used to call it *el río de las animas perdidas en el purgatorio.*"

Fargo gave him a sidelong glance, the mocking smile touching the corner of his mouth. "Now what would you be getting at, friend?"

"Nothing."

Fargo's smile fled from his mouth. "You're a damned smart *hombre*. That's your trouble. You read too much and you think too much. You'd have a hell of a lot easier time if you just did your job."

"I'm not made that way."

"Well, if you've got something to say, let's have it. If we start this job, we'll finish it. Both of us."

Fargo had his pearl-gray Stetson tilted at the usual rakish angle; his right hand rested close to gun butt. Rick gave him a measuring look, reading nothing in those blue eyes. He said: "Maybe something's biting you, Pete. You've been proddy as hell lately."

"I ain't proddy. It's just that we'll be bringing Verling's greetings to Charley Williams pretty soon. I aim to find out what kind of a partner I've got before we do."

"If you don't know what kind of a partner you've got after a year, I sure can't tell you."

They rode into Stone Saddle in cold silence.

II

Main Street lay in an irregular curve along the bench above the river, a weird collection of false-fronted frame structures, log cabins, and adobe buildings crowding the boot-worn walks. Rick's eyes scanned the street until he saw a livery stable. He asked—"This do?"—and, when Fargo nodded, he reined in to the stable, his partner behind him.

A buggy had come into town from the upriver road. It crossed the bridge below Main Street, the horse's hoofs cracking sharply on the heavy planks. Rick and Fargo gave orders for the care of their horses and stepped back into the street. As they moved through the archway, the buggy swung toward the stable and wheeled past them. The driver was a girl, slender and dark. In her severe brown suit and hat, she was strikingly pretty.

Fargo whistled softly. "Say, maybe we should have come to Colorado years ago."

Resentment rose in Rick. Fargo classed all women the same way, and this girl didn't belong in that class. He said: "Let's go hunt the steak we were talking about last night."

"Hell, there's no hurry." Fargo drew a silver dollar from his pocket. "Let's toss to see if we get a drink or the steak first."

"I'll have the steak," Rick said, and angled across the dusty street to the Commercial House.

Fargo followed, grumbling: "I wanted a closer look at that girl."

They ate hungrily, the first meal in three days that had not been camp-cooked, then stepped into the bar. It was past noon now, and the saloon was nearly empty, with only a scattering of cowhands along the mahogany. The apron eyed

16

Fargo and Rick with obvious disapproval, saying nothing.

"What's biting you?" Fargo asked in the cold voice he used when he was inviting trouble.

"Nothing," the barman said sulkily, and moved away.

"Damned ornery galoot," Fargo said. "You'd think we had smallpox."

"Maybe he heard we were coming."

The cowhands had turned to stare. Fargo glared truculently at them. He said loudly: "That bunch of. . . ."

"Let's start looking for Charley Williams," Rick cut in.

"Yeah, I reckon we'd better. Might be the Grant don't draw as much water up here as it does across the line."

It had started to rain by the time they stepped into the street.

"Got a notion where the office is?" Fargo asked.

"Not any."

"Well, we ain't asking. I don't like the smell of things in this burg."

They turned the corner, glanced down the street that rose steeply from the river, and saw the weather-beaten sign, **Isham Grant Company Office**. Fargo said: "There it is." He rubbed his cheek. "Say, I should have bought a shave."

"Williams won't care how we look," Rick said. "I'm getting wet."

Rick strode down the walk, Fargo falling into step beside him. The Grant office was housed in an ancient adobe building, probably dating back to the Indian trading days. Rick moved through the door, Fargo dropping back to follow him. Rick stopped, Fargo crowding in beside him, and both stood there, motionless.

The slender girl they had seen in the buggy was facing a man. She was thoroughly angry, and the man was grinning in a slack-jawed way as if he'd had one drink too many. He was big and shaggy, about forty, Rick judged, heavy-boned and swell-chested, with a pendulous lower lip and a predatory face.

There was a tight moment of silence, the girl and man too intent upon each other to realize anyone else was in the room. The girl said: "Get out of the way, Duff. I'm going in to see Williams."

"He ain't in, honey."

"You're lying."

"Now, now, Ruth. Did you ever know Duff Estey to lie to you?"

"I never knew you to do anything else where the Grant was concerned. I said to get out of the way."

Estey laid a heavy-knuckled hand on her arm. "You know how you could fix it so I'd let you see Williams."

She jerked away, slapping him hard with her right hand, the *crack* of the blow a sharp sound that ran the length of the room. Estey grabbed her, swearing. Then Rick was on him, right hand gripping his shoulder and swinging him around. That was when he saw the star on the man's shirt.

Rick had acted instinctively. Fargo had said a dozen times that a man who made his living with a gun had no business using his fists. That was right, and it was a crazy thing to antagonize the law the first day he was in Stone Saddle, but these thoughts, running through his mind in this short moment, were not enough to stop him.

He caught the man's nose with a vicious, turning fist, felt the nose flatten, saw the scarlet stream as the big head bobbed back. He brought his right through to the fellow's stomach, ducked a ponderous defensive blow, and drove his left to Estey's jaw. The man went back, spilling against the counter, and slid heavily down to the floor.

Fargo moved forward, gun palmed. "That's it, friend," he said to the man on the floor.

Estey sat with his head against the counter, staring blankly upward. A door in the back slammed open, and a little man ran out, bawling: "What's going on here? What's going on?"

That would be Charley Williams, Rick thought. And he'd be angry. Chances were Williams had maneuvered carefully to win the lawman's favor. Now, in a space of ten seconds, Rick had undone the Grant man's work.

"So you were there," the girl said. "I thought so."

"I didn't know you were out here," Williams said. "I assure you I didn't, Miss Dallam."

"You lie like your bought-and-paid-for deputy!" the girl cried furiously.

Williams shrugged. "I can't make you believe me if you don't want to." He looked at Rick, then at Fargo. "What is this all about? This office isn't a place for brawls, you know."

"This lady a settler on the Grant?" Rick asked.

"Yes," the girl said quickly. "My father is Major Ed Dallam. We live in Redwall. I've tried the last three times I've been in town to see Charley Williams, but he's never in his office."

"Why, I told you . . . ," Williams began.

"We're familiar with the Grant's policy of dealing with settlers," Rick said. "Maybe you don't know what it is, Williams."

"You kind of act like you don't," Fargo added. "We'll tell you about it, Charley. Grant men always talk to the settlers, if the settlers want to talk."

Williams began to swell up. He was bald except for a fringe of light brown hair; his nose was long and saber-sharp, and his purse-like mouth was pulled into a round protuberance. At this moment he was a comical, ineffectual figure, fighting down his wrath and failing to find the words he sought.

The girl had been staring coolly at Rick. She said: "I've never seen either of you before. Who are you?"

"Rick Marvin." Rick motioned to Fargo. "Pete Fargo."

Fargo lifted his Stetson. "Pleased to know you, Miss Dallam. I hope you'll accept the Grant's apologies. Charley wasn't raised right, it looks like."

"So you're the Grant gunmen." The girl bit her lips, puzzled. "It doesn't seem to make sense, does it? We had been led to believe that you two were. . . . Well, I mean we were misinformed."

"What can I do for you?" Williams asked brusquely.

"Dad wants you to come to Redwall for a meeting."

"Why, I . . . I'm too busy right now, but I'll see that someone is there."

She started to speak, then closed her mouth, saying nothing. Rick, taking this chance to look closely at her, saw that she was as pretty as he had first thought. Her skin was darkly tanned, her hair so black it held a blue sheen. She had an oval face lighted by dark eyes that were warmly friendly, but at this moment there was no smile in them or on her red-lipped mouth. Rick guessed she was about twenty, yet somehow she seemed older. Rick had seen the same harried look she wore on women's faces south of the state line, settlers' women who stubbornly stood with their men until they were evicted.

Duff Estey had pulled himself to his feet. Now, with one hand holding the bloody pulp that was his nose, he reeled into the street.

"I should have known you'd have some excuse, Williams,"

the girl said with biting contempt. "You're too busy to do anything except sit behind your desk. Why don't you admit the truth, Williams? You're afraid to come to Redwall."

"You don't need to think this kind of talk will get any better treatment for you," Williams blustered.

"Oh, shut up," the girl said wearily. She held out a tanned, strong hand to Rick. "Perhaps you'll come. I'm not sure we can prevent trouble, but we've got to try."

"We'll come," Rick promised.

Turning to Fargo, she offered her hand to him. "Thanks to both of you." Then she stepped around Fargo and went out into the rain.

Williams stalked to his office, saying: "Come on back here."

Wade Verling, the Grant's general manager, was a hard-driving man who never liked to admit a mistake. He was responsible for the hiring and firing of the principal Grant employees, and, because he never wanted to appear wrong, he hesitated to dismiss the men he had personally hired. It was his greatest weakness, and was responsible for the fact that there were almost as many incompetent men working for the Grant as there were able ones. Now, sitting on a rawhide-bottom chair in front of Williams's desk, Rick decided this Stone Saddle agent was the most incompetent of the lot.

Williams said nothing for a time, busying himself with some papers on his desk. The silence ran on, Rick trying to mask his distrust. Fargo's face was expressionless, as usual.

Williams suddenly found the courage to explode: "Damn you two for bungling fools! It's taken me a year to get on the good side of Duff Estey. Now you come along and bust his nose. I'll have a hell of a job patching this up."

Fargo straightened in his chair, threw a glance at Rick, then eased back and began rolling a smoke. It was Rick who said: "It strikes me you're in a poor position to call us bungling fools. You look like you'd fit that description yourself."

Williams's round cheeks blossomed into a bright red. "Let's come to an understanding right now . . . both of you. I'm the Grant agent up here. Not you. As long as you're working out of this office, you'll take my orders, and you'll treat me with respect."

"You'll earn our respect," Rick threw at him, "but not by using a deputy sheriff for an office boy and hiding out when some of the settlers want to see you."

Williams leaned back. "We'll say you made a mistake and let it go at that. But get this clear. You're taking my orders."

Fargo said softly: "Sure, Charley. What are they?"

"You'll go to Redwall at once. Today. Talk to Dallam. Talk to any of the rest who want to talk. Jason Galt is up there, I believe. And the storekeeper, Ben Shaw, is the president of their anti-Grant association. Talk to him."

"What'll we say?" Fargo asked in the same deceptively soft tone.

"What have you been saying?"

"This is different . . . or so Verling told me." Fargo leaned forward, cold and dangerous. "I don't cotton to being called a bungling fool, Charley. I say Rick was wrong, but if you were worth anything, the Dallam girl wouldn't have been put into the position she was. You'd have been out there talking to her instead of lying about not knowing she was here."

"Don't call me a liar!" Williams shouted. "You're fired, both of you! Go back to Raton and draw your time."

Rick rose. "That's the best news I've heard lately, Pete. Let's drift."

"Sit down," Fargo said. "You're plumb wrong, Charley. It takes Verling to fire us. We'll go back to Raton if you say so, but if we do, Verling will hear some things that'll curl his ears."

The cigar in Williams's mouth began to droop. Like many small men Rick had known, Williams was possessed by an overweening pride that made him try to cover his inner weaknesses, but it didn't go. He wiped a hand across his suddenly sweaty face.

"All right," Williams said, "go up to Redwall. Let them get a good look at your guns. Tell them we're not backing down on the line we've taken. They'll be evicted, or we'll pay for their stock and improvements if they want to sell and get off the Grant."

"That's better," Fargo breathed. "And you'll back us up, or I'll fill you so full of holes they won't find enough of you for the burying."

"I'll back you up."

"And if any of the settlers want to come down and talk business, you'll see them."

Williams nodded, fishing into the pocket of his flowered waistcoat for a match to light the cigar that had gone cold in his mouth.

Fargo rose. "Let's drift, Rick."

"Not yet. In our business you learn to read a man, Williams. I'll bet my bottom dollar that your Duff Estey would sell his grandmother out if he could make a nickel."

"He's the best I could get," Williams said in a beaten voice. "I have some political influence here, so I was able to secure Estey's appointment. I thought it was a good idea to get a man into the sheriff's office who was on our side."

"I take it the sheriff isn't?"

Williams spread his hands. "There's two hundred votes

on the head of the river. Lee Combs, the sheriff, got those votes last election. That makes him hard to manage."

"The Grant makes a point of operating within the law," Rick said. "It can't afford to do otherwise."

"I'm aware of that," Williams stated. "If the settlers start a rebellion. . . ." He motioned significantly. "Well, Combs would have no choice."

Fargo gave Williams a thin-lipped grin. "So that's the way the wind blows. Maybe we're heading into more than we know about."

"If you boys are as good as you're supposed to be, you can handle anything."

"We'll handle it," Fargo said, and turned toward the door.

"There is one thing I haven't told you," Williams said with some reluctance. "Before you go into Redwall, stop at the log cabin you'll see to your left. It has a white fence around it and a row of hollyhocks. A woman lives there named Sparky Hogan. Talk to her. Just be sure you don't let the settlers know there's anything between us and her."

"Is there?" Rick demanded.

Williams shrugged with pretended indifference. "She's on our side. That's all. I arranged for her to buy a choice piece of land from us."

They went out then, crossing the outer office and going on into the street. Rick asked: "What do you think of it, Pete?"

"You know what I think," Fargo said bitterly. "It's a damned poor thing when you have to work for a small man."

III

As they put on their slickers in the stable, Rick asked the hostler: "Where's the sheriff's office?"

"On Bridge Street," the hostler answered. "Next to the river."

"Thanks," Rick said, and stepped up.

When they were outside, Fargo asked: "What kind of notion have you got in your head now?"

"I want to have a talk with this Lee Combs. Might save seeing the inside of his jail."

Fargo said nothing. Rick gave him a studying look, but there was no reading the masked face. It was an old situation between them, Rick thinking ahead and trying to avert trouble, Fargo making no commitment about a decision which was entirely Rick's.

They turned down Bridge Street, the rain still pelting them, the thick dust turned into slippery mud. Passing the Grant office, Rick wondered whether Williams were watching. He felt his distrust of the man grow. If it came to a question of loyalty, he felt sure that Williams would disclaim any responsibility for their actions, if those actions held discomfort for Williams or the Grant.

The sheriff's office and the jail were in a long adobe building on the west side of the street. Rick reined toward it, stepped down, and tied, Fargo following.

Fargo said: "This is your show, son. Go ahead."

Nodding, Rick stepped around the hitch pole and went in. A lanky man with a droopy yellow mustache looked up from his desk. He rose, giving Rick careful scrutiny, touching the star on his vest as if he wanted to be sure Rick saw it. He said in a soft voice: "What can I do for you?"

"You're Combs?"

The lanky man nodded. "Lee Combs. I'm the sheriff, if that's who you want."

Rick came across the room, his hand extended. "You're the man I'm looking for. I'm Rick Marvin."

Combs stepped back. "I won't shake hands with a Grant gunslinger."

Rick dropped his hand, anger flaring in him. "Now what the hell's the matter with you?"

"I've heard of you," Combs said bitterly. "They say you're fast." He nodded at Fargo, who stood in the doorway. "And that'll be Pete Fargo, your partner. While you're shaking hands with me, he'll pull his iron. I don't suck into a trap that easy."

Rick turned to look at Fargo. "Ain't this the damnedest thing?"

Fargo grinned. "Your idea, son."

Rick wheeled back to the lawman. "Get this straight, mister. If we came in here to pull a gun on you, we'd do it without any folderol like shaking your hand. You never saw the day you could match either one of us."

"That may be true," Combs agreed, "but I want a chance to try."

"Don't look like we're right welcome," Rick said. "What causes that?"

"You're Grant men, ain't you?" When Rick nodded, Combs added: "All right. That's enough."

"We're not here to make trouble."

"Trouble's your business, Marvin. You ain't fooling me."

"Trouble is our business when the Grant has trouble. We don't go around making it. We're going to Redwall because Miss Dallam was in the office and asked Williams to

26

come up there for a meeting. Williams wouldn't go."

"No, he wouldn't." Combs dropped into his chair, looking at Rick, and then at Fargo. "We have had no trouble yet, but it's just waiting to get a fire lighted under it. If you two go up there, you'll be lighting that fire."

Rick shook his head. "We don't aim to be any tougher than we have to. Personally, I have a lot of sympathy for the settlers, and I'll do anything I can for them."

"You're talking crazy, Rick," Fargo said bluntly. "There's nothing you can do for 'em. They've got to get off the Grant. That's what it adds up to, nothing more and nothing less."

"I'm afraid it will be that way," Combs agreed, "but Major Dallam still hopes that Congress will step in and do something for them, so he wants to hang on as long as he can. Your bunch wants them off. The way to bring on a showdown is to provoke trouble. With Jason Galt up there, you won't have to go very far to find a fight."

"If there is any shooting, it will be their doing," Rick said sharply. "That's what we came in to say."

"And what will you do about it when the ruckus starts?" Fargo asked.

Combs rolled a smoke, fingers trembling. There was a stooped, almost grotesque slackness in his thin shoulders; worry lines were deeply etched about his eyes. He was younger than Rick had first guessed, probably about thirty, too young in years and experience to handle this thing.

"I don't know," Combs said at last. "Every hour I'm awake I curse the day I let the settlers talk me into running for sheriff. I've sworn to uphold the law, but what the big guns call law favors the Grant. The trouble is I'm not a man who can shut his eyes to the simplest principles of justice."

Fargo's laugh was a taunting sound. "Now ain't you in a hell of a fix?"

"Yes, I am," Combs said miserably. "I've done what I could to avoid trouble, but the Redwall people are ready to fight. If you go up there, they will fight. You'll be killed. Then I'll have to get a posse and go after them." He spread his hands in a weary gesture. "They're good people who deserve something better than this. Their women and children may be hurt. It might even become a rebellion that would be little short of a civil war."

Fargo laughed again. "Look, friend. I've worked at jobs like this for thirteen years. I've always been on the side that had the law behind it. I've seen the little fry holler and squall and raise a hell of a fuss, but when it comes to a fracas, that's all they are, just a big holler."

"You haven't seen these people," Combs said reasonably. "I have, but you'd never understand them, because you're not free men. You're hired gunslingers who have orders to carry out." He rose and leaned forward, palms on the desk, his unlighted cigarette crushed between the fingers of his right hand. "Damn you! Stay out of Redwall."

Rick stared at the white, bitter face, and he saw himself as this lawman saw him. Fargo's shoulders were shaking with laughter, but there was no laughter in Rick Marvin. He was seeing Juan Sandoval's face again, puzzled and hurt; he was hearing the Mexican's voice: "The law . . . she is something I do not understand."

"We've got to go up there, Sheriff," Rick said in a voice he didn't recognize as his own, "but if there is trouble, they'll make it."

Rick swung out of the room. He heard Combs say in a bitter, flaying tone: "They'll make it . . . you can be sure of that."

28

Rick went to his horse. Fargo lingered to say: "You'd better be ready to pull us out of a jam. You swore to uphold the law, you know."

Still laughing, Fargo tromped out of the sheriff's office and, mounting, swung in beside Rick. They crossed the bridge, Rick staring at the swollen brown stream. Then they were on the north side and turning upriver. Fargo said, a little grudgingly: "Well, we know what sort of a hairpin totes the star. He's sure caught in a squeeze, and I've got a hunch there ain't much sand in his craw."

"I think you're wrong," Rick said. "The part I don't understand is why he's got a deputy like Duff Estey."

"Which reminds me," Fargo said testily. "When you swung on Estey, you was the biggest damn' fool you ever have been, and I've seen you do some purty foolish things."

"Sure," Rick murmured. "I used my fists on a man when I should take care of my hands, and I sided with a girl I didn't know who turned out to be a settler."

"Hell," Fargo said hotly, "that wasn't the worst part of it. It was like Williams said. He'd finagled around until he got a man into a deputy's job who favored the Grant."

"I'm way ahead of you," Rick cut in. "Anyhow, thanks for siding me."

"No thanks coming. We work as a team, or we don't work at all. I won't make a mistake like that, but in case I do, you'd better be damned sure you back me up."

Rick nodded, saying nothing. They rode in silence for a time. It had stopped raining now, and westward the sky was clearing. There was no sound but the plop of hoofs in mud and the growl of the flood-high river to their left. Then Rick said: "Too bad you didn't get to try out the local tinhorns."

"It was, for a fact," Fargo said. "The more I think about

Charley Williams, the less I like him. There wasn't no need
for us to pull out for Redwall today."

The valley narrowed, and the mountains were blotted
from sight by the timber-covered lower ridges. In late afternoon they came into sight of the red wall, a strange phe-
nomenon of nature that gave the town its name. It ran
parallel to the range and perpendicular to the valley, a giant
upthrust that rose above the valley floor like a man-made
wall guarding an ancient city. In some places it held a
scanty covering of brush and dwarfed trees; in others the
harsh rock, red and orange, frowned in grim defiance at
those who had the temerity to invade the valley.

Neither Fargo nor Rick spoke for a long time, both
staring at the wall. Rick had lived in the Southwest all his
life; he had seen hundreds of arches and spires carved by
the blasting, sand-carrying wind, and he had seen innumer-
able mesas, piled one upon the other like irregular steps
lifting toward the high, broken country, but he had never
seen anything like this wall that, except for the one gap in
its center, divided the valley.

It was both beautiful and terrifying to Rick, and his mind
instinctively turned to the prehistoric time when the wall
had been made by some titanic force of nature, but to Pete
Fargo it was something else. He said characteristically:
"The squatters could put half a dozen men with
Winchesters in that gap and hold off an army."

"They've probably thought of it," Rick said.

The settlement lay at the foot of the wall, a dozen buildings or more, all built of logs except one two-story frame
building with the usual false front holding the weathered

letters, **Mercantile, Ben Shaw, prop**. Two roads crossed each other at right angles, making four corners that were occupied by the business buildings. Besides the store, there were a sprawling log structure marked by a swaying sign, **Dallam Hotel,** a blacksmith shop, and a saloon. Beyond the corners, facing each other across the road that led through the gap, were a schoolhouse and church.

Cabins were scattered haphazardly through the timber, many with garden patches behind them and a few flowers in front. All of them, and this was the most surprising thing to Rick about the settlement, showed the careful and loving attention that people would give their own homes if they expected to live a lifetime there. Nowhere did he see evidence of the shiftless kind of existence he had always associated with people who squatted on someone else's land and hoped to trade their nuisance value for a few dollars.

A woman called: "You're a queer pair to be riding into Redwall! Maybe if I live here long enough, I'll see Wade Verling show up in a red-wheeled buggy behind a span of Morgans."

Rick and Fargo turned, hands instinctively dipping to gun butts and then dropping away as they realized it was a woman who had spoken to them. She stood in the doorway of the first cabin, leaning against the jamb, a roundly molded, seductive figure.

"That the Sparky Hogan that Williams was talking about?" Fargo asked in a low tone.

"I reckon," Rick answered. "We'd better have a talk with her."

They reined toward her and stepped down, both a little uncertain because they judged, from what Williams had said, that she was a Grant spy, and neither had any use for spies. They stepped through the gate, Rick noting the row of hollyhocks higher than his head and now in full bloom, the white fence, the carefully tended yard. They went on up the path, both lifting their hats.

"You must be Sparky Hogan," Fargo said. "Williams told us to see you."

"I'm Sparky to my friends," she said quickly. "Missus Hogan to everybody else."

She made no motion to invite them inside, her bright blue eyes frankly appraising. She was in her middle twenties, Rick guessed, and pretty in a blatant sort of way. She wore a dress with puffed sleeves and ruffles, the color matching her eyes, but it was her hair that gripped Rick's attention. It was as vividly red as the scarlet that was spreading across the sky above the wall.

"Then we'll be calling you Sparky," Fargo said.

"I don't know about that," she said tartly. "I never liked a man who uses a gun to make his living, and I'm very sure I wouldn't like a man who dolls up so he thinks he'll knock a woman's eyes out."

Nettled, Fargo said: "I don't buy duds to knock any woman's eyes out. I buy 'em because I like 'em."

She was a tough one, Rick judged, but tough or not, there was no use fighting with her if she belonged to the Grant. He said now: "No offense, ma'am. We're. . . ."

"I know who you are. Williams said you'd be along. He didn't like it much, but it was Verling's idea. This Christmas tree with the pretty clothes is Pete Fargo and you're Rick Marvin. Now, I'll tell you what you do. Get back on those nags and hit the dirt. Keep going till you're in Stone Saddle."

Fargo's mouth hung open. He looked at Rick, as puzzled as Rick had ever seen him. "Is this the redhead talking?"

"The words came out of her pretty mouth," Rick said. "Must have been her."

She laughed, a pleasant sound to hear. "I like that, Marvin. Funny what a good-paying job does, teaming up two gunslingers as different as you two."

"Thought you didn't like men who used guns to make their living," Fargo said.

"There's a difference. Marvin looks like he's worked for a living, but I doubt that you have."

Without another word Fargo wheeled and started toward his horse. Sparky Hogan called: "Where are you going?"

"To Redwall," Fargo answered without breaking his stride.

"No," Sparky cried. "Dallam isn't there. Jason will work them up till they'll kill a Grant man."

Fargo didn't stop. Rick said: "No use, ma'am."

"Go ahead, then. Let them kill you. It's what Williams wants."

Rick asked: "Which side are you on, ma'am?"

"Neither. I'm just watching. But any fool could see that a couple of Grant leather slappers floating around here can't do anything but stir up trouble." She gripped Rick's arm and shook it. "Now go pound some sense into that locoed Fargo's head."

"We've got orders," Rick said. Pulling away from the woman, he walked to his horse.

Fargo was already in the saddle, waiting. As Rick stepped up and reined into the street, he couldn't help thinking that Lee Combs had been right. Pete Fargo and Rick Marvin were not free men; they were hired gunslingers with orders to carry out.

Glancing at Fargo, Rick could see no trace of worry on the man's dark face. He thought of Juan Sandoval, now homeless; he thought of the Mexican settlements he had seen today, and he raised his eyes to the great sheet of rock that was the red wall. Before the sun was down, circumstances might force him to kill a settler. If it did, he would never again have the peace of a free conscience.

They walked their horses into the settlement, the sun throwing long shadows behind them. Fargo asked: "What do you make of the redhead?"

"She's no spy," Rick said shortly.

"If she ain't, she's sure made a fool out of Williams."

"I'm thinking Williams was a fool to start with, but I dunno about the redhead. She may be fishing for Verling."

Fargo nodded. "I thought of that. Well, if Verling don't know Williams's caliber, he'll find out." He reined toward the hotel. "Let's get a room."

They dismounted and racked their horses, Rick saying: "Funny about that redhead. Suppose she's right about Williams wanting us beefed?"

"You're slow in the head today," Fargo said. "Sure, she's right."

Fargo swung up the path and went into the hotel. Rick stood at the hitch pole for a moment, looking back at Sparky Hogan, who was still in front of her cabin. Now she flounced around and went inside. Rick turned toward the hotel, but he didn't go in, for Fargo stomped out, his face black with anger.

"We'll be sleeping with the sky for a blanket again," he said bitterly. "That damned fool clerk in there wanted to know if we wasn't Grant men. When I said we was, he says they didn't have no rooms."

"The Dallam girl ain't there?"

"Reckon she ain't back from town." Fargo jerked his head at the store. "Come on. Let's have a palaver with this Shaw *hombre*."

They were in the middle of the street when a bell started clanging. They wheeled, saw the heavy bell in the tall frame behind the hotel, and started around the building on the run. There was no fire. Coming hard upon the heels of Fargo's admission that they were Grant men, and the clerk's refusal to rent them a room, this bell's ringing could mean but one thing: the prearranged signal notifying the settlers that Grant men had arrived.

They cleared the back corner of the hotel, a pup yapping behind them, a flock of half-grown chickens scattering with a rising crescendo of scared squawks. A boy was pulling hard at the bell rope, but the instant he saw Fargo and Rick, he let go and jumped for the back door. Fargo caught him a step from the door, shouting: "Where's the fire?"

The boy tried to jerk free, terrified. Rick said: "Hold on, Pete. The kid's too scared to talk."

"Scared? What'n hell's he scared of? All I asked him was where the fire was."

Fargo let go. The boy backed against the building, eyes on Rick. "There ain't no fire. I was just telling folks that there was a Grant man in town."

"All right, all right," Fargo said angrily. "You've told 'em. Now get inside and stay there."

"Wait, Pete." Rick motioned to the boy. "Why did you ring the bell?"

"Mister Galt told me to." The boy swallowed and ran the tip of his tongue over his lips. "He said that Grant men would come to kill us and burn our houses. He said to ring that bell first thing, and that'd give our men a chance to get here and fight." He squared his shoulders, glaring at Fargo with the full wickedness of youth soured by hate. "All right. Kill me. That's your size, ain't it?"

Fargo swore bitterly and, swinging on his heel, said: "Come on, Rick."

But Rick didn't move for a moment. He was staring at the boy, not seeing him; he was hearing Lee Combs say back in the sheriff's office in Stone Saddle: "You'd never understand them because you're not free men." And this boy, not over thirteen or fourteen, had said: "Kill me. That's your size, ain't it?"

All the contempt and fear and hatred that this lad had for the Grant was in his voice, and he had that same contempt and fear and hatred for Rick Marvin, because Rick worked for the Grant.

Wheeling, Rick caught up with Fargo. He said: "Let's drift, Pete. I don't aim to be the bait that fixes it so Williams has an excuse to send a sheriff's posse in here."

Fargo gave him his thin-lipped grin. "You're a little late, son."

Men were in the street with shotguns and Winchesters in their hands—a dozen of them, running out of the hotel, the saloon, and the blacksmith shop. For a moment Fargo and Rick faced them, feeling their hesitation and lack of leadership.

"Let's see Shaw," Rick said.

Fargo nodded, and they went on into the store. It was a long, gloomy building, the cool interior filled with the mixed smells of vinegar and lard and leather. There was an odd sense of quiet here, and for a moment Rick felt he had stepped out of a high, breathtaking wind.

A small man with mutton-chop whiskers came out of the back of the store. He said: "I presume you're the Grant men. You made a mistake coming here, you know."

"We came because Ruth Dallam asked us to," Rick said. "Miss Dallam said you people were having a meeting."

"We're always having meetings," the store man said. "I'm Ben Shaw, president of the Redwall Settlers' Association. We talk and we pass motions and we listen to Jason Galt read his last circular. Do you see any harm in that?"

Fargo had moved around the potbellied stove to stand with his back to the counter. He said, his voice very soft: "No, no harm in that."

Shaw stood with his hands pushed deeply into his pockets, a banty rooster of a man feeling his own importance and the importance of the occasion. He said: "But there is great harm in you men coming to Redwall. It would have been all right if it had been Williams, but it would have been useless because we are not leaving our homes, and the Grant Company is too greedy to give up its claim, fraudulent as it is. But you men are not like Williams. You're killers, so we assume you're here to kill us."

Rick shook his head. "You're wrong, Shaw."

"I think not. Jason Galt travels between here and Raton a good deal. He keeps us informed about what goes on below the line. You men have shot and killed Ace Traverse, Three-Shoot Phipps, and Limpy Smith." Shaw spread his hands. "I could go on naming others you have killed since you became what Wade Verling likes to call his trouble-shooters. But I will tell you this . . . you will not add another notch in your guns here."

"Did Galt say those men were settlers on the Grant?" Rick asked.

Shaw seemed puzzled. "Why, I assumed they were. Naturally Verling is not in the habit of throwing Grant money around. Why else would he have hired you?"

"We've got no reason to explain anything," Fargo said in that same soft tone. "We didn't come here to kill anybody. We came because Ruth Dallam asked us to, and Charley

Williams ordered it. The minute we show up, a kid rings the bell and your men grab their artillery and pile into the street. You call that neighborly?"

"We have no reason to be neighborly to you or any Grant man," Shaw said bitterly. "It's only a question of time until we will be evicted the same as settlers across the line have been. There's nothing we can do but fight."

Outside, men galloped past the store. Someone raised a shout of defiance, and others took up the cry, the sound of their voices a rising rumble that beat ominously against Rick's ears. He asked: "Do you think fighting will get you anything?"

"I'm sure it will," Shaw said placidly. "We've talked this over, and we decided to hang you if you came. Then we will be let alone."

Fargo laughed. "You'll hang us, like hell."

Rick glanced at Fargo, and Fargo gave a bare half-inch nod. This was the one thing in which they worked together perfectly. Rick moved back to the other counter, and drew his gun the same instant Fargo did. Shaw, caught between them, could only blink uncertainly as he stared from one gun muzzle to the other.

"We don't aim to hurt you," Rick said, "but we don't like what's going on. If you're the boss of this outfit, step outside and tell 'em to scatter."

"They wouldn't go. I . . . I'm not the boss. I mean, I just preside over the meetings. It's Jason Galt they listen to. Or Major Dallam when he's here."

"You'd better start presiding over this meeting." Fargo jerked his head at the door. "Move!"

Shaw hesitated, chewing on his lip, but he was not a man who could stand this pressure. He walked to the door, Rick and Fargo falling in behind him. Rick said in a low tone:

"Verling won't like a shooting party, Pete."

"We're in a fix," Fargo said. "Hot lead's the only way out."

They followed Shaw from the store and into the late afternoon sunlight. There had been a dozen men on the street. Now there were fifty. Someone saw them, and shouted: "There are the killing sons-of-bitches. They've got Ben."

"Get the ropes," a great voice rose above the others. "Shake out your loops. We'll hang them. They'll be the last Grant men who will ever come to Redwall Valley."

That would be Jason Galt. Rick had never seen him, but he'd heard a lot about the man. They came down the street, Galt in front, tall and arrow-backed, with a close-cropped beard and red-flecked eyes that were alive now with the desire of the moment. A violent man, Jason Galt, in a flat-crowned black hat and a long-tailed black coat, a zealous, fanatical man had somehow endowed these people with his fanaticism.

Two men had ropes. They whirled away now from the crowd toward a pine at the edge of the road and tossed their ropes over a limb.

"Better start speaking your piece," Fargo said, jamming his gun against Shaw's back. "Make it do the job, or some of your backbone will be coming out your front."

Shaw raised his hands, shouting: "Listen, men! Listen, Jason! Don't do this! They haven't come here to harm anyone. Let them talk."

"Their kind talks with guns!" Jason Galt shouted. "Get away from them, Ben. They came to take life, but it will be theirs that is taken."

Shaw began to tremble. He cried out: "He's got a gun in my back! He'll kill me!"

But his voice was a wail lost in the roar of this killer mob. They were not more than seventy-five feet away now. Rick, staring at their wild faces, knew that Shaw could not stop them.

Fargo bawled: "I'm going to give this jasper his!"

Turning, Rick jammed his gun against Fargo's side. "Let him go, Pete. Beefing him won't save our hides."

In this moment, with the last blue chip down, Rick Marvin, leather slapper, saw himself as Lee Combs and Sparky Hogan had seen him, as even Wade Verling and Charley Williams had seen him. There was no sincere belief driving him, no great motivation that could give him an excuse for taking a settler's life. He was just a man with a gun for rent. Now, with perhaps five minutes of life, Rick Marvin hated himself for what he had been, for when a man died he should die for something worth dying for.

IV

Rick heard the sullen rumble of the in-sweeping crowd. He saw relief break across Ben Shaw's whiskery face as the little man clutched greedily at this new hope. He saw Fargo turn to him, and for the first time in his life he had no trouble reading the gunman's face. First there was the blank expression of a man who has seen something happen that is too fantastic to believe. Then he did believe, and anger was in him. Hatred was there, and contempt, and the driving urge to revenge himself upon the man who, as he saw it, had double-crossed him.

Fargo's left hand swept Shaw headlong into the crowd as he swung his gun toward Rick. Instinctively Rick knocked the gun aside as a shot rocked out above the roar of the crowd. The settlers were on them then, swarming in like a plague of locusts.

Fargo bawled a bitter oath and went down under the weight of numbers. Rick laid his gun barrel across a man's head and dropped him. He rammed into the crowd, trying to get his hands on Jason Galt, but Galt was too far in the back, his commanding voice beating against Rick's ears. Then Rick, like Fargo, went down under the overpowering weight of the burly settlers.

"Bring them here, men!" Galt shouted. "The ropes are ready."

Two men grabbed Rick's legs, two more his arms, and the rest fell away as the four of them carried him toward the pine. Four more brought Fargo. Another man had led two saddled horses under the big limb.

"Fit the loops on their necks," Galt ordered. "Tie their hands and their feet. We'll let them swing until they rot. We'll let Charley Williams see them. I hope that Wade Verling will come to view them. This is your first blow for your homes."

Rick's hands were tied behind his back. Another short length of rope was knotted around his ankles. A loop was dropped over his neck, and tightened. He was boosted up in the saddle, Fargo beside him, and suddenly there was silence.

"Have you anything to say before you're swung into eternity?" Galt asked.

"Yeah, I've got something to say to my double-crossing partner," Fargo said. "You're the man who wouldn't go soft and who wouldn't quit the job when the chips were down. I hope to get to hell ahead of you. If I do, I'll sure blackball you."

"You're an evil, impious man," Galt said reprovingly. "I shall pray for your soul." He motioned to Rick. "Have you a final statement?"

"No statement," Rick said, "but I have a prophecy. Before the sun's down, you'll regret what you've done. You've had the last good night's sleep you'll ever have."

There was no break in the harsh set of Galt's face. "Do you have any confessions to make that will make your entrance into eternity easier?"

"Go to hell," Fargo snarled.

"You?" Galt motioned to Rick.

"I have nothing to confess."

"You've worked for the Grant," Galt said. "Men have died before your gun. You've carried out Wade Verling's orders. It would be better for you if you made a full confession."

"I've never murdered a man," Rick said. "That's more than you'll be able to say."

"I am sorry for you." Galt motioned to the men behind the horses. "Give them a sharp cut, boys."

"Jason . . . no, Jason!" It was Ruth Dallam's voice. She broke through the crowd, crying out: "Wait, Bert. Wait, Clarke! Why are you doing this?"

The men behind the horses had raised their quirts. Now they lowered them and swung back to face the girl.

"Strike, Bert!" Galt cried out in sudden fury. "Strike, Clarke. Strike this blow for your homes and families."

Then Ruth was facing Galt, her black eyes flaming. "Jason, you fool. You hare-brained, murdering fool!" She swept a hand toward the men behind the horses. "You talk about your homes. Don't you know they'll hang you and them and maybe every man here for murder? Are you trying to cut away every friend we have?" She shook his arm.

42

"Think, Jason. For the love of heaven, think. You'll have Lee Combs coming up here with a posse hunting every one of you down, and Lee's the best friend we have in Stone Saddle."

The man she had called Clarke wiped his sweaty face. "That's right, Jason. Lee wouldn't have no choice."

The other man, Bert, dropped his quirt and walked toward Galt. "Damn you, Jason." He rubbed his throat. "I can feel Lee Combs's rope on my neck now. I've got a wife and four kids. I might just as well starve with my family than to hang and have them starve by themselves."

Ben Shaw pushed up to stand beside Galt. "Stay out of this, Ruth. They came here asking for trouble, didn't they? What else brought them here?"

Ruth motioned to Bert. "Get these men down. I asked them to come. It's my fault they're here. Can you understand that? If you hanged them, I'd be a murderer along with the rest of you."

"Stand away, boys," Galt said. "I'll do this job if none of the rest of you has the courage it takes. Perhaps Lee Combs will hang me, but this is not murder, Ruth. It's justice. If I hang, every American citizen from California to Maine will read about it and know why I died. Then the government will act."

"Justice?" Rick asked. "You gave us no trial. You charged us with no crime."

"You were fixing to kill me," Shaw cried. "Don't deny that!"

"There would have been no threat against you if this mob hadn't started after us," Rick reminded him. "And I saved your life, remember."

Shaw lowered his head under the force of Rick's stare. He mumbled: "That's right, I reckon." Then he looked up at Fargo and motioned to him. "But he was going to shoot me. He had a gun in my back. Hang him."

"No." Ruth gave Bert a shove. "Get them down, I tell you. I asked these men to come to talk over our troubles and prevent bloodshed, and you treat them this way. I'm ashamed of you. All of you. Would you do this if Dad were here?"

"I tell you I'll do this!" Galt shouted. Picking up his quirt, he raised it over his head to slash it across the back of the horse that Rick was on. Clarke gripped his arm and jerked the quirt from him.

"There will be no hanging this day, Jason," he said evenly. "Not by you, or anyone. Ruth's right. We wouldn't have done this if Ed Dallam was here."

They took Rick and Fargo down, a dozen hands reaching up for them. Knives slashed the ropes that bound their wrists and ankles; the loops were taken from their necks.

Bert said honestly: "I'm sorry." He ran a sleeve across his face, and nodded at Rick. "You were right. If we had gone ahead, we never would have slept again."

"You'll regret this!" Galt shouted. "Once you've put your hand to the plow, you cannot turn back. What do you think they'll do to us when these men get to Stone Saddle and tell Charley Williams what we were going to do?"

"I don't know," Ruth said, "but I do know what would happen if you'd gone ahead. I owe these men a great deal, Jason."

"How could you owe a Grant gunman anything?" he flung at her. "They're murderers. They came to destroy, and you saved them."

"This pulling and hauling has gone on for a long time, Jason," she said. "I know you're honest in what you're doing, but you're mistaken. My folks were the first in the valley. Remember that. We were here before the Utes left. We were here when there was even less law than there is now." She motioned toward the hotel. "We may lose our property, and it's our home, too. If you want to count it in dollars and cents, we would lose more than any of the rest of you. If you want to count it in sentiment, remember my mother and my brother are buried here. I would give anything to keep the Grant from taking our home."

She licked dry lips, not yet sure of her victory. Rick, watching, sensed something she had not put into words. This was part of the struggle between her father and Jason Galt.

"We know," Clarke said. "You're right, Ruth. We lost our heads." He glared at Galt. "We put our hands to the plow, but we didn't turn the sod over, Jason. We can still look back."

"I want to tell you about these men," Ruth said. "They fought for me. I saw today in Charley Williams's office that they are not the kind of men we have been led to believe they are."

She told them about the fight with Duff Estey, and about asking them to come to Redwall. She said then, her tone bitter with self-condemnation: "I should have come with them, but I didn't dream you'd treat them this way. I told you I was ashamed of you. I still am. Go home, all of you."

Ruth began to tremble, now that it was over. She tried to smile, but her lips quivered. She said in a low tone: "I'm sorry. I can only apologize for them. Now let's go inside. Did you get rooms in the hotel?"

"No," Fargo said. "You've got a hairpin inside who don't like Grant men any more than these other *hombres* do."

"Then I must apologize for him, too. Come on. I'll see

that you have rooms and supper."

They walked toward the hotel, Ruth between them, her hands on their arms. Once Rick looked over her head at Fargo. The gunman was staring straight ahead. The settlement between them must come soon. Rick had made that certain when he had shoved his gun against Fargo's side. There were some things Pete Fargo could forgive, but that was not one of them.

The Dallam Hotel was a rambling two-story structure, much like any house built for a large family. Ruth guided Rick and Fargo along a hall that led from a front room that served as a lobby. Neither the man who had been at the desk when Fargo asked for a room nor the boy who had rung the bell was in evidence.

Ruth opened a door and stepped back. "I have this room for you. Or, if you want separate rooms, I can put you upstairs."

"This will do," Rick said.

Fargo gave him a sharp glance, saying nothing, his face hard.

"Supper is probably ready," Ruth said. "I'll see if I can help. You'll find a pump and wash pan on the back porch."

Rick stood by the window, listening to the girl's steps fade along the hall. The sun was out of sight behind the Sangre de Cristo range, and the darkening shadows of twilight were flowing out across the valley. Fargo stood inside the door, cool eyes on Rick. He had been roughed up by the mob, his hat was dirty, his silk shirt rumpled and sweat-stained. Although his face was as expressionless as ever, Rick sensed that his temper had been honed down until it was like a raw wound.

In the year they had traveled together, Rick had seen Fargo like this many times. It would take little to bring him to the exploding point, but he was a careful man, even when he was as bitterly angry as he was now. They were not out of the woods, even with Ruth Dallam's friendship, so it was unlikely that Fargo would force the issue until they were back in Stone Saddle.

"Guess I'll wash up," Rick said, and walked past Fargo.

Rick gave Fargo his back until he was outside, a risk that he would not have taken with some, but Fargo, like many men who lived by the gun, had his own strict code. He would no more have shot a man in the back than he would have blown his own brains out.

Rick pumped a pan of water and washed briskly. He dried with the roller towel, noting that it was cleaner than most towels he had found in such places. As he combed his hair with a short end of a comb that he found stuck between two logs, he thought that the towel was typical of the place.

Fargo joined him, and, after he had washed, they went back along the hall to the lobby, where they waited. A few minutes later Ruth called them to supper. There were just the three of them. Rick wondered again about the man and the boy, but he didn't ask. It was a reasonable guess that Ruth had told them to eat somewhere else so there would be as little strain as possible at the table.

The food was good, but Rick had little appetite. There was a tension about him he could not explain, unless it was the natural result of his handshake with death.

"Dad is in Denver," Ruth said suddenly. "I think I forgot to tell you. He should be back tonight or tomorrow. We're in a lawsuit, you know." She stirred her coffee, staring moodily at it. "It's our last chance. If the Grant wins, we'll be evicted."

"I haven't thanked you," Rick said. "It was what I'd call a rescue from the rim of hell or something like that."

She said simply: "You don't need to thank me. It wasn't as much as you did for me. I'm just ashamed. If Dad had been here, it wouldn't have happened."

"Someday I'll notch my sight on that Galt *hombre*," Fargo said, "and I'll blow his gizzard right out through his backbone. Soon as I get my hands on a gun."

"I have yours," Ruth said. "They were dropped in front of the store, and Henry brought them over. He's the boy who rang the bell. He took care of your horses, too. They're in back of the hotel."

Ruth rose and went into the lobby. She returned in a moment with Fargo's silver-plated Peacemaker and Rick's walnut-handled .44, and sat down again.

Ruth watched Rick while he checked the gun, ejected the loads, and thumbed shells from his belt into the cylinder. Then she said: "You men may think we're wealthy, but I want both of you to know how it is with us. It seems important because you'll be going back to Stone Saddle and report to Williams. Or perhaps to Verling in Raton. I'm afraid it will be a bad report."

"It sure as hell will," Fargo said, pushing his empty plate back.

"We hire a cook, a chore boy, and a man who handles the desk and works anywhere he's needed. We did have a little money. My folks came here a good many years ago, you know. In those days nobody talked much about the Grant, and the Department of the Interior said this country was open to entry. Dad and Mother came up the river in a covered wagon. I was small, but I remember the trip. I particularly remember how they talked about the valley, its beauty and the timber and the deep soil. They said this was what they had been looking for, so they stayed."

Fargo leaned back and rolled a smoke. "I think I'll get a drink."

"Just a minute," said Ruth sharply. "I want you to hear what I have to say. I think you owe me that much."

Fargo shrugged. "Go ahead."

"We made some money. This is a good potato country, and Harvey buys them from us for his restaurants. There has always been good hunting and fishing, and quite a few Stone Saddle men come here to stay. Charley Williams was one of them. As you know, the Grant changed hands, and the new owners have been trying to get us off. Dad took it to the courts. That was his way of fighting." She gestured as if it had been a hopeless cause from the first. "You know what lawyers charge. There may be no bottom to the Grant pocketbook, but there was to ours. We're a little past the bottom now."

She paused, a hand going up to her throat, the lamplight falling across her tanned face. "I don't expect to swing you to our point of view, but I want you to see that much of the right is on our side. I suppose our system of government can be blamed for the whole thing. The Grant was confirmed by Congress a long time ago, about Eighteen Sixty, I think, but the boundaries were not set down definitely. According to the old Mexican law, these grants were to be no more than eleven square leagues. If the Isham Grant had been held to that, we would have been all right. But through some political fraud, the Grant Company was able to secure many times that. Now the Supreme Court has decided in favor of the Grant."

"Then why bring this suit you have pending now?" Rick asked.

"Dad's lawyer thought there was a chance. A new survey, I believe, but I'm afraid it's the old story of power and wealth against the little fry."

"You haven't got a chance," Fargo said brutally. "The little fry never has. That's why I'm on the side of the big boys."

"But there are moral questions involved," she said earnestly. "I had hoped to make you see that. We hold a patent on this land. We settled here in good faith, because we took the government's word. Then the Grant Company, which has never done a thing to develop this country, threatens to evict us. The Grant wants money. We want homes. It's very simple. It's a question of fraud on one side, and the faith of its citizens on the other."

Fargo rose. "I guess I'm smarter'n you folks, ma'am. I learned a long time ago to take the world the way it is. Now I'm gonna get me that drink." He moved to the door. "Coming, Rick?"

"No. Go ahead."

Fargo's grin was suggestive. "It's a simple matter with you, too, ain't it? Well, don't forget what I said the other night about your bank account in Santa Fé. A fancy coffin. Or maybe a purty woman."

Fargo went out, and Ruth looked at Rick. "What did he mean?"

"Just talking to hear the wind blow," Rick said morosely.

"He must have meant something."

"He did. About what I'm going to do with myself." There was a restlessness in him. "I've heard all that about the Grant, but never quite the way you said it." He told her about the Sandovals, adding: "It'll be the same up here. I always figured that if you had the law on your side, you were all right, but I've been wrong. I'm done working for the Grant Company. When I get to town tomorrow, I'll tell Williams."

She gave him a questioning look, making no effort to hide her doubts. "Why did you go to work for the Grant in the first place?"

He shrugged. "Money. I started with a gun and six bits in my pocket. Now I've got a little money in the bank. I never worried as long as the law was on my side. The law is on the Grant's side. Fact is, I never did much thinking about it until I sat there in court and watched 'em take Juan's home away from him. Now I feel like I'd had a hand in it."

"What will you do?"

"I don't know."

He leaned forward, elbows on the table, his eyes locked with hers. He knew what he wanted. It was here, the treasures he had hoped someday to possess. Here was a woman he could love, the sort of woman who could always be a challenge to a man because she would deserve the best that was in him. The land was here, too, the kind of place he had pictured in his mind, a good stock country with a valley where he could raise hay and winter his cattle. But there was no use telling her this, for she was Major Dallam's daughter, and he was a leather slapper who had taken orders from the Grant. Whatever his intentions were, he could not expect her to believe in him. In her eyes there was no difference between him and Pete Fargo.

He rose and rolled a smoke, trying to hide the regret that was in him. Then he knew he was not hiding anything, for she said: "Rick, there's no use being sorry for what's behind us. It's the trouble that's here now that we've got to do something about. It's greedy men like Charley Williams who make it. And Duff Estey. Jason says Verling is the same. Is that true?"

Rick shook his head. "He's concerned about the Grant,

51

that's all. Nothing else matters to him."

"I have no right to ask you for help," she went on, "but I'm going to ask anyway. Isn't there something you can do for us?"

He shook his head. "I told you I was quitting the Grant. A man can stand so much. No more. I'd like for you to think that I'm different from Fargo. He sold both his gun and his soul. I just sold my gun."

"I think I can see how it is." She began tracing a design on the tablecloth. "But from working with the Grant, you must know its weakness." She looked up. "Or would telling me the Grant's secrets go against your code of honor?"

"As far as the Grant goes, it don't have any weaknesses. If it did, I'd tell you."

She began tracing the design again. "I suppose not. It has power, and that's enough. Verling and the rest know how to use power." She shook her head. "We don't have any weapons to fight back with."

"You can buy your land," he said. "Maybe I can help you with Verling."

"Buy the land we've already paid the government for?" She shook her head. "No, Rick. That we'll never do. We've bought our land, and we were given a patent for it. Now the courts tell us a patent means nothing. These men who own the Grant never held an axe in their hands or dug a stump out of the ground or plowed a furrow, but we've done those things and made the land valuable. Now they offer us a pittance for our improvements and kick us off."

"But it's your home. The only way you can hold it is to buy it again. I think I can help you, if you don't let Galt go crazy again. He's the worst enemy you've got."

"No, he isn't. He's mistaken, but he's sincere, Rick. I

know you can't believe that after what happened, but I know he is. He would have taken your life, and he'd give his own just as freely if it would do any good."

"It wouldn't," Rick said doggedly. "That's just it. Williams would like to see trouble up here. I tell you you've got to get rid of Galt."

"We can't. The settlers love him because they know he's sincere. A few of them will follow him into anything."

Rick squeezed out his cigarette. "I'll see Verling. Your job is to hold Galt in line."

"I'll try."

He turned toward the hall door, and then swung back. "Just how does Sparky Hogan fit into the business?"

He saw Ruth's face tighten. "Why do you ask?"

"Williams said to see her. He talked like she was with the Grant, but when we stopped, she told us to go back to town. She acted like she was on the settlers' side."

"I can't tell you anything about her. She's in the community, but she's not a part of it." Ruth paused and bit her lip. Then she added: "She's pretty, but so is a mountain lion if you don't get too close."

That, Rick saw, was as much as she would tell him. He bade her good night, and went along the hall to his room.

V

It was a dark night, relieved only by the faint star shine that lay upon a silent earth. Rick smoked another cigarette beside the open window, the breeze cool and rich with pine smell. The black sky seemed to press downward with the weight of all eternity; the valley lifted upward into the mountains and met to flow together in one great swell of soil and granite.

He took off his boots and coat and unbuckled his gun belt. He lay down, his gun within easy reach, and tried to sleep, but he could not. The truth is not easy to recognize; right is never completely right or wrong entirely wrong. There was something to be said for the settlers, and something to be said for the Grant. Rick lay motionless in the darkness, weighing both sides in his mind. Still he could come to no decision.

There was Ruth, who was good. But Jason Galt, who was with her, would have hanged two men today because such a hanging would focus public opinion on this Grant issue. There was Charley Williams and Duff Estey, who were evil. But Wade Verling was with them, and Verling represented men who had invested their money in the Grant. Some of them might be ruined if the Grant went broke, the same as the Dallams were being ruined.

He must have slept at last, for he came to with a start, aware that someone was outside his window. He reached for his gun, gripped it, and swung his feet to the floor. It came again, a tapping that must have been the sound that had awakened him. Silently he moved toward the window and stood beside it, the gun in his hand. He asked: "Who is it?"

"That you, Marvin?"

It was a woman's voice, vaguely familiar, but at the moment he could not place it. He said—"Yes."—and opened the door slowly.

"It's Sparky Hogan." She was in the room then. "Put that iron up. Soon as I pull the blind down, light the lamp."

He hesitated for a moment, uncertain of her. He heard the rattle of the shade being pulled down, then her impatient voice. "Hurry up. Light that lamp. I don't like to talk to a man in the dark."

"What kind of a damned fool stunt is this?" he said roughly.

She laughed. He thought again, as he had thought when he had talked to her in front of her cabin, that it was a pleasant sound. "You know Fargo wouldn't object to a woman being in his room, but you're different. Or maybe it's just that you wouldn't want Ruth to find me here."

"Might be."

"Well, roll your conscience over and light that lamp. I've got talk to make. Then I'll get out."

He struck a match and lighted the lamp on the bureau. When he had replaced the chimney, he turned to look at her. She was wearing the same dress with the puffed sleeves and ruffles; her hair was as fantastically red as he remembered it. She was pretty, all right, but without the blatant boldness he had seen in her in the afternoon. There was a smudge of dirt across her nose, and she seemed almost subdued by comparison.

"How does it feel to be a walking dead man?" she asked.

"I'm still scared," he answered.

She nodded grimly. "You ought to be. Well, I tried to tell you how it would be, but you and that fool Fargo were too smart. In case you haven't figured it out, you're just plain lucky to be alive. I didn't think Ruth would pull it off."

"You watched it?"

"Sure, I watched it. I watch everything around Redwall. That's why I'm here."

He motioned to a chair and sat down on the bed. He still didn't see where she fitted or what she was working for. He said: "Let's hear that talk you want to make."

She dropped into the chair, her shoulders slack. "Maybe you've learned something, if you're as sharp as Wade thinks you are. You'd better believe me this time. Get out of here, now! Fargo will get himself shot full of holes, but it won't be any great loss."

Rick shook his head. "I'm leaving in the morning."

"You're leaving now, friend. I know what's going on around here. I've got big ears. I poke into everybody's business. If I get caught, Jason Galt will hang me like he aimed to hang you." She shrugged. "Only I'll be leaving before long, too."

He gestured impatiently.

She smiled grimly. "I hate myself, Marvin. Funny what a woman will do for a man. Likewise it's funny how you can change your mind after you're here and you see what these people are like. Some of them had a meeting tonight, just a few of the hare-brained fools who will follow Galt to hell-an'-gone. Galt still aims to hang you, and with level-headed men like Clarke and Bert somewhere else, he'll do it if you stay. Galt still yaps about striking for home and liberty."

"I'll stay till Fargo goes," Rick said stubbornly.

She threw up her hands. "He's in the saloon taking all the settler money he can and getting drunk. You're worth saving. He isn't. You see, I know Wade Verling very well, Marvin. I'm quoting him."

"Damn it," Rick said angrily, "where do you fit into this business?"

She folded her hands, sitting motionless for a long moment, her eyes fixed thoughtfully on him. Finally she said: "I'll tell you something that nobody knows but me and Wade. I'm going to marry him. Fact is, we'd be married now if he hadn't seen this was his trouble spot and sent me up here to find out what was going on. Not Charley Williams's version, but the truth. I've got it, but I haven't the proof I need. That's why I've been hanging on."

He said: "Why?"

"Williams is the snake in the brush," she said savagely. "Williams is filling his pocket with rental money, and I've got a hunch it stays right in his pocket. He uses Estey to keep some of the settlers scared. The ones down the river don't have any gumption, and they're paying rent to the Grant Company. The rest of them, the ones you saw with Galt today, won't pay anything. They think fighting's the answer, so they hang on. I've written to Wade, but you know how he is. Once he's hired a man, he hates to admit he made a mistake."

Rick nodded, knowing that what she said was true. "Maybe Williams keeps things stirred up so Verling won't think he's collecting anything."

She said: "You catch on fast, friend. It's my hunch Williams is about ready to pull out with his pockets full of Grant *dinero,* and I don't know how to stop him. Funny thing, Marvin. These settlers hate me, but I like them. The ones around here . . . not the yellow bellies down the river who've kowtowed to Williams. I don't like any man who won't fight for what's his." She shook her head, smiling a little. "I even like that crazy Jason Galt. Doesn't make sense, does it? I'll bet old Moses was a lot like Galt when he was leading the children of Israel out of the land of bondage."

"Why don't you get Verling up here, and we'll talk to him?" Rick asked.

"I aim to. It's time we hung Williams with his own rope. These are real folks, Marvin, and they're getting a rough deal. I want Wade to see how it is with them." She got up. "Not that you can blame these people. I've watched them

57

fret and stew about what the Grant will do next. The way they figure, the devil is the Grant. Williams and Wade and you . . . anybody else who's hooked up with the Grant . . . are working for the devil. That's why they hate me. They think I'm a Grant spy, and I am, but what they don't know is that I'm starting to see it their way."

Rick rose and re-buckled his gun belt around him. "I'll go get Fargo and we'll travel."

She had moved to the window and raised the blind. "Maybe it's too late."

He came to stand beside her, hearing the thud of hoofs. He could see dark shadows moving along the road in front of the hotel.

"Now what in hell do you suppose they're up to?" she asked.

Rick heard the door open and spun toward it, hand sweeping downward to gun butt. Then it fell away. It was Pete Fargo who had come in.

The gunman had been drinking. He swayed in the doorway, his eyes on the woman. He said: "Well, I'll be damned."

"Throw a loop over your tongue, Pete," Rick said evenly.

"I ain't throwing a loop on my tongue," the gunman said savagely. "This has been a long time coming, mister, a damned long time. I was afraid you'd go soft, talking about that Mex like you did. Wouldn't quit your job when the chips were down, you said."

"I didn't. I ain't quitting till we get to town tomorrow."

"So you figure you'll quit tomorrow?" Fargo's lips were slack. His left hand trembled as he wiped it across his forehead. "Now why would you be quitting, bucko? The pay's still good."

Fargo was as drunk as Rick had ever seen him. He had often said: "A man who lives by the gun ain't got no more business with whisky than he has using his fists on somebody's jaw."

"Yeah, the pay's good," Rick said, "but I've had enough of it."

Fargo took a step forward. "You know something, son? You're the first hairpin who ever stuck a gun in my direction and lived. I didn't like that."

"You know where you'd be if I hadn't?" Rick demanded.

"I ain't talking about that. I'm talking about you shoving your cutter at me. I don't stand for that from nobody. You double-crossed me. If you'd stood up there and used a little hot lead on that bunch, they'd have run like rabbits."

Sparky whirled toward him. "You're talking like a fool, Fargo. Those boys don't run like rabbits. You might have downed a few, and then they'd have blown you over the range in a dozen places."

"Why, hell, they're just sodbusters, ain't they?"

"No, they're more than that," Rick said. "The way Galt had them worked up, they'd have kept coming if we'd made every slug count. If you could think straight, you'd see that I saved your life."

"That's right," Sparky said. "Now quit your yapping, Fargo. Marvin saved your ornery hide, and that's all there is to it." She turned her back to the window and swore softly. "Well, they did it."

"What?" Rick asked.

"They've burned my cabin. Now Duff Estey will have himself a time rounding up the bunch that did it. That fool Galt played right into Charley Williams's hand. They'll fill the jail in Stone Saddle, and Williams will convince a few more they'd better start paying rent."

Rick looked over her shoulder at the red pillar of flame, the hope that he could do something with Wade Verling dying in him at the same time. Even if Verling were a less stubborn man, he would find it hard to believe anything good about the people who would commit this lawless act against Sparky Hogan.

Fargo had come to the window. He stood motionless, breathing hard, shocked sober by what he saw. He said: "Maybe they ain't like rabbits at that. I didn't think they'd do anything after the way the Dallam girl curried their hides."

"I had some nice things there," Sparky said in a low tone. "I'd done a lot of sewing for the house Wade was going to buy for us in Raton. It's gone now."

Rick shook her shoulder. "Why did Galt do that?"

"I told you what they thought of me. They aim to clean anybody out that they think is on the side of the Grant. Next they'll come here and tear this hotel apart trying to find you."

"You can't stay here," Rick said.

"No, not if I want to live long enough to marry the boss."

Wheeling, Rick blew out the lamp. "Come on. We'll saddle up and hit the dirt."

"I can't go," Sparky said. "My horse is in my shed."

"We'll take Ruth's."

"No. Jason would make horse-stealing out of it. Anyhow, Ruth may need her horse. I'll stay and take my medicine."

"Now who's being the fool?" Rick pushed her toward the window. "I'll take you up behind me."

"I ain't running . . . ," Fargo began.

"I'd think you'd had enough of a taste of a rope," Rick said. "Come on!"

"Yeah, maybe I did, but I'm coming back."

"I aim to be back, too," Rick said grimly, "just to see if I can pound some sense into Galt's head."

They went out through the window, Rick first, then Sparky, and Fargo, still grumbling. They skirted the pool of light falling from a back window of the hotel, and ran toward the shed.

"There's a lantern inside," Sparky said. "Wait. I'll find it."

Rick paused in the doorway, hearing nothing. He shut the door as Fargo lighted the lantern. Quickly Rick and Fargo threw saddles on their horses. Fargo stepped up, saying impatiently: "Let's slope out of here."

The door squeaked, and Rick jumped away from his horse, pulling gun and letting it drop back when he saw it was Ruth. Sparky blew the lantern out an instant later, saying angrily: "Damn it, Ruth, do you want that bunch to know we're pulling out?"

"I didn't know," Ruth said. "I heard someone out here. I came to see who it was."

Rick led his horse from the barn, Sparky following. She said: "You saw what they did, didn't you?"

"Yes," Ruth said tonelessly. "I should have had Bert and Clarke stay here tonight. I didn't think Jason would do anything else."

"He'll keep doing this kind of thing till he's dead," Sparky said grimly, "and I'm thinking that won't be long the way he's going. Let's ride, Marvin."

Rick said: "Just a minute." He stood in front of Ruth, thinking of a dozen things he wanted to tell her. He put his hands on her shoulders. "I'm coming back."

"There's a trail back of the shed that circles the settlement. It joins the road below here a piece."

"I know about it," Sparky said. "You're wasting time, Marvin."

Rick could not say to Ruth what was on his mind. A man had to prove himself before he could tell a girl he loved her, and she had every reason to distrust him. She had asked for his help, but there might be nothing he could do for her.

Then she was in his arms. He never knew exactly how it happened, but her arms were around his neck, her lips seeking his. As long as Rick Marvin lived, there would be no greater moment than this. For those seconds he forgot himself, forgot his resolution to wait until he had proved to her that he was something more than a leather slapper with a rented gun.

But finally Rick let Ruth go, saying softly: "I'll come back soon, I hope. I'll see Verling. I . . . well, I didn't aim to do that. Not until I could bring you some kind of help."

"You have," she said simply. "You've given me hope."

She ran back to the hotel. Someone was yelling: "Ruth! Where in blazes are you, Ruth?"

Sparky whispered fiercely: "Now will you move?"

Rick gave her a hand up and swung into the saddle. She put her arms around his waist, and it was only then that he sensed the fear that gripped her, fear that must have been in her all these months as she had watched this trouble come to a head.

She said: "The trail's straight ahead. Take it slow."

Rick reined into the opening in the pines, Fargo falling in behind. The darkness was complete then, for the trail narrowed as it swung toward the hill to the north. There was no sound but the thud of hoofs in the pine needles and the soft whisper of the wind in the treetops.

Presently the pines thinned, and the trail curled southward toward the road. For a time the lights in the hotel and the fire from Sparky's cabin had been lost to sight. Now Rick could see them again. He reined up, saying softly: "Wait, Pete." They sat listening, but there was no sound that indicated the presence of any of Galt's men.

"It isn't far," Sparky said. "The road's just yonder."

Rick sat his saddle, hardly aware of Sparky's tight arms around him. It seemed to him that, if Galt had really planned to take Fargo and him tonight, he would probably have put guards here on this trail, or at least in the road. But Sparky might have been wrong. Perhaps the burning of the cabin was no more than a warning.

"All right," Rick called in a low tone to Fargo.

They went onto the road, still walking their horses. Then, with no warning, a man yelled: "They're here, Jason." Before the echo of his shout had died, a gun cracked, the bullet snapping past not a foot from Rick's head.

VI

Rick's action was instinctive. He cracked steel to his horse, calling to Sparky to hang on. Other settlers back along the road had taken up the cry. There was a moment of confusion, for there seemed to be no organization among Galt's men, nor did Rick hear the preacher's commanding voice above the others.

Fargo swept by, shouting derisively: "You'd better dust, son!" There was more firing behind them, wild bullets that sang harmlessly through the night. Rick didn't return the fire, for he wasn't one to waste lead, and any shooting he did would give the settlers a target. Besides, he had Sparky Hogan to look out for.

After two miles Rick began to hope there would be no pursuit and pulled his horse down. Burdened double, the animal could not hold this pace. There was no sound of Fargo's horse. He would be far ahead by now, a fact that brought disappointment to Rick. He had no illusions about the gunman. Their differences would be settled with powder smoke, but as long as they were in enemy territory, they should have stood together.

Sparky had not relaxed her grip around Rick's middle. She asked worriedly: "You think they've quit?"

"Dunno," he said. "How far are we from the line?"

"Ten miles or more," she answered. "We'll be safe then."

Rick laughed shortly. "I ain't sure about that. Jason Galt's behind us, and Charley Williams and Duff Estey are ahead. It's going to take a pile of funerals for anybody to be safe hereabouts."

It was after midnight now. They rode on through the darkness, the river making its steady growl to their right. They came to a Mexican plaza, the adobe houses indistinct shadows between them and the Purgatory. A dog barked, a high yap that stretched Rick's nerves a little tighter. A door was flung open, and lamplight washed across the bare yard. A man stepped from the house and moved quickly out of the pool of light. In one quick glimpse Rick saw that he carried a Winchester.

"These are the Grant people," Sparky said. "Some have come in the last year or so, and the rest have been here almost as long as the Dallams have been at Redwall. All of them have either bought land, or pay rent to the Grant."

"That hairpin must be a little worried," Rick said.

"They all are. They're not fighters. Peace is all they want. Galt's been talking about chasing them across the line. If it comes to that, Wade won't be selling any more

Grant land in the East. People will buy land, but they don't want to buy a fight with it."

Rick thought about that, seeing in it a point that Wade Verling could not overlook. The Grant must make money to survive. It was conducting an expensive selling campaign in the East, and had been for more than a year. A bloody fight here on the Purgatory, making headlines in the Eastern newspapers, would go a long way toward cooling off prospective buyers. That may well have been the thought in Jason Galt's mind.

Sparky's arms tightened convulsively around Rick. "Horses," she whispered.

He reined up, hearing the drum of hoofs on the road behind them and knowing that his horse did not have another hard run in him. He asked: "You know the man we saw back there?"

"Pablo García. He's the most important man in San Marcos."

Rick swung his horse back toward the plaza. Sparky's fingers dug into his hard middle. She cried out: "Marvin, what are you going to do?"

"Go back. We can't outrun them."

"García can't help. He wouldn't dare. Have you gone crazy, Marvin?"

"I reckon. But it's the only thing we can do. Verling won't listen to anybody if you get shot."

"But these people won't fight, I tell you."

"Maybe you'll be surprised."

He put his horse into a run, momentary panic striking at him. They were finished if he didn't beat Galt's men to the plaza. The low bulk of the adobe houses appeared directly ahead of them; the long finger of lamplight still lay like a yellow pool on the yard. The dog renewed his frantic yappings, others joining in.

"Don't shoot, García!" Rick called.

He reined his horse around to the dark side of García's house. He swung down, pulled Sparky after him, and lunged around the corner of the building. García was crouched there, his Winchester covering them. Galt's men were close now, so close that there was no time for argument.

"Who is it?" García asked.

"I'm a Grant man. Anybody inside?"

"I'm alone."

Rick pushed Sparky toward the door. "Get inside. Blow out the lamp."

"What is this, *señor?*" García demanded. "We want no trouble."

Sparky slipped past him into the house, and, when the lamp died, Rick said: "Friend, you've got trouble. That's Galt's bunch coming."

"You brought them?" García cried.

Galt's men had thundered up. They stopped in front of the house, vague blurs in the blackness, the air heavy with the dust their horses had kicked up. Leather squeaked as riders shifted in saddles. There was this moment of indecision, then a man called: "García, are you hiding Rick Marvin?"

Rick crouched against the adobe wall, uncertain what turn this would take. Chasing a man on the run was one thing; digging a badger out of his hole was something else. If Galt was with them, they'd come after him, but it was Rick's guess that Galt was not there, or he would have been the one to call out. There was a slim chance he could bluff them, and he made his play that way.

Rick said: "I'm here, but nobody's hiding me." His six-gun was in his hand. He cocked it now, the sound an ominous click in the stillness. "Vamoose, the whole damned bunch of you."

Still they hesitated, caught between their fear of him and the orders Jason Galt had given them. The silence was tight and oppressive. There was not even the squeak of saddle leather. Then, without warning, a gun spoke. It was the signal that touched off the explosion.

Rick had no choice now. Still crouched against the building, he gave his answer in lead, spacing his shots so closely that they made one continuous roll of sound, every bullet ripping into that mass of men and horses. Instantly Galt's men were thrown into confusion.

It was over as suddenly as it had begun. Galt's men broke and fled back along the road to Redwall. They kept up a sporadic fire for a time as they raced away, aimless shooting that was a waste of bullets. Rick reloaded his gun, holding his position against the wall until the firing stopped and the drum of flying hoofs had died to the west.

"All right, García?" Rick asked.

"*Sí*, I am all right. And you?"

"Fitter'n a fiddle string. Well, looks like they didn't have the belly for hot lead they thought they did. Light the lamp. There won't be no more trouble."

García went into the house. A moment later, Rick heard the sputter of a match as it flamed to life. He moved through the door as García lighted the lamp. Replacing the chimney, he flashed a smile at Rick, white teeth gleaming in the lamplight.

"I am happy to meet you, *Señor* Marvin. Juan Sandoval has written about you. He counts you as a friend, and Juan's friend is my friend."

García held out his hand. Rick took it, instinctively

67

liking this man, as he had liked Sandoval. "Funny, running into somebody up here who knows Juan."

"Not funny, *señor*. All of us in San Marcos know him. We wanted him to come north with us, but he is stubborn. He would stay where he was and fight the Grant." García shook his head. "She is no good, fighting the Grant."

"Juan lost his place," Rick said, "just before I came north."

García's brown face was now without its smile. He stroked his black mustache, eyes showing the hurt that Rick's words had brought to him. He said: "I had not heard."

Others, aroused by the firing, had come to stand in the yard in front of García's door. They formed a half circle at the edge of the lamplight, silent men, frightened and uneasy.

"It was a fool thing, you coming back here," Sparky said, motioning to the men outside. "You know what you've done to them?"

"I know what may happen," Rick said somberly. "I hope to hell I can stop it."

García was speaking to his neighbors in Spanish, telling them to go back to bed, that there would be no more trouble. Slowly they faded into the darkness, obeying without argument.

When they had gone, Rick said: "I'm sorry I brought this onto you, García, but there wasn't much else I could do. From what Missus Hogan tells me, you'd had some trouble with the upriver bunch before."

"Threats, *amigo*," García said. "So far that is all, but now they will come again."

"If they do, tell 'em I'm to blame for what happened tonight."

"I will tell them. But that Galt,"—García shook his

68

head—"he is a wild man."

"Keep guards out. Don't let them surprise you." Rick paused, searching for the right words to say what must be said, for he was remembering Sparky had told him that these people wanted nothing but peace. He said slowly: "García, sometimes a man has to fight for what is his."

"That is true, *señor,* but with us it is strange. We have paid our *dinero* to the Grant, so we will have no more trouble that way." He motioned toward Redwall. "There is our trouble. We have not slept well for a long time."

"You may still have trouble with the Grant," Rick said bluntly. "I've got a hunch Charley Williams stuck your money into his own pocket. Did he give you any receipts?"

"Receipts?" García stared at him blankly. "*Señor* Williams said nothing about receipts. I saw him write it down in a book. He said we are not to pay again until next year."

Rick swung to Sparky. "What kind of proof have you got that Williams ain't turning this money over?"

"Proof? I don't need any. I know how much Wade's been getting, and I know everybody in the lower valley has paid. Add it up and it makes a pile. Where did it go if Williams didn't steal it?"

"Looks to me like Verling had better talk to these people, just the same." Rick turned back to García. "If we get Verling up here to see you, will you tell him what you've told me?"

"*Sí, señor,*" García said, puzzled, "but I don't understand."

"We'll iron this out if we have to get Williams's scalp to do it. I'll tell the sheriff what happened, so it'll be up to him to give you protection." He jerked his head at Sparky. "Let's drift."

Rick led his horse to the front of the house. He helped

Sparky up and swung aboard. García stood in the doorway, the lamp throwing his long shadow into the yard. For a moment Rick looked at the man's dark face, heavy with trouble, and he felt the weight of a new burden.

"Keep a guard out," Rick warned again.

"We will," García said gravely. *"Buenas noches."*

"So long," Rick said, and rode away into the darkness.

There was little talk between Rick and Sparky Hogan. They rode slowly, the miles falling behind with the hours, and presently gray light began showing in the east. The valley had widened out, and now the ridge lines were distinct on both sides of the river. Another hour brought them to Stone Saddle.

It was full daylight when they swung across the river to the sleeping town, hoofs cracking sharply upon the plank floor of the bridge. Rick turned up Main Street and reined in to the stable where he and Fargo had left their horses when they had first ridden into Stone Saddle.

Dismounting, Rick held up his hands for Sparky. She dropped to the ground, and, if it had not been for Rick's grip, she would have fallen. She swayed uncertainly, and by the thin light washing in through the open door he saw how completely weary she was.

Rick stripped his horse and rubbed him down. "Give him a double feeding of oats," he told the sleep-eyed hostler who had shuffled down the runway. Then Rick walked out to where Sparky was waiting for him.

"They'll have good beds at the Commercial House," she said.

Nodding, he turned with her along the walk. Rick had been giving thought to her position with Verling all the way from San Marcos, and he wasn't sure that Verling would believe either Sparky or Pablo García unless there was some solid proof to back them. Verling would hate to admit he'd been mistaken.

They crossed to the hotel, the street still muddy from the rain, and signed the register. The night clerk pushed two keys across the desk. "Your usual room, Missus Hogan." He nodded at Rick. "Number Twenty-Four."

They went up the stairs and along the hall until they reached Sparky's room. She unlocked the door and, turning, leaned against the jamb, her shoulders slack. He thought how completely he had misjudged her at first. He knew now that she was inherently fine and honest, and that both his and her happiness depended upon what happened within the next few hours.

"Don't have trouble with Fargo," she said. "Wade needs you. Integrity is something the Grant can't buy."

"I'll handle Fargo," he said, and turned away.

"Rick." When he swung back, she said: "Wade lives for the Grant. I know that anything I can give him is incidental, but for his own good I've got to show him he can't keep on pushing. If I can make him see that, there will be a big place for you with the Grant."

"No, I'm done with the Grant," Rick said, and walked away.

He found his room, went in, and locked the door. Taking off his hat, coat, and gun belt, he fell across the bed. For a moment he laid there, his body aching with weariness. He thought of Ruth, of the unspoken promise her lips had given him, and he found peace in that thought. Then he slept.

VII

It was mid-afternoon when Rick woke. He lay motionless for a time, fighting the need for more sleep. He knew he should get up, but he found no reason great enough to bring him upright. Then someone knocked at his door.

Rick swung his feet to the floor, wondering if this were Fargo. He buckled his gun belt around him, unlocked the door, and pulled it open. Sparky Hogan came in without invitation, saying irritably: "You must have been the sleepiest man in Colorado."

He yawned. "I reckon."

"Heaven and hell may wait for you while you sleep, but a woman won't. We're eating breakfast."

Moving to the window, she stood with the sun directly across her shapely body. She had changed to a tailored black suit; her red hair was pulled back from her forehead and softly plaited behind her head. In Rick Marvin's eyes, she was an attractive and thoroughly desirable woman.

He poured water into the cracked basin on the pine bureau. He said: "You know, Wade Verling is a lucky man."

"You can tell him that," she said gravely. "He'll be here tonight. His train gets in about midnight."

"You wired him?"

She nodded. "I just got his answer. I don't think he's very happy about coming."

Rick washed, and combed his hair. Still facing the fly-specked mirror, he said: "You can tell me it ain't none of my business, but how'd you get to be Missus Hogan?"

"By marrying Mike Hogan. My family history is short and not very sweet. Mike was a leather slapper, and a lot like Pete Fargo. He was shot two years ago in Las Vegas,

72

and I'll admit I didn't shed a tear when they planted him."

Rick put on his hat. "That why you don't like leather slappers?"

"I didn't say I didn't like them. It's what's inside a man that counts. Mike just walked through one empty day after another." She moved to the door. "Come on."

"A mite late for breakfast," Rick said as he locked his door. "I'll just skip it and have two dinners."

They went down the stairs and across the lobby to the dining room. As they took a table near a window, Rick said: "Say, I've got to tell Combs to get some men to San Marcos."

"He's out of town," Sparky said. "Left early this morning. There was a killing down the river."

Rick swore softly. "I wonder . . . ?"

Sparky nodded. "So do I. Now Estey's the law, and Charley Williams can call the turn."

Rick stared unseeingly at the menu, bitter disappointment in him. Lee Combs was not a strong man, but Rick judged him to be an honest one. With Major Dallam gone, Combs was the only one who might keep Jason Galt from making some wild and senseless play that would throw the law against the settlers. Burning Sparky's cabin was bad enough. A massacre of innocent people at San Marcos would wipe out the last thin chance of keeping peace.

A waitress took their order and disappeared through the swinging door. Rick rubbed his face, the sickness of impending failure crawling into him. "Damn it, I don't know what to do. Maybe I'd better hightail back to San Marcos."

Sparky shook her head. "If anything would make Galt go clear off his nut, your being there would do the job." She glanced at the lobby door and quickly brought her eyes to Rick. "We've got company. Take it easy."

Charley Williams and Pete Fargo had come into the dining room. Seeing Sparky, Williams came toward her, ignoring Rick. Fargo paced beside him in his cat-like way.

Rick settled back his chair and waited, meeting Fargo's cool stare. He said: "You missed a good fight last night, Pete."

Fargo grinned. He was freshly shaved and had bought a new shirt. His pearl-colored Stetson had been brushed and was cocked at a rakish angle. His china-blue eyes were faintly mocking as he asked: "Needed some help, did you?"

"We made out."

"Missus Hogan," Williams said sharply, "you undertook a certain task in Redwall."

"That's right," she agreed.

"Well, you failed miserably," he said angrily. "Not once have you brought me any vital information concerning the settlers' plans. Now your presence here is a danger to us. I'm asking you to leave the country. If you will come to my office, I'll pay you whatever you have coming. I refuse to have anyone working out of my office who disregards my authority to the extent of wiring Verling to come here to investigate my actions."

"That's what makes me dangerous, isn't it, Williams? Well, keep your money. I'm staying."

"How'd you find out about that wire, Charley?" Rick asked.

"My business," Williams answered stiffly. "I understand you've quit the Grant, Marvin."

"Not exactly. I'll make my report to Verling."

"If he comes," Williams said.

"He'll be here. Or maybe you didn't know about his wire to Missus Hogan."

"I knew about it, but I think Missus Hogan will see the

74

light. If she wants to stay in the Grant's employ, she'll send another wire telling Verling she was mistaken."

"You're all balled up, Charley," Rick said testily. "First you tell her she's fired. Now you say she can keep her job. Make up your mind."

"It's made up," Williams snapped. "If she doesn't keep Verling out of Stone Saddle, she is fired. Savvy?"

"I savvy," Sparky said, "but your bluff isn't good enough."

For a moment Williams stood there, short legs spread, his mouth pursed.

"We might as well drift, Charley," Fargo said.

"I'm wondering about one thing, Pete," Rick said. "You've always been a smart *hombre,* full of talk about being on the right side of the big fellows. Charley's finished, you know. How come you're stringing along with him?"

Fargo gave him a thin smile. "Charley ain't finished. You're the gent who's got his money on the wrong horse." The smile fled, leaving his face barren and ugly. "Gonna be around for a while?"

Rick had never been able to read the gunman's face, and he could not now, but he sensed what was in the man's mind. Fargo never forgot a debt, nor did he like to harbor a doubt about another man's gun speed being greater than his own. Fargo was wondering whether the test should come now.

"I'll be around," Rick said as Fargo and Williams turned to leave.

Sparky drummed her fingers on the table, suddenly thoughtful. "I've been wondering how Williams knew about my wire. Duff Estey was in the street when I went to the telegraph office. He must have got a copy of the wire I sent, and one of Wade's answer."

Rick nodded. "I reckon it was that way."

Sparky leaned forward. "Why is Fargo so sure Williams isn't finished?"

"I don't know," he lied.

He looked away, unable to meet her eyes. He could not tell her that Fargo was certain Verling would continue to believe Williams no matter what Sparky said. But he doubted that Sparky Hogan was fooled.

It was nearly five o'clock when Rick finished his meal and left the dining room. He stood on the spur-scarred walk in front of the hotel while he rolled and fired a cigarette. Stone Saddle, soaking-wet the day before, now steamed under a harsh sun. The puddles were gone from the street, and the mud was crusting over.

There were few people on the boardwalks, few horses and rigs racked along the street. It was, Rick thought, as if people sensed the impending trouble and were staying under cover until it came to a head. An idea stirred in his mind, and he turned toward the nearest livery stable. There were three stables in town. He asked in each if Charley Williams kept a horse there. He had his answer in the third one. "You bet he does." The liveryman jabbed a thumb at the fifth stall. "That bay gelding yonder. Fastest animal on the Purgatory."

The bay was a trim, leggy animal with the lines of a race horse. He would be, Rick thought, as fast as the stableman said.

"Heard he had a fast horse," Rick said. "Wonder what he wants for him?"

"Hell, he wouldn't sell. I know for a fact he's turned down some mighty good offers."

"I reckon he's got a good thing, racing him against every cowhand who comes through who thinks he's got a fast animal."

The stableman shook his head. "That's a funny thing. Far as I know Charley ain't ever put that bay in a race. Why he keeps him is a mystery to me."

"Yeah, does seem funny. Well, won't hurt to ask Williams what he'll take for him."

"You're wasting your wind, friend."

Rick grinned. "You never know," he said, and turned back through the archway.

Charley Williams was not a sporting man who went in for horse races. Now that Rick had established that, there was only one answer to the mystery of why Williams kept a fast horse. He was prepared for flight, if the time came when he was certain his goose had laid her last golden egg.

The question now was whether Williams would find enough strength in Fargo's backing to see this through, or whether he'd be content with what he had and make a run for it. Rick walked slowly, thinking about it. Then he saw Ruth Dallam ride out of the street that led to the depot. She was the last person he expected to see, for he had supposed she would stay in Redwall, doing whatever she could do to block Jason Galt.

She saw him, too, and brought her horse to a faster pace. Rick ran toward her, thinking of a dozen things that might have happened, all of them bad. She reined up when she reached him, asking worriedly: "Are you all right, Rick?"

"Sure. What fetched you to town?"

"I wanted to know about you. You must have used a

shotgun on those men at San Marcos last night. There were five in the bunch, and four of them were hit."

"Any of them bad?"

She shook her head. "They'll be all right, but they'll be in bed a while."

"They had no business chasing us," he said defensively. "What do you think Verling would do if Sparky had been shot?"

"I'm not blaming you," she said quickly. "But it's bad because it gives Jason the talking point he's been looking for."

"What's he going to do?"

"He's got the settlers behind him again," she said hopelessly. "They'll come down the river and drive García and his people off the Grant. He swears he'll hang any of them that resist."

Rick's eyes looked into the girl's dark ones; he saw the misery that was in her. Her lips, that had held a warm smile for him, were now pressed into a thin line. She said: "Oh, Rick, I don't know. I just don't know. I tried to talk to them, but what could I say that would mean anything, after they had seen the men you'd shot?"

Angry words formed in his mind, but he did not give voice to them. There was nothing he could say. Right or wrong, the shooting at San Marcos had done exactly what Ruth said it had. "I wish your dad was here," Rick said.

"He will be. I was just down at the telegraph office. His train gets in at six." She shook her head. "But it's too late for him to do any good. We lost our suit, and that was our last chance."

He knew, then, why she had lost hope. Even though she had not really expected to win the lawsuit, it had been a thin reed that she had held to, the one thing which could have proved to the settlers that Jason Galt's way was wrong.

"I'm sorry," Rick said. "I ain't sure it's too late for him to do any good, though. Maybe he can stop Galt. If he can't, I will."

"You can't stop them now."

"They'll be stopped," he said grimly. "I don't aim to let no long-tongued preacher drive the San Marcos people out of their homes on account of something I did." He looked at his watch. "That train's getting in pretty quick. I'll be at the depot to meet your dad."

She straightened as if his words had revived hope in her. "I was hoping you would. That's why I came uptown to find you. I wanted to see you. Then when I did, I couldn't bring myself to ask you." She bit her lip, hesitating, and then said: "He won't like you, Rick. Not at first."

"Maybe not, but he'll listen. Now you get back to the depot. I've got a chore to do. I'll be there before six."

He swung away, not looking back, and turned down Bridge Street toward the sheriff's office. If Combs were back, there might still be a chance. But the sheriff was not there. Duff Estey sat in Combs's swivel chair, his feet crossed on the spur-scarred desk, a neat bandage on his battered nose.

Estey rose when he saw Rick, right hand dropping to gun butt. He said: "If you're looking for trouble, Marvin, you sure as hell came to the right place."

"I've got plenty of trouble. Where's Combs?"

"He rode out this morning."

"When do you expect him?"

"How the hell would I know?"

Estey grinned at Rick, a wicked grin that invited trouble. Probably the only thing holding him back was Williams's order to avoid trouble. That would be Williams's way, to let this play out until Jason Galt had enough rope to hang himself.

Rick took a long breath, knowing what he must do. He could not let the San Marcos people be sacrificed. He told Estey what had happened the night before and what Galt aimed to do. He said then: "I promised García the sheriff would protect him. Since Combs ain't here, you'll have to do it."

Estey burst into a booming laugh. "Marvin, you sure played hell, didn't you? I'll take care of San Marcos, and, when Galt shows up, I'll take care of him. Williams figgered that them burning Missus Hogan's cabin would make Combs do something, but this is even better. I won't have to wait on Combs."

Rick heard the long shriek of a train whistle, muted by distance. He swung toward the door, then paused when Estey said: "Don't you come messing around San Marcos, and don't figger on Verling pulling you out of a hole. You dug the hole, and afore I'm done, I'll shovel the dirt in on top of you."

Rick went out and took the street to the depot, wondering what lay behind Estey's threat. Williams and Fargo and Estey were far surer than they had any right to be. Verling was proud, stubborn, and unreasonable, but he was smart. There was a chance he'd see through them, a chance he'd believe Sparky Hogan and Pablo García.

Then Rick had a sudden thought and stopped, jarred by its impact. Suppose they met Verling at the depot? Suppose they never gave him a chance to listen to Sparky and García? If he disappeared, it would be weeks, or months, before the Grant stockholders appointed another general manager. Williams's goose could go on laying its golden eggs indefinitely.

Again the train whistle pierced the evening stillness, and Rick went on, running now. He swung around the depot, saw Ruth, and went to her. There was another horse racked beside hers, and, when he came up, she said: "I got Dad's horse out of the stable. We'll start for San Marcos right away."

The train came in, the engine snorting as steam hissed and smoke rolled out in a dark smelly cloud. Ruth cried— "There he is!"—and ran to her father.

Rick waited until they came over to him. Ed Dallam was heavily built, but with no fat on him. His eyes, shadowed by black brows, were dark and piercing; his mustache and short beard were black and wire-stiff. He carried his dignity as easily as Ruth carried her grace and beauty. Ed Dallam had a natural capacity for leadership, but he was not burdened by the fanaticism that was so much a part of Jason Galt.

"Dad," Ruth was saying, "I want you to meet Rick Marvin."

Dallam hesitated, his eyes reflecting the dislike that Rick's name aroused in him. "Marvin? What's a Grant gunman doing here with you?"

Rick said quietly: "I'm not with the Grant now. Leastwise not with Charley Williams."

"Rick isn't like Pete Fargo," Ruth said quickly. "He's . . . well, he's fine and good." Suddenly she took Rick's hand. "Dad, we love each other."

Major Ed Dallam looked for a moment as if he were going to choke. Before he could say anything, Rick put his arm around Ruth. His voice was more defiant than he intended when he said: "You've heard some lies about me, I reckon. We'll talk about them later, but right now you've got a job. Ruth can tell you what's happened while you're riding to San Marcos."

"Hell's bells, I'm going to eat supper before I ride any-where!" Dallam shouted indignantly. "As for my girl loving a gunslinger. . . ."

"Dad!" Ruth cried.

"You can say what you've got to say later," Rick said sharply. "Right now your job is to stop Galt. He's fetching a bunch of your settlers downriver to wipe San Marcos out. I told Estey. . . ."

"Estey?" Dallam scowled. "Nobody but Charley Williams trusts that ornery pup. Where's Combs?"

"He ain't in town. I told Estey because he's all the law there is. He said he'd fix Galt, which I reckon he will if you don't stop him."

"That fool Galt," Dallam said irritably. "Estey will make up a posse of all the thugs he can pick up in the dives of Stone Saddle. It'll be a massacre."

"You haven't got time to stand and augur about it," Rick said impatiently. "You've got to stop Galt before he does something that makes outlaws out of your settlers. Verling's coming in on the night train. I've got a hunch Williams aims to get him before he has a chance to hear what we've got to say, so I'm going up to Meridian and take him off the train."

"Rick, you can't do that." Ruth faced him, very pale. "They'll kill you."

He gave her a little shove. "Go along with your father, Ruth."

Still Dallam hesitated, dark eyes filled with resentment. "So help me, I never thought I'd see the day when a gun-slinger would order me around."

"Damn it," Rick shouted, "I'm doing all I can to save your hides! Handling Galt is your chore."

They went then. He watched until they disappeared.

VIII

Rick ate supper with Sparky. He wasn't hungry, but there was an hour to kill and he wanted to tell Sparky what he aimed to do. Williams would certainly make no move to leave town until it was dark. If he actually held the same confidence that seemed to be in Duff Estey and Pete Fargo, he might stay and play it out. But he was a coward, and a coward's way was to run.

Sparky listened, nodding somber agreement. Meridian was the first station above Stone Saddle. The train would make a brief stop there.

"I hadn't thought of it," Sparky said, "but murder would be the easiest way out for them."

"I figured on taking him off the train," Rick said, "but it would sure go against his grain if I used a gun on him. I guess I'd better just get on and talk to him."

She nodded again. "You think Williams has the money in the Grant office or his house?"

"It should be one place or the other. I'll watch the office. You watch his house. If he fetches his horse, you get over and tell me. I'll be in the alley."

She drank her coffee, frowning as she thought this over. "I'd have time. His house is just a block from the Grant office."

Rick rose. "If he's gonna make a break, he'll be jumpy as hell. Be careful."

"Go on," she said. "I want to go up to my room, but I won't be long."

Rick left the hotel, swinging sharply to get out of the light. It was almost dark now, with only a faint glow in the western sky, but lamplight fell in irregular pools from open doors and windows. He hugged the walls of the buildings, walking rapidly, and turned into the first alley. Anyone watching would have seen him, but the street seemed deserted.

A moment later Rick reached the back of the Grant office. There he hunkered in the weeds. A slow hour dragged by, and then another. Rick was never one to wait, and now he found it torture. There was one weakness in his plan, and the more he thought about it, the bigger it seemed to be. He would have to leave town about eleven to reach Meridian before Verling's train got in, and it was possible that Williams would wait until after that to make his flight.

One by one the house lights died. Overhead stars burned in a tall black sky. The town quieted. The heat of the day was gone, and a chill, pine-scented wind ran across the valley, whispered around the eaves of the buildings, and rustled the dry grass. Then, before Rick knew anyone was in the Grant office, a thin line of lamplight showed around the green shade of the one window in the rear wall.

Rick moved silently to the window, but he found that the shade fitted so closely that he could see only a small part of Williams's office. He heard desk drawers open, the clink of gold, the drawers being slammed shut. A sense of triumph set his heart pounding. He'd guessed right. He'd have the deadwood on Williams when the man left the office.

The lamp died, and Rick heard Williams shut the door into his private office. He was going out through the front, the way he'd come in. Rick raced around the building, stumbled in the darkness, caught himself, and went on. He reached the front just as Williams was locking the door.

The Grant man heard Rick and whirled. The light was very dim, but Rick caught the movement of Williams's arm as he tried for the gun in his shoulder holster. Rick gripped his arm, threw a shoulder against him, and jammed him against the door. He held him there while he pulled the gun and tossed it into the street.

Williams recognized him then. He cried—"Marvin!"—in a high, scared tone.

"Shut up," Rick ground out.

There was no sound from Williams except the heavy labor of his breathing until Rick had finished searching him. He found nothing but a wallet with a few gold coins and some change. There was no money belt around him.

"Where is it?" Rick demanded.

"Where's what?"

"The money. The Grant money."

"So you're just a common thief," Williams breathed. "I should have known all the time. You and your pious talk!"

Rick gripped his arm again and shook him. "Stop that! What are you sneaking in here for this time of night if you weren't aiming to make a run with the Grant money you've been holding out?"

Williams's courage rushed back into him. "So that's it? You thought you'd have something to tell Verling when he got here. Well, you're wrong, Marvin."

"Shut up, I said." Rick shook him again. "What were you in there for?"

Williams hesitated, as if trying to decide which course of action would be the safest. He cowered against the wall, breathing hard. He said finally: "It's on the ground. I dropped it when I heard you."

Rick hesitated, wondering if the man were lying. He might have a sleeve Derringer he'd use when Rick stooped to see what was on the ground. It was no time to take chances. Rick drew his gun and pronged back the hammer. "Pick it up. Try anything, and you're a dead duck."

"Go easy with that iron," Williams whispered. Stooping, he picked something up and handed it to Rick. "That's what I came for. I expect to keep Verling in my home when he gets here, and I wanted him to have a look at the Grant books."

Rick eased the hammer down and dropped his Colt into holster. He struck a match, and by the light of the tiny flame he saw that Williams held a ledger in both hands. He said: "Open it."

Williams obeyed as Rick struck another match. The pages to which Williams had opened at random were filled with names. There were dates and sums of money paid. Rick turned a sheet. Then another. They were all the same.

Rick dropped the match. He said heavily: "All right."

Williams edged along the wall, then suddenly whirled and ran. Rick remained motionless, staring into the darkness until the sound of the man's steps died. Then he turned and walked toward Main Street, disappointment choking him. He had been so sure he'd have the evidence he wanted, but there was no crime in taking a ledger home. What Williams had said sounded plausible enough.

Rick saddled his horse, telling the hostler he'd be back, and rode into the street. He turned toward Raton Pass, following the same road he had traveled with Pete Fargo not many hours before. He thought of the things that had happened in those hours, but mostly he thought of Ruth Dallam, of his life with her if he could do the job he had set himself to do.

He rode slowly, his mind turning to Pablo García and the San Marcos people, and he wondered if Ed Dallam would be able to stop Galt. He wondered, too, if the people on the Grant would ever get the justice they deserved.

Meridian was just ahead now, a cluster of small buildings along the track. He dismounted, leaving his horse in a clump of brush above the road. From up the cañon he could hear the approaching train. Rick saw the headlight far up the track, throwing out a yellow tunnel into the blackness.

Then a thought struck Rick. Sparky had been certain that only a little money had been forwarded to Verling. Williams was insisting that very few of the settlers on the Grant had paid, yet those pages of the ledger had shown the names of the settlers and the amount each had paid.

Rick cursed himself for a fool. That ledger was the very proof he needed. He had no idea why Williams had kept it correctly, but he had, and Rick should have taken it to show to Verling.

Rick heard the scuff of boots behind him. A warning chill struck his spine as he wheeled, right hand sweeping down to gun butt. The train was close now, slowing down for the brief stop here at Meridian, and the whistle cried out, shrill and piercing to Rick's ears.

He glimpsed the shadowy figure of a man as his gun swung upward, but he didn't fire, nor did he hear the other man's shot. He spilled forward into total blackness.

He didn't know that then he was dragged away from the track into the brush. He was unaware that the man who had shot him climbed aboard the train as it braked to a car-banging stop, and moved along the aisle until he found Wade Verling.

IX

Rick's first impressions were hazy and chaotic. His head ached with steady throbs that threatened to crack his skull above the temples. He was lying down, a lantern on the ground beside him making a murky splash in the darkness. A man was talking in a reassuring voice that seemed to flow out of a black void beyond the fringe of light.

"Now you're fretting, ma'am. He'll be coming around. That slug didn't do no more than give him a headache. If it had been a little lower, it would have been different."

Another voice, hardly more than a whisper: "He could have been killed. It wasn't worth it. It wasn't worth it."

Ruth Dallam! She was here, kneeling beside him, holding his hands. Everything came back to him in a rush of memory. Charley Williams. Wade Verling who was to have been on this train. Jason Galt. Pablo García and his people.

Rick tried to sit up, asking: "How did you get here, Ruth?"

She pushed him back. "Don't move. Just lie there. Oh, Rick!"

The man said again: "I tell you he'll be all right, ma'am. Looks to me like a right tough *hombre*. Your face was a sight, mister. That's what got her all wrought up. Afore we washed the blood off, you looked like a stuck hog. You know, I thought I heard a shot just as the train pulled in, but there was so much whistling and banging around, I couldn't be sure."

The man was a railroad worker, Rick guessed. He was squatting on one side of him, Ruth kneeling on the other. Tears rolled down her cheeks; she turned her head so that he would not see she was crying.

Rick put a hand up to her face. He said: "I love you, Ruth."

She leaned down and kissed him, crying unashamedly now. The man clucked sympathetically. He said: "What'd I tell you, ma'am? He ain't hurt long as he's interested in lollygagging thataway."

"How do you happen to be here?" Rick asked.

88

"I was afraid for you," she said. "You know I didn't want you to come. I kept telling Dad I ought to come up here, but he said I was crazy." She swallowed and wiped her eyes with a handkerchief. "Finally I told him his place was at San Marcos and mine was here. I just rode off and left him. When I found you, I . . . I thought you were dead."

"That she did, mister," the man said. "Came knocking on my door and caterwauling like a sick calf, she was."

"Who did it, Rick?" Ruth asked.

"I couldn't tell. I just got a glimpse of a tall man before he let me have it."

"Fargo?"

"I think so." Rick reached for his Colt. "My gun . . . ?"

"Here it is. I found it beside the track."

This time, when he tried to sit up, she didn't press him back but still knelt beside him, dark eyes filled with the same deep worry he had seen that afternoon in the Grant office in Stone Saddle. He checked his gun, promising himself that if he stayed alive, he would lift that worry from her within the next few hours.

"I left my horse in the brush."

"He's still there," the man said. "I'll get him."

"You can't ride," Ruth said. "I'll find a wagon, and you can lie down. Even a buggy would be better than sitting a saddle."

"I'll be all right." He squeezed her hand, winking at her. "One slug wouldn't bother a solid bone noggin like mine."

"You're stubborn, Rick."

He grinned. "Maybe I am. You don't know whether Verling was on the train?"

"No. Rick, don't go back to Stone Saddle. I've been through this for so long. Let's take our happiness while we can."

He shook his head. "We'd never have any happiness by riding away from our trouble."

The man came with his horse then. Rick jammed his gun into holster and got to his feet. He lurched uncertainly toward the horse, gripped the saddle horn, and steadied himself.

"You can't, Rick!" Ruth cried.

He turned to look at her. He said: "Ruth, remember you asked me if there was something I could do for you? Well, there is, and I aim to do it."

"But I didn't know then, Rick. I couldn't know how much I'd love you."

"It's good to hear that, but the trouble is I sold my soul along with my gun. I told you I didn't, but I know now I did. I've got to be damned sure I buy it back." He pulled himself into the saddle, sweat breaking through his skin. For a moment he swayed there, one hand gripping the saddle horn. Then the nausea passed. "Get on your horse, Ruth. Time to ride."

She stood motionless, hands clenched at her sides. Suddenly, as if realizing she could not change him, she turned and walked to her horse.

"Thanks for giving me a hand, friend," Rick said.

"You don't need to thank me, mister," the man said. "Glad to do anything I could."

Rick rode along the track to where Ruth sat her saddle. The wind was cold, biting at them like the prick of a thousand knives. They swung into the road and turned toward Stone Saddle. Behind them along the crest lightning was flashing in weird patterns across the sky, and thunder rumbled again and again. It smelled like rain, Rick thought. Then he quit thinking about anything. His head hurt too much. He was sure of just one thing. He had to get to San

Marcos. Verling could wait.

Presently the lights of Stone Saddle showed ahead. Now, in the small hours of the morning, there was only a scattering of them, lamps in the hotels and lanterns hung in livery stable doors. They rode slowly, Rick's eyes instinctively sweeping the street, but no one was in sight.

He reined up before the Commercial House. There was something he must do, but he had to wait a moment before he could remember what it was. He said: "I've got to see Sparky Hogan."

Ruth started to object and changed her mind. She said: "I'll wait here."

Rick swung down and walked into the lobby. The clerk glanced up inquiringly and, when Rick asked—"Missus Hogan in her room?"—the man shook his head.

"She went out right after supper. I ain't seen her since."

She had probably met Verling at the depot. Rick went back to his horse. It wasn't likely Williams would keep her since she already had a room in the hotel, and Verling would be too tired to sit up this late talking to her. But there was nothing he could do now. He was only one man, and he needed to be a dozen.

They reined away from the hitch rack and turned down Bridge Street, Ruth watching him closely. She asked: "Sure you're all right, Rick?"

"Sure I'm sure," he answered irritably.

She said nothing more. They crossed the river and swung upstream, riding faster now. Presently a gray light crept into the sky, and the ridges on both sides of the road made sharp black lines against the sullen clouds that had swept in from the west.

Rick's head still hurt, but he was thinking coherently, thinking of the year he had ridden with Pete Fargo on the other side of the state line. There had been no need for him to do his own thinking then. All he'd had to do was ride around and pay threatening visits to settlers who questioned the Grant's title to the land. But this was different.

It was full daylight when they made a turn in the road and San Marcos lay before them. It seemed entirely peaceful, much as it had been the afternoon Rick had ridden through it with Pete Fargo. The river, nearly as high as it had been that afternoon, made a steady growl as it gnawed at its dirt sides.

A long sigh of relief broke out of Ruth then. "Everything's all right, Rick. I was afraid there'd be fighting."

Rick didn't say so, but he knew everything wasn't all right. There was nothing he could point to. Just a feeling that came to him at times like this, a prickle of warning that slid down his spine. It was not unusual. He had felt it before, and he had known other men to have the same feeling when something wasn't right, men who lived by the gun and had trained themselves to be alert to every subtle hint of danger.

He said: "Stay here."

She looked at him sharply. "Something wrong?"

He nodded, giving no explanation. He knew now what it was. There were no dogs to bark a welcome, no chickens scratching in the bare dirt yards, no brown-skinned children running from house to house.

They were close to the village now. Still Rick could see no sign of threatening violence. San Marcos was as empty as if a plague had struck and its people had deserted it.

Ruth understood then. She cried out: "Rick, everyone's gone."

"Damn it, I told you to stay back."

It broke, suddenly and unexpectedly. Jason Galt was the

one who ran out of the fringe of willows along the creek, as tall and straight as when Rick had first seen him with the mob at Redwall.

Galt shouted: "We thought we were rid of you!"

Someone grabbed at him, but he jerked away. Other men appeared along the river. Major Dallam called: "Get under cover, Ruth!"

Galt went down with the first shot. Estey, Rick thought, apparently in García's house. The instant Galt fell, Rick heard the snap of a bullet. Others tugged at his coat. One slapped through the crown of his hat. He knew at once that his only chance lay in an unexpected and bold attack. If he turned, he'd get it in the back, and Ruth was in the open beside him. One way to divert the bullets from her was to focus them upon himself.

Riding low in his saddle, Rick cracked steel to his horse, yelling: "I'm coming after you, Estey!" He put his horse behind an adobe house, and came on around the other side, taking a zigzag course toward García's place. His gun was in his hand, but he held his fire. He flashed into view for a moment, reached a second house, and was out of sight again. He circled behind the house, and this time, when he came into sight, he raced straight at García's place.

The very temerity of his charge seemed to unnerve the men in the house. Bullets were all around Rick, as thick and ugly of sound as hornets prodded out of their nest. He reached the door and lunged inside.

Duff Estey loomed in front of him, big and shaggy, gun in hand. He fired, his slug slapping into the adobe wall. Then Estey went down like a great oak under an axe with Rick's bullet through his head.

There were others in the room. Two were facing the river, as if expecting a rush from the settlers. The third had been standing beside Estey. Now he squeezed trigger until his gun was empty, throwing out his bullets in the frantic way of a man who hopes that, if he fires enough times, one of the bullets is bound to do the job. His hope was a futile one, for he took Rick's second shot through his chest, and he sprawled over the deputy's body, sagging as limply as a half-filled sack of wheat.

The others had whirled. It was then that Rick was hit, the slug slicing along a rib. There were too many! Rick knew that, crouched there just inside the door. He had time to take only one of them, his bullet slamming the man against the wall. His feet slid out from under him, and he sat down hard. The fourth man was throwing down for the finish shot when García, tied up like a calf for branding, raised his bound feet and struck the man in the thighs.

Rick had not known before that García was in the room. He fired high, because he didn't want to risk hitting García, and missed. The man staggered across the room. Then he recovered his balance and fired, his bullet ripping through the rough planks of the floor a foot from Rick's head. But Rick had had the time he needed, and his bullet caught the man just below the jaw. He fell in a stumbling, loose-jointed way, arms flung out, and lay still.

Rick crawled to his feet, jerked his knife from his pocket, and, dropping his gun into leather, slashed the ropes that bound García. He stumbled outside, breathing deeply.

Ruth was there, crying: "You crazy wild man!" And Ed Dallam, frankly admiring, said: "You did a good job, Marvin."

"My friend Juan wrote that you were fast with a gun," García said. "Now I have seen."

Rick leaned against the adobe wall, slack-muscled and tired and sick from pain. Other settlers had come up—

Shaw, the Redwall storekeeper, Bert and Clarke, the men who were to have quirted the horses out from under Rick and Fargo in Redwall. Other faces he remembered, but somehow they were different now, stripped of the hate and the passion Rick had seen in them before. He understood how it was. The culmination of long-threatened violence with its gunfire and death had its way of humbling men.

"Two things to think about in doing a job like that," Rick said wearily. "Do what they don't expect and don't waste any lead."

"You saved my life, *amigo*," García said.

"You saved mine," Rick told him. "There was just too damned many."

"It was nothing," García answered.

Then Ruth saw the bloodstains on his shirt just above his belt. She cried: "You're hit again. He's been shot once already, Dad."

"We've got a doctor here from Stone Saddle," Dallam said. "He's been up to Redwall looking after the boys that got shot here the other night. We'll have him take a look at you, Marvin."

"Just lost a little meat," Rick said, making light of it.

A man came running from the river, calling: "Jason wants to talk to you, Major! He says he's dying."

Dallam hurried his steps toward the river, Shaw and the others stringing behind him. Rick held back, Ruth on one side, García on the other.

"What happened here last night?" Rick asked.

"Galt came," García said with more bitterness than he had shown before. "He said we must leave, but I would not go. *Señor* Estey came then with many men. When they saw the settlers, all but the four went back to Stone Saddle."

"Afraid?" Rick asked.

García spread his hands. "How can you tell when a man is afraid?"

"The townsmen sympathize with us," Ruth said. "Maybe they didn't want settler blood on their hands."

"Perhaps," García said. "I do not know. Estey said he would give them fifty dollars a day, but only the three stayed. Estey made me prisoner. He would kill me and say Galt did it." García glanced at Rick, shaking his head. "We wanted peace, *amigo,* but I did not forget what you said . . . a man must fight for what is his. So I would not go."

There was nothing Rick could say. He saw how it had been with Estey. The deputy had wanted a killing so he could make outlaws of the settlers. He had determined there would be a killing, even if he had to do it himself.

When they reached the men standing around Galt, Dallam motioned to Rick. He shouldered his way through the settlers until he reached the dying man. Galt lay under a blanket, red-flecked eyes bright with the fire that burned in him.

"You're still alive, Marvin," Galt said. "Perhaps I was wrong about you. The Almighty has a purpose for all of us. Your mission has not been completed, or you would be dead. But my work is finished." Galt turned his eyes to Dallam. "I knew the courts would fail us, and I believed my way was the only way. Now it is you who must save their homes for them."

Galt closed his eyes. There was silence except for the dying man's raspy breathing. Then his eyes fluttered open. He said very softly: "Leaving you brings me one regret. I will miss you all. But I think my death will help you to hold your homes. See that news of it gets to Washington."

Then Jason Galt died with a smile on his lips, without bitterness, without fear.

Rick turned away, forgetting his weariness and his pain. Now he felt no regret for Galt's passing. More than once he had been close to death since he had come to the Purgatory, because of the man's dogged pursuit of the line he had chosen. Still there could be no question of his honesty, and for that Rick could respect his memory.

The thunder had stopped. It began to rain.

X

Most of the settlers returned to Redwall with Galt's body, the desire to fight gone from them. The doctor had washed and dressed Rick's wounds, saying: "It's a miracle you're still on your feet, Marvin. When I see things like this, I wonder about what Galt said of your mission not being completed."

"The job ain't done," Rick said somberly, and let it go at that.

They cooked and ate a meal, the settlers sobered by the knowledge that all the bloodshed so far had accomplished nothing. García promised to come to Stone Saddle as soon as he had gone for his people. Rick told him to shut the door of his house, and leave it shut until the coroner came from town.

There were a dozen settlers who had stayed, among them the most reasonable of the Redwall men. It had come to the point where there would be a compromise settlement with Verling, or they would leave the Grant peacefully, but above everything else Rick was aware of one great change. He was accepted now. His fight with Estey and his men had accomplished that.

"What is your suggestion?" Dallam asked.

"First I'd like to say that I aim to settle somewhere on the river," Rick said, "so whatever deal we make with Verling concerns me."

He saw the warm smile on Ruth's lips. He saw her father nod approval as if he had lost the contempt he had felt for the man he had called a Grant gunman. But it was Ben Shaw who said: "We'll be proud to have you for a neighbor, Marvin."

"Thanks," Rick said. "I ain't sure Verling is in town, but I guess he is. My notion is for Major Dallam to go with me and talk to him, but here's where the rub comes in. Verling can't hand you your land with his blessing. I hope to get him to sell to you at a reasonable figure."

"We won't pay nothing!" a settler bellowed. "A penny an acre would be too much."

"Then nothing can be done for you," Rick said.

"But we settled here years ago!" the man cried. "We hold patents."

"I know," Rick cut in, "but that ain't the point. Verling can evict you and sell your places to new settlers. Your improvements will let him ask a better price. In other words, the work you've done will make more money for the Grant."

He felt their resentment, saw them shuffle uneasily and look at each other. They were huddled under a cottonwood, wet and disgruntled, but they were seeing the logic of what Rick said.

Dallam motioned to the man who had objected. "A week ago I felt the same way, Jim, but not now. The trial in Denver and what has happened here have convinced me that Marvin is right."

Ruth nodded agreement.

"You'll go with me and talk to Verling?" Rick asked Dallam.

"I'll go," he said.

"And the rest of you will take any deal that satisfies him?"

They nodded reluctantly. Shaw said bitterly: "I hope to hell that everybody in Washington who had a part in this steal knows what they've done."

"Let's ride, Major," Rick said.

He walked to his horse, Dallam and Ruth beside him. When Rick had swung into the saddle, he saw that Ruth, too, had mounted. He said: "You ain't going with us, Ruth."

She looked squarely at him, her chin held defiantly high. "Rick Marvin, do you think I'd stay here when Fargo is in Stone Saddle?"

"All right," he said heavily, and reined into the road.

"When I got here," Dallam said, "Jason had the San Marcos people moving out, but García wouldn't budge. Jason swore he'd hang him. I spent most of the night arguing with Jason about it. Estey's outfit moved in, but most of them turned tail and lit out for town. Estey stayed, figuring that he wouldn't have any real trouble with a bunch of farmers. Me and Jason got our bunch down to the river without a ruckus. Estey ordered us to go back to Redwall, but Jason wouldn't go." Dallam lifted his pipe, shielding the bowl from the rain with his left hand. "Plain enough what Williams wanted Estey to do. Once we made some crazy wild move, we'd be outlaws. Then Williams could keep on telling Verling what a time he's having."

"But they shot Jason!" Ruth cried.

"He was a leader. Estey probably figured that we'd start shooting after Jason was plugged. He'd have us then. Estey was supposed to be the law." Dallam scowled. "I'd like to know how much Williams got away with."

"Plenty," Rick said. "What I want to know is why Galt jumped up so they could drill him."

"He was a strange man," Dallam said. "He thought that if he got killed, his death would shock the officials in Washington into doing something for us."

"He was wrong," Rick said. "This job calls for living, not dying."

Dallam nodded. "That's right. Now tell me something. Why did Estey try to shoot you?"

"Something personal," Rick said.

They rode in silence then, each thinking of what still lay ahead. It stopped raining, the storm moving eastward, and presently the sun was beating at them again from a clear sky. García caught up before they reached Stone Saddle, and the four rode into town together.

Rick swore when he found that Lee Combs had not returned. He said: "That sheriff is the poorest stick of a lawman I ever saw."

"He was the best we could get," Dallam said.

Rick nodded at Ruth. "You go to the hotel. Find out where Sparky is. It ain't right, her being gone."

Ruth hesitated, frowning, then turned away. Dallam asked: "What's your plan, Marvin?"

"Find Verling. That's all the plan I've got." Rick motioned toward the Grant office. "He'll likely be there if he's in town and still alive."

Rick walked into Williams's office without knocking. Williams and Fargo were seated along the wall, Fargo as immaculate as ever. If the gunman was surprised to see Rick alive, he gave no indication of it. Wade Verling sat at the desk, big hands folded in front of him. He stopped in the middle of a sentence when Rick appeared in the

100

doorway, his lips tightening.

"Howdy, Wade," Rick said softly. "I see you got here."

"And I see you ain't got a skirt to hide behind," Fargo taunted.

Rick felt the quick lash of anger. He checked it at once, for this was no time to let his temper go.

Verling glared at Rick as though thoroughly outraged. He was a rock-jawed man, paunchy from too much desk work and too little exercise, but there was an appearance of bigness about him, a sense of unleashed power that, if let go, would steamroller everything in front of him.

"Marvin, you've raised high hell around here," Verling burst out. "You know what our methods are."

Rick moved across the office to stand at the desk, Dallam and García stopping just inside the door, both uneasy as they stared at Verling's angry face. Fargo eased forward, smug and self-satisfied. Williams shoved his thumbs into the armholes of his flowered waistcoat and pressed against the wall, trying to hide his worry.

"Yeah, I've raised hell," Rick said bluntly, "but it wouldn't have been necessary if you'd come up here and looked around instead of leaving everything to a thief like Williams."

Williams let out a squall of rage. Verling's lips pressed a little tighter; his cheeks became redder. He whispered—"So."—as if he didn't have breath to say more.

Rick motioned to Dallam. "Wade, meet Major Ed Dallam, who's been picked to represent the settlers on the head of the river." He nodded at García. "That's Pablo García. He's got something to say about the rent money he and his neighbors have paid Williams."

"This is a waste of time," Williams squealed. "Pay Marvin off and let him go."

But there was a shrewdness in Verling, as well as stubbornness. Now he waved a hand to silence Williams. "Marvin, I thought you were a man the Grant could be proud of, but. . . ."

Rick leaned across the desk. "Wade, you're a damned sharp *hombre*. Either me or Williams is a crook, but you know I haven't had a chance to rob the Grant. Williams has."

"I won't listen to this," Williams sputtered.

"Shut up, Charley." Verling motioned toward Dallam and García. "Why did you bring these men?"

"García wants to tell you that he and the others on the river have paid their rent money. Missus Hogan told me you'd received mighty little money from the Purgatory. I say Williams has been stealing it, and he's been the cause of the trouble with the Redwall bunch."

"How and why?"

"By refusing to talk to them or hear their complaints. Why? Well, Wade, that's mighty damned plain. As long as there's trouble, he can lump all the settlers together and tell you he ain't collecting from any of 'em."

"Nobody's paid. Or damned near nobody, and I mean both the renters and the Redwall bunch that's squatting on Grant land." Verling opened a ledger that was on the desk. "Has García got any receipts to prove he's paid?"

García came to the desk. "No, *señor*." He tapped the ledger. "*Señor* Williams took our money and wrote it in a book. Like this one. I saw him."

"The fact of the matter is that you all owe us a hell of a lot of back rent . . . which I aim to collect." Verling gave Rick a malicious grin. "Take a look, Rick."

Rick opened the ledger. He turned a page, then another, and went on to the end. The names were here just as they

102

had been on the ledger Williams had taken from the building the night before. The ledger looked exactly like the one he'd seen, but there were only a few places where **Paid** was written after a name.

"Last night I saw another ledger," Rick said. "It was the right one. Where is it, Williams?"

"You're lying!" Williams yelled. "I tell you he's lying, Mister Verling."

"Rick, are you making out he kept two ledgers?" Verling asked incredulously.

"That's it. Williams didn't think you'd come. He tried to bluff Missus Hogan into wiring you to stay in Raton."

"That's another lie!" Williams cried. "I welcome your visits, Mister Verling."

"He had to get rid of the right one when he saw that Missus Hogan wouldn't bluff," Rick went on. "I couldn't figure out last night why he'd kept a correct account, but it's plain enough now. He didn't want to give receipts, so he let the renters see him write in the other book. If they asked for a receipt, he could say the book was proof they'd paid."

Fargo grinned derisively. "Purty thin, ain't it, Wade?"

"Pretty thin," Verling agreed.

"Have you talked to Missus Hogan?" Rick asked.

"I haven't seen her," Verling said. "I don't know where she is."

Rick had guessed Williams and Fargo might murder Verling, but that had not been their plan. They had Sparky Hogan. Either they had killed her or were holding her prisoner. Rick pinned his eyes on Williams, sick with the knowledge that he had made a mistake that might prove fatal. It had been safer for them to take Sparky out of the picture than Verling. Without her, there was no chance that Verling would believe García.

103

"Where is Missus Hogan?" Rick asked, his tone hard.

"How the hell would I know?" Williams shouted. "Don't accuse me of kidnapping a woman."

"Dry up," Fargo said testily. "Let him talk. His lies make me laugh."

"This has gone far enough," Verling said. "Missus Hogan is probably in Redwall. In any case, I'm satisfied with the way Charley has been running things, and I'm not satisfied with you, Rick. We'll have to evict these people at once."

Dallam moved to the desk, very pale and trembling in his anger. "Verling, I had hoped you'd listen to reason. We hold a patent on that land."

Verling threw out a big hand. "I've heard of you, Dallam, and I've heard of Jason Galt. You're done making trouble for us, both of you."

"Galt's dead," Dallam said gravely. "Murdered by a sidewinder that Williams was able to get appointed deputy."

"You don't expect me to show regret over Galt's death, do you?" Verling asked harshly.

"No," Dallam said between clenched teeth. "I suppose it means nothing to you that we've cleared and farmed land that the government told us was open to entry."

"Damn it!" Verling bellowed. "You lost your case in Denver. Congress has confirmed our title, and the Supreme Court has decided for us. If you want your homes, you'll pay for them."

"Why, you're as big a robber as Williams," Dallam broke in. "I came here to meet you halfway, but by hell. . . ."

"Get out." Verling jumped up and shook his fist in Dallam's face. "So help me, I'll have you evicted as fast as the law can work."

They faced each other, both fighting for self-control. García had moved back to the door. Rick edged away, watching Fargo for the first hostile move, and all the time he was telling himself that there must be a way to break Williams. He had heard the clink of gold last night when he'd been standing in the alley, but Williams had not moved it from the building—not when he'd taken the ledger. Williams would probably consider it safer in the Grant office than in his own home.

"Sit down, Wade." Rick knew where it was now. He should have thought of it sooner. "If you evict these people, you'll have a civil war on your hands."

Verling wheeled to face him. "It's Grant land. They can't fight a United States marshal."

"They can't win, but they can fight," Rick said coldly. "If there is trouble, the kind that makes news, how much Grant land will you sell?"

Verling, as angry as he was, could not help seeing the logic in what Rick said. He rubbed a cheek, saying reluctantly: "It won't be good, and that's a fact. If they force it, there's nothing I can do."

"But there is," Rick said. "Make Dallam a reasonable offer."

"I'll make no offer. If Dallam and his neighbors want to buy the land they're on, they pay the same as anyone else would."

"How much salary does Williams get?"

"Twenty-four hundred. Why?"

Williams was on his feet now, suddenly frantic. "Kick him out, Mister Verling."

Fargo, too, had risen. "Yeah, I think we've had enough gab."

But Rick stood motionless at the end of the desk. For the

first time he saw doubt come into Verling's face. He asked: "Suppose there was money hidden here? Big money?"

"Then I'd believe you," Verling said.

"One more thing. Williams has a fast horse. He's racked outside. Know why?"

"No, but he's got a right to own a horse."

"Sure, but ain't it damned funny that he'd have the fastest horse on the Purgatory when he never uses him in a race?"

"It's his business."

"It's his business to make a fast getaway when he figures his string is run out."

Without warning, Rick jerked a drawer out of the desk, upset it, and drove a boot through the bottom. Gold ran out in a yellow stream, ten- and twenty-dollar pieces.

Williams shouted: "Fargo, you promised this wouldn't happen!"

But Fargo was in no mood for talk. His hand darted downward for his gun. Rick had kept the gunman within his range of vision, and now, with Fargo's first hostile movement, Rick reached for his Colt.

Both guns came out of holsters in the same instant and everyone else in the room dived out of range, the fast draws of men who had practiced much and whose lives depended upon their guns. The two shots roared out together, so closely that one sounded as if it were the echo of the first. Fargo, always so sure of himself, showed disbelief on a face that had seldom showed any expression at all. Then there was fear, the fear of a man who had brought death to others but had never believed it would come to him in this manner.

Rick watched without emotion while Fargo began to wilt. He stood as if frozen while Fargo gave at knee and waist. He fell and lay still, and only when Rick knew the last spark of life was gone from Pete Fargo did he swing to Williams.

Williams had sprawled in the corner as he had desperately struggled to get out of range. Now he sat with his thin shoulders against the wall, mouth drawn into the tight little protuberance, saber-sharp nose wiggling like a captured rabbit.

"Is Sparky alive?" Rick demanded.

"She's in the closet in my house," Williams whimpered. "She's tied up."

Then Rick's knees would hold him up no longer. He dropped his gun, one hand going to his shoulder where Fargo's bullet had tagged him. He grabbed at the desk and, missing it, went down.

It was night when Rick came to. A low-turned lamp stood on the bureau, and Ruth sat in a rocking chair beside his bed. He turned, painfully, for he ached in every nerve and muscle. He said: "I knew you'd be here."

"I'll always be here, Rick," she said simply.

"What happened?"

"Sparky wasn't hurt. She went back to Raton with Verling. He's sending another man up to take this office. Williams is in jail. Combs got back right after your fight with Fargo."

"Your land?"

"Everything's all right, Rick. After Williams confessed, when he found out how big a mistake he'd made with Williams and Fargo, Verling was a changed man. He agreed to sell us our land at a dollar an acre." Ruth smiled. "It helped when Sparky took some of his hide off with her tongue. Her red hair, you know."

"Funny about Fargo," Rick said thoughtfully. "He always wanted to be on the side of the big fellow."

"He couldn't turn down the offer Williams made him," Ruth said. "Williams had twenty thousand dollars hidden in false bottoms in that desk. He had promised Fargo half of it."

There was silence, then, for Rick was thinking of many things. Sparky Hogan would live in the big house in Raton. Pablo García and his people would keep their homes without paying their rent twice. The Redwall settlers could buy their land for a mere token payment. But most of all he was thinking of his years with Ruth, the good, rich years in a country where his roots would go down.

Ruth bent and kissed him. He put an arm around her; he felt the softness of her body and the inherent goodness that was in her.

There were these two worlds, the one of economic necessity, with its ruthless demands and its temptations. Pete Fargo had surrendered to it. But there was the other world that had to do with a man's heart and the fullness of his soul. That was Rick Marvin's world.

The Fence

"The Fence" by Wayne D. Overholser first appeared in *Ranch Romances* (2nd June Number: 6/11/48). It was subsequently reprinted in *Triple Western* in the issue dated June, 1953. This is its first appearance in book form.

I

Jim Hallet could look back upon a series of decisions, bitter, sometimes brutal decisions, which had influenced the course of his life, all of them building toward the stand he must take this day. Now, his hard-muscled back pressed against the door jamb of the sheriff's door, the hot summer sun winking back from his star, and he watched the Wyatts approach town, thinking of what he would say to Boone Wyatt. He had made his decision after a worried, sleepless week, knowing what it would cost him, and knowing he could not change it.

There was no other family like the Wyatts in the Stillwater country, nor, for that matter, in all of eastern Oregon. White-haired, old Latigo Wyatt, as slim and arrow-straight at seventy as he had been at twenty, always rode in front with his granddaughter, Kitsie, when they came to town. Latigo's son Boone, Kitsie's father, forked a roan behind him, Kitsie's twin brother Stub at his side. They were the Wyatts, the royal family of the valley, proud of their name, their wealth, and of Wagon Wheel, the biggest spread in that corner of the state. All of them were certain of their high destiny, and all but Kitsie intolerant of opposition.

Gramp Tatum, younger than Latigo and looking ten years older, lurched along the path from his shack in the sagebrush west of town, reached the boardwalk, and stumbled toward Jim's office. He sat down in the doorway as if the last of his strength had seeped out of him. He said: "I sure need an eye-opener, son. Can't seem to get waked up this morning."

Usually Jim sent the old man on about his business that

was mooching drinks in the Bonanza Saloon, but today was Saturday, and Gramp's luck hadn't been good lately. "Go get your eyes opened," Jim said, dropping a dollar on the walk in front of the old man.

Gramp picked it up and slid it into his pocket. He muttered—"Thanks, son."—but he didn't stir. His eyes were on the dust cloud to the south. He said with deep sourness: "There they come just like they've been coming for twenty years. You could set your watch by 'em. Ten o'clock every Saturday morning, and for why? Just so folks will bow and scrape in front of 'em. Sure makes Latigo feel good."

Jim said nothing. He wished Gramp would move on. He had no sympathy for the old man. Gramp had made his decision years before when he had refused to fight back. Latigo had stomped on him and broken him and beaten the pride out of him. It was Latigo's way with any man who stood in front of him, but some had fought and died. That, to Jim's way of thinking, was better than crawling, belly down, through the dust. For the third time that morning he lifted his gun and checked it and slid it back into his holster. He would not surrender even for Kitsie.

"Yeah, bow and scrape and forget you was ever two-legged and walked like a man," Gramp said with more violence of feeling than Jim thought was in him. "That's what I've been doing every Saturday just to get a damned lousy drink out of Latigo or Boone."

Then the old man did a surprising thing. He brought an ancient cap and ball revolver out from under his ragged coat, fondled it for a moment as a small girl might fondle her favorite doll, and put it back. He looked up at Jim, lips pulled away from toothless gums in a wicked smile. He said without the slightest trace of braggadocio: "Someday I'm gonna kill that old rooster."

112

"They hang old men for murder," Jim said.

Gramp got up, faded eyes staring at Jim from under hooded brows as if arguing the sheriff's intent. He was as sober as Jim had ever seen him. "Here's one old man they'd never convict of murder," he said. "I ain't sure it'd be murder salivating a Wyatt no-how."

Gramp lurched on toward the Bonanza in his peculiar stilt-like walk, rheumatism and whisky having combined long ago to stiffen his legs. Jim watched him until he disappeared into the saloon, wondering if his unexpected threat of violence was perhaps symbolic of what lay ahead.

Jim was still there in the doorway when the Wyatts reached town and turned eastward along Main Street. Latigo nodded and called courteously: "'Morning, Jim."

" 'Morning, Latigo," Jim said, and lifted his Stetson. " 'Morning, Kitsie."

She smiled and said—"How are you, Jim?"—in a cool, impersonal tone. Neither of them thought that Latigo or her father, Boone Wyatt, guessed their feelings for each other. The four of them rode on to rein up in front of the bank and rack their horses. Boone and young Stub had not even glanced at Jim. There was an understandable pride in Latigo that was never offensive. In his son and grandson it became snobbish arrogance. They might have spoken condescendingly to Jim if he had spoken first, something Jim would never do.

Still watching, Jim saw Latigo go into the bank where he would have a long conference with Zane Biddle. They would decide, Jim thought with biting sourness, which of the Poverty Flat ranchers would lose their spreads and which Biddle would let go another year. Latigo would do the deciding, and he would reach his decision on the basis of how each one of the Poverty Flat boys had treated him.

Kitsie went into the Mercantile where she would examine the new dress goods that had come in. Later she would drop over to Nell Craft's place. Nell made her dresses, and her kitchen was the one sanctuary where Kitsie and Jim could meet.

Stub went into the Bonanza where he would drink too much. Then he'd get into a poker game and lose anything from fifty to a thousand dollars to Chris Vinton, the only Poverty Flat rancher who consistently paid his interest at the bank when it was due. Usually Boone trailed along with his son, obligingly paying his losses when the game folded.

It was Boone's habit, while young Stub was throwing good money away over the green-topped table, to spend his time at the bar, drinking sparingly and basking in the respect given him by the Poverty Flat boys. But today Boone did not follow Stub into the Bonanza. Instead, he came directly toward Jim, a scowl lining his face, thick legs driving hard against the boards of the walk in sharp, echoing cracks.

Latigo Wyatt, for all of his pride and restlessness, was a likable man, but Jim found nothing likable in Boone. He was in his middle forties, heavy-shouldered and bull-necked, and anything but constant yessing brought his temper to an instant boil. He had spoiled Stub, had tried to make a boy out of Kitsie and, failing, piled dislike upon her, except when Latigo was around. Kitsie, in manners and disposition, was a throwback to her grandfather with none of Boone's truculence in her.

Jim stepped out of his office and strode toward Boone, knowing that this was the moment in which he must take his stand. A year ago he had been riding for Wagon Wheel when the sheriff, Bill Riley, had been killed by a dry-gulcher's bullet. Latigo had secured Jim's appointment, and everybody, except Jim himself, conceded that he was a Wyatt man, a mistake he had found no occasion to correct until today.

Boone was ten feet away from Jim when he bawled: "What kind of a damned ninny of a sheriff are you, Hallet?"

Boone Wyatt bullied everybody except his father whom he feared and his son whom he pampered. Others took it, the Poverty Flat cowmen, Zane Biddle, and the rest. Even Jim had taken it because of Kitsie, but all the Stillwater folks had been pushed nearly as far as they could be pushed, and Jim was quite a bit ahead of the others.

"I'm a good sheriff," Jim said clearly, spacing his words so that each hit Boone Wyatt like the slap of an open palm. "What kind of a damned cheap thief are you, Wyatt?"

They had stopped, a pace apart, and for an instant Boone looked as if he had ceased breathing. He stood spread-legged, head tipped forward, his face as set and hard as if it had been worked out of granite. Morning sunlight beat upon it, and in that sharp, unrelenting light Jim saw doubt flow across the full-jowled face, saw arrogance wash out of him. It was, Jim thought, the first time since Latigo Wyatt had brought his herd and family north from California a generation before that a Wyatt had been talked to like that.

There was this moment of silence between them while Boone made up his mind. It was not fear that troubled the man, Jim saw. It was a case of battered pride, of mental struggle while Boone decided upon the best way of holding his shattered dignity, and Jim knew that regardless of what happened between them he would receive from this moment the full force of Boone Wyatt's soul-deep hatred.

"Reckon I didn't hear it right," Boone said.

"You heard. Or maybe you want me to repeat it."

"Once was one time too many. Write out your resignation, Hallet. We'll have no sheriff in office who tries to cover his incompetence with insults."

"I won't do that until the county court asks me for my resignation," Jim said flatly. "You can get them to call a special meeting. Maybe they'll fire me, but, if you call that meeting, I'll tell them what you tried to do to Ernie Craft. I'll write the story and take it to the newspaper. I'll send it out to the Portland dailies. I'm calling the Wyatt hand, Boone. What are you going to do about it?"

Fury grew in Boone Wyatt, the kind of fury that insulted dignity raises in a man. It showed in the squeezing together of his meaty lips, the corded jaw muscles, the beat of his temple pulse. For a moment Jim was afraid that he had gone too far, that Boone would draw his gun. Then Boone shrugged casually as if the affair was of no importance. He said: "Why should I do anything, Hallet? I get madder'n hell when a fly buzzes in my ear, but I never heard of a fly hurting a man."

Boone swung on his heel and strode along the boardwalk to the Bonanza. Jim, staring after the man, felt doubt stir in him. He had declared his independence. He had protected Ernie Craft against a phony rustling charge, something Bill Riley would not have done. Riley had been a Wyatt man. When Latigo or Boone wanted a settler moved away from the edge of Wagon Wheel range, Riley could always find a way if the banker could not. Now the Wyatts knew how Jim Hallet stood, and the answer to what they were going to do would not be long in coming.

The sheriff loitered in front of Hoke Foster's saddlery, rolling a smoke and lighting it, letting his presence show his defiance to Wyatt rule. He saw Kitsie leave the Mercantile and walk around the corner. She would go, he knew, to

Nell Craft's house, and impatience tightened his nerves.

Jim smoked his cigarette out, tossed it into the dust, and crossed to the hotel. Again he paused, gaze raking the street. Boone had disappeared into the Bonanza. Stub was still inside, and Latigo had not come out of the bank. Usually Jim waited an hour or more before he followed Kitsie to Nell's house, but he didn't wait today. He had made his decision. Kitsie must make hers.

He paced along the boardwalk, turned the corner, and went directly to Nell's house. It was a white cottage set behind a picket fence, the yard in lawn, a tall row of red hollyhocks along the front, the only house in town that showed pride of ownership.

II

He pulled the bell cord and waited. A moment later he heard Nell's quick steps. She opened the door, said—"Jim, you're early."—and he stepped inside. She was a small, brown-eyed woman, almost forty, who had somehow missed marrying in a land where women could take their pick, but although she disdained romance for herself, she did all she could to further Kitsie's.

Jim followed Nell into the kitchen, doubt crowding him again. He stood in the doorway looking at Kitsie, Stetson in his hand, a tall, slender man with a strong chin, a thin beaky nose, and smoky-gray eyes that said things to Kitsie he could not put into words. Kitsie, turning from the sink where she was peeling potatoes, smiled to tell him she understood.

"Aren't you running a big risk coming here so soon?"

Kitsie asked. "And through the front door?"

"I aimed to run a risk," he said with unusual violence.

Kitsie put down the knife and gave him a straight look. Jim took a long breath. No matter what she said or did, or what the rest of the Wyatts did, he would never stop loving her. She was twenty, four years younger than he was, a tall, high-breasted girl with blue eyes and red-gold hair that reminded him of a sunset behind a field of ripe wheat, and full lips that were quick to smile but now had been turned sober by his tone.

She came to him, asking: "What is it, Jim?"

"It's got to be one way or the other," he said more roughly than he intended. "Seeing you for an hour once a week in Nell's kitchen ain't enough. Pussyfooting in and out so nobody will know I've seen you ain't no way for a man in love to do."

"But there isn't any other way, Jim. Not now."

"Yes, there is."

"What?"

He pulled her to him, knowing that his hands were as rough as his words, but still unable to help it. He said: "I've loved you since the day I rode into Wagon Wheel and asked Latigo for a job. You were standing under them poplars, your hat hanging back of your head, and I looked at you and knew I wasn't going anywhere else. Not unless you went along."

"I guess I loved you then, too, Jim," she breathed. "We didn't need any more hands. If I hadn't asked Grandad to hire you, he'd have sent you on."

"Then if you love me, you'll marry me," he said.

"When?"

"Today."

"Today?"

Her eyes widened as she looked at him. He felt the pressure of her breasts against him, smelled the fragrance of her hair, and he was stirred as he was always stirred by her nearness. The need of her was pressing him and adding to the violence that was in him, but he could not turn back. This was decision day. He would not be a slave to Wyatt pride and greed, even for the girl he loved.

Kitsie drew away from him and walked to the window. She stood there, staring at the zinnias Nell had planted along the base of the house. She said, without turning: "You know we can't, Jim. What's happened?"

"I just told your dad what I thought of him for trying to frame Ernie Craft for rustling," he said. "From now on it'll be me against the Wyatts. I've got to know where you stand."

She whirled to face him, suddenly and terribly angry. "Jim, are you crazy? My father wouldn't frame Ernie Craft for rustling."

"You think I'm lying?"

"I think you're mistaken."

"No." He told her what had happened between him and her father. Then he said: "When I was buckarooing for Wagon Wheel, I knew Latigo and your dad would get Bill Riley to give anybody a kick who settled within shooting distance of Wagon Wheel range, but it wasn't any of my business. Now that I'm wearing the star, it is."

Her tanned face had gone white; her mouth was pressed so tightly that it was a long-lipped line. Utterly miserable, she said: "But why would Dad want to get rid of Ernie Craft? He never bothered anybody."

Jim shrugged. "He claims the settlers eat Wagon Wheel beef."

She threw out her hands in a gesture of disbelief. "It

doesn't make sense, Jim. There is only a handful of settlers, and we've got a lot of cows."

"There'd be more settlers if Latigo and Boone hadn't kept pushing," Jim reminded her.

She nodded reluctant agreement. She had, he thought, known it all the time, but she had kept her eyes closed to it, and it worried and bothered her. The things Wagon Wheel did were not governed by limits of justice and moral right. The only consideration was how far the Wyatts could go without inviting the Poverty Flat cowmen to strike back, and Jim had often thought that if Boone Wyatt ever dictated Wagon Wheel policies, even that would not be a limiting factor.

"I can't marry you today, Jim," she said finally. "You know that."

"Why?"

"A girl just can't get married any day her man says so. There's things to do."

"Like what?"

"A wedding cake to be baked," she said defiantly. "And I'd have to get Nell to make a dress."

He wiped her objections away with a sweep of his hand. "It's you and me that's important, Kitsie. Not cakes and dresses." He swallowed and forced himself to say: "And it ain't the Wyatt men and it ain't Wagon Wheel. That's what you've got to decide. It's whether our love is as important to you as a ranch that's become a god to the Wyatt men."

She stood straight and tall beside the window, hands clenched at her sides, knuckles white with tension. "You can't say that," she cried. "It isn't true. You have no right to doubt my love, but how can I marry you after what you said to Dad?"

"How could I marry you if I go on my knees to him like

the other men in the valley do?" Jim demanded. "Chris Vinton is crazy about you. He'd bow and scrape to get a chance at part of Wagon Wheel. So would Zane Biddle. Your dad would like Biddle for a son-in-law. A banker who's taken orders from Latigo ever since he opened his bank. Do you want a man like that?"

"No, but I don't want a man who calls my father a cheap thief."

"All right. Maybe I said too much, but that ain't the point now." He came to her and took her hands. "Look, Kitsie. We've both been cowards, and it's gone against the grain all the time. Sneaking in here to see each other. Afraid to tell Latigo or Boone how we felt. Trying to be satisfied with a kiss and one hour a week with you. If you love me, you wouldn't ask me to wait. We've waited and waited and kept on waiting. For what?"

"For something to change," she whispered.

He laughed, a hoarse, humorless sound signaling the misery that was in him. "You think your dad will ever change? Or Latigo? The only thing that would change them would be for me to come up with a million dollars, and I never will. So what'll happen? We'll put it off and off until you get tired waiting and you'll marry Zane Biddle, which same is what your dad wants."

"But not Granddad. He wants me to be happy. Oh, Jim, we've got to keep on waiting and having faith. Something will happen."

Something would happen, but it wouldn't be what they'd want. He was certain of it. He couldn't tell her why; it was a feeling that had been in him from the moment Boone Wyatt had walked along the street toward him that morning.

He put his arms around her and held her hard against his

body; he felt her softness and her strength. "We can't wait, Kitsie. It's your family or me. There's a fence between us. Which side are you going to be on?"

She stared up at him a moment, suddenly angry. "If there is a fence, you built it!" she cried. "Let me go."

But he didn't let her go until he had kissed her. She stiffened and tried to break free, and her fists beat against him.

Then, as she had that first time he had kissed her when he had been riding for Wagon Wheel less than a week, she went slack, her arms coming around his neck, her body molding to him. There was this moment when she could not get enough of him, and she could not give him enough, a moment when the rest of the world faded into nothing and there were just the two of them. It was passion, mad and wild and crazy, but so real that there was no doubting what was in her heart.

Then Nell Craft's cough broke dimly into their consciousness. He let Kitsie go, anger stirring him. Nell had never done anything like this. She stayed out of the kitchen as long as Jim and Kitsie were together. But now, when Jim looked at her, his anger melted, for he always held a pity for her. She was a hungry-faced woman whose eyes held a lingering ghost of a long-dead past.

"Excuse me," Nell said, "but I wanted to tell you something, Kitsie. Don't let your grandfather's or your father's notions make you lose the only thing in life that is worthwhile."

"I don't understand," Kitsie said.

"You will after it's too late. And don't doubt what Jim said about your father trying to frame Ernie for rustling. I was home last Sunday when Jim came out. He found the hide where your father said it would be."

III

The doorbell gave out its metallic jangle. Someone was pulling the cord repeatedly and angrily. Nell moved across the kitchen to the door that opened into her living room, her thin face hard-set by the worry that gripped her.

"You won't keep your secret now unless Jim wants to hide," Nell said, "and I don't think he will. Your father and your brother are outside."

For a moment Jim forgot to breathe. He looked at Kitsie. He heard Nell close the kitchen door, heard her cross the living room. He saw fear squeeze Kitsie's face, saw the beat of her throat pulse, and knew that the same thought was in her mind that was in his. If he killed her father and brother, their last chance for happiness would be gone.

"Why don't you hide?" she whispered. "Or go out through the back?"

"We'll face it," he said harshly.

Boone Wyatt's loud insistent voice came to Jim. He heard Nell arguing. Then the stomp of booted feet as the Wyatts crossed the front room, the jingle of spurs, and he opened the door before Boone reached it. He said coldly: "Looking for someone, Boone?"

Wyatt stopped abruptly, surprised, and Stub, a step behind him, said: "Well, I'll be damned. Looks like Gramp gave you the right hunch."

"Get out, Hallet," Boone said thickly. "Kitsie, it's been a long time since I took a blacksnake to you."

"And you'll be dead a long time if you do now," Jim said in cold fury. "If you didn't get me straight a while ago, Boone, you'd better get it this time. You Wyatts figure you run the valley. Maybe so, but you sure as hell don't run the sheriff's office, and you don't run me."

"He talks tough," Stub breathed, his hostile intent plain to read.

He was slender like his grandfather with Latigo's fine handsome features, but he had been pampered by Boone until his sense of reality was completely distorted. Now, just a little drunk, he was bound to push until he had trouble.

Jim stepped through the door, pausing when he was a pace from Stub. He said: "Boone, since we're facing our cards, we might as well do a finish job. Kitsie and I are in love. We're asking your permission to get married."

"Married?" Stub howled. "So that's it. Well, maybe it's time."

There was no mistaking the boy's insulting meaning. Jim took one quick step, grabbed Stub's shirt with his left hand, and jerked young Wyatt toward him. "Back up, kid."

"Back up, nothing!" Stub bawled his defiance. "A two-bit sheriff don't marry no Wyatt. Kitsie knows that. She's just playing with you. She'll marry Zane Biddle."

"That's right," Boone said with biting triumph. "Just on the off chance she ain't playing with you, you'd both better know that, if she marries you, all of Wagon Wheel goes to Stub. She'll starve on your wages, Hallet."

Stub laughed in Jim's face. "She ain't used to starving, tin star."

Jim released his grip on Stub and wheeled to face Kitsie. "Tell them. You're almost twenty-one."

"Old enough to have some sense," Boone flung at her. "Better know what you are, Kitsie. If it's the wrong thing, Hallet will be dead by night."

"That wasn't necessary, Dad." Moving around Jim, Kitsie came to stand beside Stub. "You were right. I was just playing with him."

"Oh, Kitsie!" Nell cried. "You fool!"

"Shut up!" Boone wheeled on Nell, triumph working through him like a drink of whisky. "You tell your mule-headed dad to get out of the country. There's other ways of working on him if the sheriff don't want the job." Boone strode to the front door. "Come on."

Without a word or a glance at him, Kitsie followed her father out of the house. Stub lingered long enough to prod Jim with a grin, his flushed face alive with malice. "Wyatts take their fun where they find it, mister. Even the women." Still grinning, he followed his father and Kitsie out of the house.

Jim stood motionless, staring at the door Stub had slammed shut. It was as if a light had gone out in the room, as if there was no hope anywhere, for life had tricked him with a gaudy promise that it had never meant to keep.

He moved toward the door, stiff-legged, thinking that the smart thing would be to ride out of town and keep riding. He owed the country nothing. He had been a drifter from the time he'd been a kid until he had stopped to ride for Wagon Wheel, and the only reason he had stopped then was because Kitsie's red-lipped smile had warmed him with its promise. Yet, now that he faced this decision, he knew he would stay. His stubborn pride would hold him.

He opened the door, and then turned to look at Nell. "Thanks for trying. Tell Ernie not to budge unless he's scared."

"He's not scared. He'd rather die there than let the Wyatts run him off. He said he didn't think there was a man in the county strong enough to stand against the Wyatts like you have."

Jim grinned thinly. "My hide won't turn a bullet. When Latigo's out of the way, Boone will bring his outfit into town and fix me good."

He moved through the door and paused when Nell cried: "She loves you, Jim! Don't do anything foolish."

"She's sure got a funny way of showing it," he said, and went on into the hot sunshine.

He moved mechanically to Main Street, trying to tell himself that Kitsie had done what she had to do and what he had expected her to do, and at the same time knowing in his heart that she shouldn't have done it. He had thought she possessed strength enough to stay with him. She didn't love Chris Vinton or Zane Biddle or any of the rest who had courted her. She had reason to hate her father, and he knew she had only contempt for her brother. That left Latigo, and like any drowning man reaching for a wild hope Jim saw in the elder Wyatt a slim chance of turning Kitsie back to him.

Reaching the corner of the Mercantile, Jim paused, looking at the bank and wondering if Latigo were still there. He decided that the old man had had time to finish his palaver with Zane Biddle and moved on toward the Bonanza. It was then that he noticed the long string of horses racked in front of the saloon. Again that strange monitor in the back of his mind jangled its warning bell. There were always a few Poverty Flat cowmen in town on Saturday mornings, but this was too many. Without actually counting the horses, he judged that every rancher on the Flat was in the Bonanza.

Jim swung across the street, reaching into his mind for an explanation and finding none. He shouldered through the batwings and stopped, for the dozen men at the bar swung away from it to stare sourly at him, their hostility a pushing force laid against him.

There was a short moment of silence. Then Chris Vinton said: "We don't want no Wyatt hands in here, Hallet. You'd better git."

This was trouble. Jim read it in their faces, in their stiff,

126

unnatural postures. To back up now under Vinton's threat would be a fatal mistake. Striding to the bar, he said— "Whisky."—and turned to Vinton, smoky-gray eyes locking with the other's green ones.

Vinton was close to thirty, Jim judged, a barren-faced man who had courted Kitsie with grim persistence and weekly beat young Stub at poker. He had a ten-cow spread in the poorest part of the Flat, was seldom home, and made his brag that he was the fastest man with a gun on the Stillwater. Jim guessed that he might be, for he wore his gun low and tied down as a professional would. There was always a smoldering bitterness in Vinton's eyes as if he were looking for a fight.

Jim, raw temper making him as proddy as Vinton, said in a flat tone: "Get this through your thick head, Chris. I'm not a Wyatt man. As long as I'm sheriff, I'll enforce the law which same won't be Wyatt law and it won't be Poverty Flat law."

Vinton laughed. "You're a liar, Hallet, and a crook to boot."

Jim stepped away from the bar. "You want us to think you're a purty tough hand, don't you, Chris? All right, we'll see how much of your talk is wind."

They might have set it up to go that far and no further, hoping to break him under the weight of their bluff. Jim was never sure. In any case, that was as far as it went, for Vinton did not draw, and the rest of them moved along the bar, Buck Deeter saying: "No cause for a ruckus, Jim. Chris, shut your tater trap."

Deeter owned the Staircase, the biggest spread on the Flat, and was a man Latigo considered important enough to be elected county commissioner, although he had not been in the valley long. He was tall and swarthy with strong white teeth and dark eyes that liked to laugh. A good man, Jim thought, and a level-headed one.

Not trusting Vinton, Jim said: "All right, Buck, but there is a place where a sheriff stops being a sheriff and starts looking after his own end. That time comes when a cheap-talking tinhorn calls him a liar and a crook." He watched them closely, right hand near gun butt, left hand on the bar beside his drink. "You're all proddy as hell. What's biting you?"

Even Lippy Ord, usually grinning and wanting to talk, was sourly sober. He said: "The Wyatts, Jim. You back up, you bow and kowtow to 'em, and after a while you see you've either got to quit calling yourself a man or do something about it. We're aiming to do it today."

Old Gramp Tatum lurched along the bar. "That'sh right, Lippy, old shon. Shoot 'em dead."

Somebody laughed, a high shrill laugh that was more of a release for taut nerves than an expression of humor.

Deeter said: "This ain't a question of law, Jim. You'd best stay out."

"Mebbe he's aiming to look out for the Wyatts," Vinton sneered.

Too much had happened this day. Jim shoved Lippy Ord aside, the last shred of his self-control breaking, and drove a fist against Vinton's mouth. Men tumbled away. Gramp Tatum sprawled on the floor. Vinton stumbled over him, took another blow on the side of the head, and landed on his back.

"Wait . . . ," Deeter began.

"Let 'em alone," Lippy Ord cut in. "Chris has been spoiling for a fight. Maybe he'll get enough."

Vinton rolled and came to his feet, cursing and spitting blood and teeth. He drove at Jim, fists swinging in round, aimless blows. Jim moved in close and hit him in the stomach. Vinton snapped a fist into Jim's face. Jim felt the shock of it and tasted his own blood. Vinton got his arms around him, hung there, and tried to knee him. Turning, Jim took a blow on his hip, battered Vinton in the ribs, but still Vinton clung to him.

For a moment they danced away from the bar toward the poker tables, Vinton's arms around him, chin hooked over his shoulder, squeezing and trying to bring Jim to the floor. They slammed into a poker table and overturned it, cards and chips cascading to the floor. They stumbled on to the opposite wall and fell against it, Vinton releasing his grip.

Jim's knees slid out from under him, and he went down. Vinton tried to fall on him, knees aimed at his ribs, but Jim rolled clear and came to his feet. Vinton struggled up, crazy with frustration, and lunged at Jim. It was a wild, reckless attack without a thought of defense, the kind of attack that only a furious man driven by a goading sense of futility would make. Jim swung aside and chopped him down with a single sharp-cracking fist to his jaw. Vinton fell, belly down, and this time lay still.

IV

Jim stepped away, rubbing his knuckles and opening and fisting his right hand, a sense of having done a foolish thing rushing through him. This was a poor time to risk a broken hand. He looked at them, Lippy Ord and Buck Deeter and the rest of them, gauging their temper and letting them feel the weight of his anger.

He said: "Let's have it. What got you boys on the prod?"

All of them stirred uneasily, eyes dropping, and he saw that they were changing their estimate of him. Deeter, turning his back to the bar, poured a drink as he said: "You're the law, Jim. Stay out of it until a crime has been committed."

Jim stooped and, jerking Vinton's gun from holster, slid it into his waistband. He straightened, gaze again running along the line of men. He said with a blunt directness: "Bill Riley was a Wyatt man. We all know that, but you likewise know that none of you has been in trouble with the law since I took the star."

"No reason we should be!" Lippy Ord cried. "It's the Wyatts who ought to be in trouble. If our cows get on their side of the deadline, they raise hell. If their cows work up on the Flat, we ain't supposed to do nothing but sit and watch 'em eat our grass, which we ain't got enough of for our own beef."

"Just what are you fixing to do?" Jim pressed.

Again he felt that sullen uneasiness grip them. He knew that someone had worked them into a killing temper, but at the same time he sensed that they wouldn't tell him who it was or what their plan was.

"All right," Jim said coldly. "If there's murder done, some of you will hang." He jerked a thumb at the motionless Vinton. "If you're loco enough to let a loud-mouth like Chris talk you into something you'll kick yourself for later, there'll be some widows on the Flat afore morning."

Jim wheeled to the batwings and immediately turned back when Buck Deeter said: "What are you fixing to do, Jim?"

"I'll have a palaver with Latigo. You boys have got plenty to holler about, and it's time somebody was giving it straight to the Wyatts."

Lippy Ord nodded. "Fetch Latigo over if he wants to palaver, but we'll shoot Boone if he opens his mug."

"I'll get Latigo," Jim said, and, pushing the batwings

open, stepped into the street.

The bank was empty, except for the teller who stared at Jim through the grillwork of his window.

Jim asked: "Where's Latigo?"

"Mister Wyatt is in conference with Mister Biddle," the teller said with distaste as if Jim's familiarity in calling the elder Wyatt by his first name was sacrilege.

Jim pushed back the swinging gate next to the wall and stepped through. The teller called sharply: "I said they were in conference."

"I aim to join the conference." Jim winked at the fuming teller and drummed his knuckles against the door marked **Private**.

"Who is it?" Zane Biddle called.

Without answering, Jim opened the door and stepped through. Biddle rose from his desk, pink-cheeked face showing the surge of anger. He was a round-bellied little man with blue eyes and a nose that twitched when emotions pressed him. He was Santa Claus without the whiskers, Jim thought, and probably a fake one, despite his protestation that his bank existed to serve all of the Stillwater country fairly and impartially.

"I didn't tell you to come in," Biddle said sharply. "Get out. We're busy."

"This is official business." Jim shut the door and winked at Latigo. "Want the money grabber to stay, Latigo?"

Latigo Wyatt had never held Biddle in high regard, and it amused him now to see Jim prodding the man whom other folks held in almost as much awe as they held the Wyatts themselves.

He chuckled and nodded. "Let him stay, Jim, unless you aim to burn his ears off."

Without invitation, Jim pulled up a chair and, sitting

131

down, began rolling a smoke. He said: "You've got trouble, Latigo."

Wyatt reached into his pocket for his stinking black briar and filled it. His cream-colored Stetson was pushed back on his head; his white hair reached almost to his shoulders. Anyone who didn't know would have guessed him far short of his seventy years, for his blue eyes were bright and sharp, his face weather-stained but less lined by age than most men of middle life.

When Latigo had his pipe going, he pinned his eyes on Jim, and said with characteristic confidence: "My troubles are all over, son. It's the other gents that have troubles now."

"I'm one of them other gents," Jim said. "I want to marry Kitsie, only Boone's got other notions."

Biddle pulled in a sharp breath, but Latigo laughed. "What does Kitsie say?"

"I thought she loved me," Jim said, his misery momentarily breaking through his mask of self-control. He told Latigo what had happened at Nell Craft's house. With sudden distaste, he jerked the cigarette from his lips and threw it into the spittoon. "Damn it, Latigo, I don't have no million dollars or a million cows, but I'd make her a better husband than some of these gents who do."

Latigo turned his gaze to Biddle and laughed. "You sure said something that time, son. You and Kitsie didn't fool me much. I seen you making calf-eyes at each other ever since you started riding for us."

"That was why Boone gave you the sheriff's job," Biddle blurted, the tip of his nose working like a rabbit's. "She's young and romantic, and it'd be easy to make her lose her head, but if you really loved her, you'd want her future arranged for."

"I'll arrange for it," Jim flung at him. "She'll have a lot

more fun with me than she would with a fat banker with soft hands."

Biddle had been standing behind his desk. Now he jerked a drawer open, wounded dignity whipping him into an action he would never have taken at another time. Jim came out of his chair to face Biddle.

"Zane, if you touch that gun, I'll kill you."

"Sit down, both of you," Latigo said testily. "You love Kitsie, Jim. I ain't saying she don't love you, but I do say she ain't likely to marry you. She's Boone's girl, not mine. If it was me, I'd favor you." Taking his cold pipe out of his mouth, he reached for a match. "What was this trouble you think I've got?"

"That's for you to hear and not that cottontail. Let's go somewhere."

Latigo laughed again, eyes turning to the silent, raging Biddle. "He's sure got you pegged, Zane. Cottontail. Yes, sir, cottontail with pink cheeks and a wiggly nose." He sobered, nodding at the door. "Suppose you go find something to do out front while me and the sheriff palaver. Trouble." He snorted. "Maybe some trouble would spice things up. Been damned dull lately."

Holding his shattered dignity around him like a worn garment, Biddle rose. "You are welcome to use my office, Mister Wyatt," he said, and, going out on tiptoe in his cat-like walk, he closed the door softly behind him.

"I'm gonna hand it out straight, Latigo," Jim said bluntly. "A lot of folks don't like you, but they know you'll keep your word. That's a notion you never got across to Boone and Stub. They think they're little gods, and they try to make everybody else think the same. That's why you've trouble."

"Now hold on . . . ," Latigo began, quick anger sparking in him.

"Nope, I ain't holding on. I told you I was gonna hand it out straight. Nobody's supposed to talk to the Wyatts like this, but I'm doing it. I seen how it was when I rode for Wagon Wheel. I seen more of it when I started toting the star. Trouble is you're blind 'cause you're on top."

Anger and puzzlement struggled in Latigo for a moment. "What'n hell are you talking about?"

Jim leaned forward. "You bully and you shove and you kick any man in the pants who don't agree with what you Wyatts say. Like Gramp Tatum. Or Buck Deeter. Or any of the rest. It goes for a while. They get madder and madder and scareder and scareder, but all the time their pride's working on 'em."

"Pride," Latigo snorted. "They don't have none. You've got it, and I've got it. So's Boone and so's Stub. So's Kitsie. It's the one thing I was damned sure they had to have, and I taught it to 'em, but Gramp Tatum. . . ." He brushed the thought away with a wave of his long-fingered hand and dug for another match. "Or Zane Biddle. Hell of a fish hook! They don't know what the word means."

"They've got it," Jim said earnestly. "It just ain't our kind of pride, but after so much pushing it gets to working on 'em. Then they're dangerous."

Latigo laughed. "You're spooked, Jim." He struck the match and sucked the flame into the pipe bowl. "They're weaklings. In this country, a weakling's got to stick with the strong if he wants to live. Us Wyatts are strong, Jim. So are you. That's where we're likely to have trouble. When I gave you the star, I knowed you'd never be a Bill Riley. At the same time, you ain't smart if you start getting bullheaded."

"Who did give me this star?" Jim asked curiously. "Biddle said Boone did to get me away from Kitsie."

"We talked it over," Latigo admitted. "I figured that

you'd make a good sheriff, and Boone wanted you out from under Kitsie's nose." He rose. "If you're trying to scare me, Jim, you're barking up the wrong tree. I'm too old to scare."

"I ain't trying to scare you. I'm just trying to get you to see some sense. The Poverty Flat boys are in the Bonanza, and they're sure on the prod. I dunno what got 'em that way, but if you don't go over and powwow with 'em, you've got some fighting to do before you leave town."

Latigo peered his disbelief in a snort of contempt. "They'll have their hands full if they start anything, son. You tell 'em that."

"You afraid to talk to 'em in the Bonanza? Afraid to find out what's eating on 'em?"

"Afraid?" Latigo bawled the word like an enraged bull. "Hell's bells, you know better'n that. Come on. I'll talk to 'em, and I'll use a language even them limp-brained sons can understand. I'll poke some hot lead down the throat of the first yahoo that opens his mug."

V

Latigo stomped out through the bank and into the street, Jim behind him. Biddle, Jim saw, was gone, and he wondered why the banker had not stayed. He caught up with Latigo in the middle of the dust strip.

He said: "Let 'em get it out of their systems, Latigo. Maybe just talking will do the job. You know how it is when a bunch gets steamed up. Sometimes a palaver lets the steam off."

"I don't give a damn whether the steam's off or not,"

Latigo snapped, "but if they want to stop at talking, they'd better be damned careful what they say. I wouldn't let anybody else talk to me like you've done. . . ."

A gun cracked from somewhere across the street. Before the echoes of that first shot died, Latigo Wyatt had stumbled and fallen on his face into the street dust.

For an instant Jim Hallet stood paralyzed, a dozen thoughts rushing through his brain, thoughts that were compressed into a space of a clock tick. He had expected it to happen, but not this way and not this soon.

Another shot racketed into the hot stillness, the slug kicking up dust at Jim's feet. Stooping, he grabbed Latigo's shoulders and, lifting them, dragged the old man across the street to the boardwalk in front of the Bonanza. He never expected to make it. That second bullet had been aimed at him and had missed. A man who would cut down Latigo with a single shot wouldn't be likely to miss again. But the hidden killer did miss. The third bullet was wide by three feet. Jim had Latigo off the street when another gun spoke three times, fast. He was facing the Bonanza, and he didn't know whether the slugs geysered the dust or not.

Jim laid Latigo on the walk. He knelt beside him, vaguely aware of the scared faces of the Poverty Flat men who had bulged out of the saloon but still held back. He heard the thump of running steps and knew that Doc Horton had grabbed his black bag, as he always did when he heard gunfire, and was on his way. He was dimly conscious of these things, for his attention was focused on Latigo. The old man was dying, and he knew it, and the knowledge brought a gaunt weakness to his face. He had killed others, but like many arrogant men he had never expected to die. Now, for the first time since Jim had known him, he was afraid.

"They done it, boy." Latigo's hand gripped Jim's arm. "Boone ain't man enough to run the Wagon Wheel. I never thought the day'd come when I wouldn't be around. You're my kind, Jim. You've got to help him."

Jim nodded. Latigo was right about Boone, but Boone wouldn't see it.

Doc Horton was there then. He tried to nudge Jim away, asking briskly: "Hit bad?" Jim didn't move. It was only a matter of seconds, and Latigo had something more to say.

A lesser man would already have been dead. Latigo's grip on Jim's arm was vise-like; blood bubbled on his lips. Somewhere he found the strength to say: "You marry Kitsie. Don't let that damned pussyfooting Biddle get her." Then his grip went slack, and his arm fell away. Latigo was dead, and the long shadow that he had thrust over the valley for so long passed with him.

Jim rose. "Get him off the street, Doc." He nodded at Lippy Ord and the others who stood in the doorway. "Give him a hand, boys."

They came silently and respectfully, awed by the suddenness and violence of death when only a few moments before they had been idly threatening this man who lay before them. Jim, with his eyes ranging over them, saw that not all of them were there. Chris Vinton was gone. Buck Deeter. Gramp Tatum. A braggy kid named Bud Yellowby who had squatted recently in the fringe of the timber.

"The girl," Lippy Ord muttered. "Don't let her see him, Jim."

Jim turned. Kitsie and Stub were hurrying along the walk. He moved toward them, blocking their path and gripping Kitsie's arm. He said: "It's Latigo. Get her out of town, Stub."

"He's . . . dead?" the girl breathed.

Jim nodded. "He's gone."

"Who did it?" Stub demanded, facing him angrily.

"I don't know."

"Why in hell ain't you finding out?"

"I'll find out. Right now I'm trying to keep this from happening again. Somebody aims to rub the Wyatts out."

Kitsie began walking to the hotel. She had strength to hold back her feelings, but Jim knew how she had loved Latigo, and he knew how much his death would hurt her, a hurt that would grow with time. But Stub didn't stir. He was staring at Jim, violently hating him and still realizing that Jim was his one protection. Latigo had been the keystone. Now neither Boone nor Stub was strong enough to hold Wagon Wheel together, and Jim, watching Stub, sensed that the boy knew it.

"Where's Boone?" Jim asked.

"I don't know."

"I'll get your horse. Go to the hotel and stay off the street."

The Wyatt horses were racked in front of the Mercantile. Jim strode quickly to them, fear prickling his spine. The killer might still be in one of the rooms over the Bonanza or in the hotel. Or on one of the roofs behind a false front. He had not located the dry-gulcher when the shots were fired. As he turned, leading Kitsie's and Stub's horses, he raised his gaze to rake the windows and false fronts, but there was no flash of fire, no snarling slug, nothing to indicate where the murderer had hidden or whether he was still there.

The Poverty Flat men were knotted in front of the Bonanza. As Jim swung toward them, he saw that Buck Deeter had appeared.

Deeter called: "Anything we can do?"

"You've done plenty," Jim said, and moved on.

Jim tied the horses in front of the hotel and went in. None of the Wyatts was in sight. He climbed the stairs and turned along the hall to the front corner room that Latigo had kept rented for Kitsie, but before he reached it, the door opened, and Zane Biddle stepped out. His pink-cheeked face was held very sober as he closed the door.

"I was just offering my condolences," Biddle said. "I trust you will be careful what you say. Kitsie is terribly hurt."

Anger rose in Jim. He had never liked Biddle, and the man had plenty of reason to dislike him, but Biddle's feelings for him were strictly masked behind the sympathetic soberness of his face.

"Thanks for the advice," Jim said, and started to move on toward the door, but Biddle stepped in front of him, a fat, moist hand laid on his arm. He whispered: "Do you know who fired the fatal shot?"

"No."

Biddle looked over his shoulder at the closed door, and then along the hall. He brought his mouth close to Jim's ear. "Where was Boone at the time the shot was fired?"

Jim straightened, his dislike of Biddle growing. "I don't know."

Again Biddle looked over his shoulder and brought his lips back to Jim's ear. "Don't tell them I'm suggesting this to you, but I knew the situation in the Wyatt family better than anyone else. I know Boone hated his father, largely because of Latigo's attitude toward Stub's gambling losses. Boone insisted on paying them, and Latigo didn't like that. He told me today that he was the only one who would draw on the Wyatt account from now on."

Jim's mind reached ahead of Biddle. What the banker had just said gave Boone Wyatt plenty of motive for murder. Wagon Wheel would go to him with Latigo out of the way, and he was the kind of passion-ruled man who might easily be touched off into doing exactly what Biddle was insinuating.

"I'll find out about Boone," Jim said.

"It was just something I thought you ought to know," Biddle said smugly.

Biddle had turned away when Jim asked: "Where were you when Latigo was shot?"

Biddle jumped as if he had been stung. He wheeled back to face Jim, suddenly angry. He opened his mouth to say something, and then closed it. His hands fisted at his sides. When he had regained control of himself, he said with biting scorn: "I suppose it is your duty to investigate everybody, but I assure you I had no reason to kill Latigo. He was the main source of revenue for my bank."

"I asked you where you were."

Biddle jabbed a thumb at the door. "In there with Kitsie when the shot was fired. Ask her if you don't believe me." Turning, he walked down the hall, the tip of his nose working, shoulders back, an aroused and insulted man.

Jim watched him until he disappeared down the stairs, a grim smile touching his lips. A pudgy man acting insulted had always been a comical sight to him, but he saw little humor in Zane Biddle now. He stood there a moment, letting the seed of suspicion that Biddle had planted grow in him. He wondered at the man's motives, but whatever they were, he knew he could not ignore what the banker had said.

Jim tapped on Kitsie's door. He waited, uneasiness working in him. The moments that lay ahead would be hard on Kitsie, but he saw no way to soften them. She opened the door and stood there, straight-backed and motionless. Without waiting for an invitation, he stepped into the room.

140

It was a sort of sitting room with expensive furniture, a thick rug, and red velour drapes on the windows. A door to the left opened into a small bedroom. The man who had built the hotel years before, when the land was new and held an unkept promise, had called it his bridal suite, but Latigo had promptly rented it permanently because, as he put it, nobody else in the valley was important enough to have it. Later, when Kitsie had grown up, it became her personal quarters whenever she came to town.

"Well?" Kitsie did not move, her tone sharp.

"Where's your dad?" Jim asked. "Does he know?"

"I have no idea," Kitsie said.

Stub, sitting beside the window, rose and crossed the room to Jim. He was still a boy, although old enough to be a man, and he could not grow up fast enough now that he faced a man's job.

He said, his voice breaking a little: "Get out."

"Just a minute, sonny." Jim crossed to the door that opened into the bedroom, looked in, and swung back. "Where was Biddle when that shot was fired?"

"In here, talking to us," Kitsie said, "if it's any of your business."

She wouldn't lie. Jim was as sure of that as he could be sure of anything that depended upon the uncertainty of human behavior. He crossed the room to her, ignoring Stub. He said: "Kitsie, I didn't love Latigo like you did, but I liked him and I respected him. I'm going to get the man that killed him."

"Go ahead."

"I need your help. Where was your dad at the time Latigo was shot?"

"I don't know. I told you that. He came up with Stub and me after we left Nell's place. We talked, and he left. He

141

didn't say where he was going."

"How long was that before the shooting?"

"I don't know. Fifteen or twenty minutes. I don't see what it's got to do with. . . ." Then she saw what was in his mind, and she froze, eyes wide. "You don't think he could have killed Granddad? Jim, why did I ever think I loved you?"

He said: "Stub, I told you to get her out of town. Your horses are in front." Turning from her, he left the room, his face hard-touched by the misery that was in him.

VI

Again Jim Hallet faced a decision, as brutal as any he had faced in the past. As sheriff he must question Boone Wyatt, perhaps arrest him if he resisted answering. Then he remembered Kitsie's frozen, wide-eyed face, and a dull hopelessness crawled through him. Only a few hours before she had come to town loving him, looking forward to meeting him, to going to Nell Craft's place as she had week after week. It had been a good world, bright with hope, hope that had lasted even after he had faced Boone in the street, after Kitsie had walked out of Nell's house with her father, for hope is hard to kill when a man is in love. Then Latigo had said that, if Kitsie were his girl, he would favor Jim, and hope had flamed again. Now Latigo was dead, and duty laid a club against Jim's back, offering him no reward.

For half an hour Jim searched the hotel rooms that faced the street, the alley, and roof tops behind the false fronts. For all of Boone Wyatt's top-heavy pride and loud-mouthed arrogance, Jim found it hard to believe that he had killed his father. He kept remembering Chris Vinton had not been with the Poverty Flat men in front of the Bonanza when Latigo had been shot. Neither had Buck Deeter nor the Yellowby kid. He could count Gramp Tatum out. The old man was drunk and sleeping it off in the alley.

The half hour brought no clue. No tracks. No empty shells. No hint of where the killer had stood and no hint as to his identity. Jim had asked the Poverty Flat men to stay in town. Now he returned to the Bonanza, not liking this task and sensing that it would bring him nothing.

They were all there, idly talking, a few drinking, some trying to interest themselves in a game of poker and failing. Jim moved directly to Vinton and asked: "Where were you, Chris, when Latigo was shot?"

Vinton's battered face held no apparent resentment. He said: "In the back room with Deeter and Yellowby. We had a little poker game going." His bruised lips shaped into a crooked grin. "I was ready to pull on Latigo any day in the year, but this time I didn't have my gun. Remember?"

Jim nodded. Vinton's Colt was in his waistband where he had placed it after the fight, but there were other guns. He swung to Deeter, but before he could put the question, the Staircase man nodded. "He's giving it to you straight, Jim. We were having a game."

Without being asked, the Yellowby kid said: "That's it, Sheriff."

Jim's eyes swept the line of men along the bar, a bitter sense of frustration rushing at him. Maybe Deeter and Yellowby were lying to cover up for Vinton, but he couldn't prove it. Not yet. Yellowby was weak. He had thought Deeter was on the level, but now he was not sure. There was no sympathy on their faces, no friendliness.

"Damn it," Jim said in sudden anger. "I was bringing

Latigo over to talk to you when somebody cut him down. Facing him with a gun in your hand is one thing, but drilling him like you done is murder."

"You don't know any of us done it, Jim," Deeter said quietly. "You'd be smart to go easy on that talk till you do."

"That's right," Lippy Ord said. "I rode in today, mighty sore about the way Latigo had treated us. Wouldn't have taken much to have made me pull on him, 'specially if we found out Biddle was closing us out like he done some of our neighbors in the past just on Latigo's say-so. Now I kind o' wish he was alive. We're gonna be worse off with Boone running Wagon Wheel."

"Not if our brave sheriff can see past his nose," Vinton said pointedly.

Jim swung toward the gunman. "Maybe I'm blind, Chris, but I aim to keep looking. That slug was mighty near dead center, and you claim to shoot straight."

"I do, but I didn't plug him. Keep looking, Jim. Maybe you can think of somebody else who wanted Latigo out of the way."

"Boone!" the Yellowby kid shouted. "Plenty of gents would kill their old man just to get their hands on something as big as Wagon Wheel."

"He knew we were in town," Deeter added, "and he knew we wasn't right friendly toward Latigo. It'd be natural enough to push it off on one of us."

A stomach-sinking sense of frustration crawled through Jim. What they said made sense, and they were clearing each other. It left nobody but Boone and Gramp Tatum, who was blind drunk. Jim felt as if the rush of events was washing him downstream, and he was helpless before the force of the current. Again Kitsie's set, cold face came before his eyes. Then he thought of something else.

Boone was not much of a man alongside Latigo, but he was a man. With him out of the way, young Stub would be running Wagon Wheel, and that would mean a quick end to what was now a great ranch. Whoever had killed Latigo may have planned for Boone to be taken out at the same time. These men all had reasons to hate and fear the Wyatts, but Jim still didn't know what had finally stirred them into a violent temper and brought them to town today looking for trouble.

Jim reached for tobacco and papers, dropping his eyes as he rolled a smoke. He said softly: "How come you boys thought of Boone?"

They stirred uneasily, looking at each other, and then the Yellowby kid saw his chance to play big. He bawled: "Hell, Sheriff, Biddle told us about Latigo stopping Boone from drawing on the Wyatt bank account!"

Vinton jabbed Yellowby with an elbow. Yellowby squalled an oath and jumped away. "Ain't no secret. We know Boone Wyatt wants Poverty Flat for summer range, and the way to get it is to shove us off."

"Damn you, Bud, keep . . . ," Vinton began.

"All right, Chris." Jim slid the cigarette between his lips. "Let the kid alone. He's got the guts it takes to talk if nobody else has."

"Yeah," Deeter murmured. "He let something slip. You know why we're on the prod and you know it was Biddle that got us to thinking of Boone. Does it tell you anything else?"

The Yellowby kid had been pushed back. They formed a tight line in front of him, watchful, grim. They had united, Jim saw, and it was natural for them to consider a lawman their enemy because valley law had been Wyatt law for a generation. They all might be guilty of murder, or just one or two, but the thing had worked so that now they were against him regardless of who was guilty.

"Don't tell me much, Buck," Jim said, "except that you boys are gunning for Boone. That might not be good."

"It's good enough to save our outfits." Deeter jabbed a forefinger at Jim, strong white teeth flashing as a vagrant ray of sunlight slanted across his swarthy face. "You're supposed to be the law, but you claim you ain't a Wyatt man like Bill Riley was. You'll prove it when you lock Boone Wyatt up."

"I'll have to find him first." Jim moved toward the batwings, cold cigarette dangling from the corner of his mouth. He turned suddenly so that he faced them, calling sharply: "Yellowby, come here."

Yellowby hesitated, narrow face mirroring indecision, gaze swinging to Buck Deeter.

Jim said again: "Come here, Yellowby."

"You've got nothing against him," Deeter said. "Stay here, Bud."

"I can see a dead man walking," Jim breathed. "The kid talks too easy. Yellowby, you're coming with me. I'll kill the first man who tries to stop you."

"We pegged you wrong, Jim," Deeter breathed. "You're a little tougher than we guessed. That makes you the dead man walking."

"Want to make a try, Buck?"

It was a challenge, cold and hard. Jim, standing loosely by the batwings, his beaky-nosed face signaling his intent, was not a man to be taken lightly.

Deeter shrugged. "I ain't asking for a fight, Jim. I want to see you turn Boone Wyatt up. Then we'll know what to do."

"Yellowby, climb on your horse. Get out of town. Keep riding."

The kid broke the batwings in an awkward, adolescent run. He went past Jim, not stopping to say—"Thank you."—and dived through the door. A moment later hoof thunder rolled in from the street.

"Yeah, we pegged you wrong," Deeter murmured. "You've got good eyes."

"I can see, all right." Jim's gaze probed Lippy Ord. "I've counted some of you boys as my friends, and I've figured you was square. Maybe I pegged you wrong, or maybe you're being pushed in a direction you don't want to go. I'll soon find out."

Jim backed through the door, watchful for the first hostile move, but none came. He stepped quickly away from the saloon and turned toward the hotel, pondering Boone Wyatt's disappearance and finding no logical answer, but he was sure of one thing. What the Poverty Flat boys did would be determined by Jim's action when Boone did appear.

VII

The stage from Ontario was rolling in. Jim paused in front of the hotel to wait for it. It was a custom with him to meet the stage whenever he was in town, partly because it was the one contact between the Stillwater country and the railroad to the east, but mostly because it was a good thing for the sheriff to be familiar with the comings and goings of the people in his town.

The two Wyatt horses were at the hitch rail. Staring at them, Jim wondered uneasily why Stub and Kitsie were still in town. It was dangerous—at least, for Stub. If Jim judged

147

the temper of the Poverty Flat men accurately, they would finish the job that had been started with the murder of Latigo.

The stage was there then, trace chains jangling, dust drifting up past the coach when it stopped in a white, suffocating cloud. There was one passenger, a young woman, close to twenty-five, Jim judged, and attractive in a round-bodied way. She stepped away from the stage to get out of the dust, saw Jim, and came toward him in a hip-swinging walk.

"You're the sheriff, Jim Hallet, aren't you?" she asked. "I'm Honey Nolan. I still go by that name, but I'm really Honey Wyatt."

He lifted his Stetson, wondering how she fitted into the Wyatt family. "Pleased to meet you, ma'am," he said.

She smiled at him, dark eyes moving appreciatively along his lean, hard-muscled body. She straightened her blue bonnet that was gray with dust, and after unbuttoning her tan duster she shook it. Her white silk shirtwaist and dark, tight-fitting skirt showed the curve of her hips and thighs.

"Some country you've got, Sheriff." She laid her bold gaze upon him, smiling. "Where's Latigo?"

"Latigo?" Jim braced himself, remembering that she'd said her name was Wyatt.

"Yes, Latigo." She stood spread-legged, hands on her hips. "Look, star man, don't tell me I swallowed a bunch of lies when Latigo Wyatt said he was the big gun in these parts. Why, he claimed he had more cows than you could count and more land than I could ride around all day. Not that I like the land, but I took Latigo for better or for worse, and I guess I took his land with him."

"Latigo's dead. Shot this morning."

"Dead?" She stared at him blankly. "No, Latigo couldn't

148

die. He wanted me to come out here when we got married. Trouble was I had a contract signed up and couldn't come. But he couldn't die. He's the kind of man who lives forever."

"He's dead," Jim said. "His grandson and granddaughter are upstairs. You want to see them?"

"Latigo dead. A sweet time for a bride to get home." She swung back to her valise and picked it up. "Sure I want to see my grandchildren, but I doubt like hell that they'll want to see me."

Jim reached for her valise and took it out of her hand. "This way," he said, and turned into the lobby. He wondered what would be the end of this. Kitsie had had too much to stand already. She shouldn't have to face this, but he saw no way to avoid it.

Honey Nolan kept pace with Jim along the hall to Kitsie's door in a leggy, graceful walk. Jim knocked. The door swung open, Stub crowding out, a cocked gun in his hand, fine-featured face quivering with fear.

"Put it up," Jim said testily.

Stub's gun arm sagged. "I thought it was Vinton or Deeter or some of them." He holstered his gun and sleeved sweat from his face. "Sorry."

"Stub, this is Latigo's wife," Jim said.

"Latigo's . . . wife!" Stub stared at the woman in the dazed way of a man so shocked that thought processes were paralyzed. "You're crazy, Hallet. He never married again."

Kitsie was standing across the room, talking to Zane Biddle. She heard and came to the door. She said: "Come in."

Honey Nolan stepped boldly into the room. "So you're the grandchildren. Latigo was mighty proud of you, and I don't blame him. Sure sorry to hear what happened. I haven't seen him since we were married a year ago in Boise, and then to get here on the day. . . ." She broke off as if she felt too strongly about it to go on.

Jim shut the door. He said: "It seems a little too pat for you to get here the day Latigo gets plugged."

Honey whirled to face him. "What do you mean by that, star man?"

"I mean a dead man ain't in no shape to deny marrying you."

"If you mean . . . ," Honey began.

"We had not heard Granddad was married," Kitsie cut in quickly. "He was an old man, over seventy. It hardly seems possible he would get married, or that he would not tell us if he did."

"He was younger than any man of seventy I ever saw," Honey said, her fists clenching at her sides. "Maybe he wasn't proud of me. Maybe that's why he didn't tell you, but I married him in good faith. He wanted me to come and live with him as soon as I could. You're not going to put me out this way."

"I don't believe it!" Stub shouted. "Got your marriage license?"

Honey dropped down on the bed and began to cry. "I didn't think I had to bring a marriage license to show my husband I was married. I didn't know Latigo would be dead when I got here. I never dreamed the man I loved. . . ."

"Just a minute, Missus Wyatt." Biddle moved toward Kitsie, pink-cheeked face showing concern. "I'm afraid she's right. You see, Latigo did marry her."

"Why didn't he tell us?" Kitsie asked.

The tempered steel that had been in Latigo had come down to Kitsie. She had complete control of herself; her grief was hidden deeply within her. Jim, watching her from

150

the door, knew that Kitsie had become Wagon Wheel. The absent Boone didn't count. Stub, scared almost to the point of hysteria, didn't count. It was Kitsie who had the hard core of courage, the grim determination. It would be Kitsie who would hold the empire Latigo had built.

For a moment neither Biddle nor Honey Nolan spoke. The woman had stopped crying, and her gaze touched Biddle's face.

She asked then: "Who are you?"

"The banker, Zane Biddle. I'm the one who has been sending you the checks." He turned to Kitsie. "As you know, Latigo didn't like to write, so he left even the letter writing to me. Or most of it."

"Why didn't you tell us?" Kitsie asked again.

"I could not betray Latigo's confidence," Biddle said. "I have been so shocked by his death that I never gave it a thought, but I can assure you that this woman is the one he married. I have her picture. It's over in the bank. She sent it to him about three months ago when her show was in Denver. All of her letters were sent to him through me because he didn't want any of you folks to see them. He was, well, worried over what you'd say."

Jim remembered that Latigo had gone to Boise about a year ago, and he had come back feeling happier than usual. He claimed to have had a big hand in a poker game that had more than paid for the trip, but he could have married this Honey Nolan. If he had, he would probably have worked it the way Biddle said.

There was a moment of silence. Stub had gone to the window and was looking down into the street, worrying, Jim saw, more about his safety than anything else. Biddle stood beside Kitsie, his gaze on her, one hand nervously patting his bald spot. Honey, wide-eyed, stared defiantly at Kitsie.

"I won't stay where I'm not wanted," Honey said. "I suppose I'll have to go back."

"I think it would be wise," Biddle said gravely. "I assure you that you'll be taken care of financially. That is the way Latigo would have wanted it."

"No," Kitsie said flatly. "She could bleed Wagon Wheel dry, and you were just telling me that our cash was very low."

"Your herd will soon be on the trail to Winnemucca," Biddle said, "and I'll be happy to advance you all the money you need. I've done that for years, and Latigo's death will make no difference."

Kitsie shook her head. "No. If . . . if . . ."—she floundered for the right word—"if Missus Wyatt wants to be taken care of financially, she'll come home. She'll work along with the rest of us, and she'll live our kind of life." She fixed her blue eyes on Honey. "I'm sure Granddad would want it that way."

"But I don't know anything about ranch life," Honey began.

"You'll learn. It'll be your living the same as it's ours, and you'll have to work for it."

"Stub never worked for his living," Biddle pointed out.

Stub swung away from the window. "Shut up, Biddle."

"You shut up." Kitsie did not raise her voice, but her words slapped him into silence. "He's right, Stub. From now on, you're working. Granddad planned on that or he wouldn't have stopped the rest of us from cashing checks. And no more poker." Kitsie turned to Jim. "We're leaving now. We would have gone sooner, but Stub was afraid of the Poverty Flat men. Are they still in the Bonanza?"

"All but Bud Yellowby," Jim replied. "I'll see you get out of town."

"Get a horse for Missus Wyatt, will you, Jim?"

"I can't ride a horse," Honey cried. "Latigo told me I wouldn't have to."

"Get a buggy," Kitsie said. "We'll be down in five minutes."

Kitsie had changed in the few hours since he had kissed her in Nell Craft's kitchen. He turned to look at her again, puzzled by it. Her face was as gray as the desert that ran a hundred miles to the west; she was as immovable as the Steens Mountains to the south. He thought, and it was like a slashing knife blade in him, that she didn't need him, that she was a Wyatt, and that many of the qualities that had made Latigo a success were in his granddaughter.

"I'll get a buggy for you," Jim said.

He stepped into the hall. Kitsie followed, shutting the door behind her. "I understand some of the things I didn't when I talked to you this morning. Dad told me the same as you did, that he had framed Ernie Craft. Then he said he'd have to get rid of you because you wouldn't take orders."

He looked down at her, wanting to take her in his arms and kiss her, to tell her he loved her and would always love her. But he didn't. She didn't want it. She was looking squarely at him, holding him away with her eyes.

"I'm still looking for Boone," he said.

"You should have sense enough to know he didn't kill Granddad. Keep looking and you'll find him." She swallowed, fighting to hold her tone level. "I think you'll find him dead."

"Why?"

"They're after the Wyatts, aren't they? There would be no sense in killing one without killing the other, would there?"

"I'll get the buggy," Jim said, and turned away.

They were on the street, waiting, when he drove the buggy from the livery stable to the hotel. Kitsie stepped in and took the lines. She said—"Thanks, Jim."—in a cool, distant voice. "Get in, Missus Wyatt."

Biddle, standing on the walk, said: "I'll be out this evening, Kitsie, and I'll bring Missus Wyatt's picture and her letters. It should be proof enough."

That was when the Poverty Flat men, Buck Deeter and Chris Vinton in front, left the Bonanza and strode along the boardwalk, Deeter calling: "Wyatt, get away from them women!"

Stub began to tremble, his face going as gray as the dust of the street. He started to reach for his gun and then let his hand drop away.

He cried: "I've got no reason to fight you, Buck!"

"We've got plenty of reason to fight the Wyatts," Deeter grated. "Make your play."

"There'll be no fighting," Jim said. "Get on your horse, Stub. Buck, if you pull, I'll drill you between the eyes."

They stopped, doubt tugging at Deeter. Vinton, still wanting to push, bawled: "Hell, he's just a bluff, Buck!"

"I don't think so," Deeter said. "Latigo was a good judge of men. Looks like Hallet is still working for the Wyatts."

"I'm sheriff, Buck," Jim said.

Stub was on his horse and reining him into the street. He

knew now he'd get clear, and a sudden rush of courage made him shout: "Us Wyatts ain't backing up none, Deeter! We started to move Ernie Craft, and we'll move him. Then you'd better get off Poverty Flat." Stub cracked steel to his horse and went out of town on the run.

Honey stood beside the buggy, paralyzed by fright. Zane Biddle, backing toward the hotel, showed concern, but Kitsie's face mirrored only contempt. "It's funny how brave you are, Deeter, now that Granddad's gone. We won't bother Ernie Craft, but Stub was right about one thing. This valley is too small for you and Wagon Wheel. Get in, Missus Wyatt."

Jim took Honey's arm and helped her into the buggy. They wheeled away, Kitsie's horse tied behind. When they were gone, Jim moved warily toward Deeter. He said: "This morning I figured you boys had a lot on your side, but I reckon I was wrong. The Wyatts don't look like angels, but I never knew one of them to dry-gulch a man. When I find out which one of you done it, I'll get him."

Deeter swung his dark eyes to Biddle and then brought them to Jim, his bold, confident smile on his lips. "You won't last long, tin star. With Latigo gone, Wagon Wheel will fall apart, and we'll move in. Poverty Flat, one hunk of bunchgrass for a cow. Hell . . ."—he spat into the dust—"we aim to get some good graze." He swung away, saying: "Let's ride, boys."

The Poverty Flat men mounted and left town in a rolling cloud of dust. Jim, staring after them, thought how much this day had changed everything. The Wyatts had sowed their seed and reaped a harvest of lead. He turned to Biddle who was watching him thoughtfully through narrowed eyes.

"A banker's neck will stretch same as a cowman's," Jim murmured, and, stepping around him, went into the hotel.

VIII

It was late afternoon with long shadows slanting across the dust strip, and it was cooler. This was the first moment Jim had had to relax since he had faced Boone Wyatt that morning, and he remembered he had not eaten, except for a slim breakfast shortly after sunup. He turned into the hotel dining room and ordered a steak.

"Jim." A quavering shout washed in from the street. "Jim, where the hell are you?"

The front legs of Jim's chair came down hard against the floor. It was Gramp Tatum. Jim rose and tapped on the window. Gramp saw him, and lurched through the lobby into the dining room. His beard was matted with dirt and filth, and he stank of the cheap whisky he had drunk that morning.

"Jim. My gun." He held out the old cap and ball revolver Jim had seen that morning. "It's been fired. Three times."

Jim took the gun, staring at Gramp and not understanding until the old man swallowed and pointed a shaking finger down the street. "Boone Wyatt. Shot three times, but I didn't do it. So help me, Jim, I didn't do it."

"Where'd you find Boone?"

"I didn't find him." Gramp gripped Jim's arm. "It was Lucky. In the storeroom back of the Bonanza. Hidden behind some beer barrels. Jim, I tell you I didn't do it."

Jim slid the gun into his waistband. He said—"Come on."—and left the dining room.

Gramp had to run to keep up, repeating over and over that he hadn't done it. Jim said nothing more until he reached the saloon. The barman, Lucky Donovan, motioned to Jim when he came in and led the way to the storeroom. There, wedged between the walls and some beer barrels, lay Boone Wyatt with three bullet holes in his chest.

"I didn't touch him," Donovan said.

Boone's gun, Jim saw, was in his holster. There was a window opening on the alley, but there were so many tracks in the dust that none meant anything.

"I didn't hear no shooting, except when they got Latigo," Donovan offered.

Jim nodded, saying nothing, but he remembered that there had been three more shots that morning after he had dragged Latigo to the walk. Gramp Tatum stood in the doorway, trembling and chattering that he hadn't done it.

"Shut up," Donovan said.

Gramp lowered his tone but kept on muttering.

"The window opens easily," Jim said thoughtfully. "Somebody could have shoved him through and then crawled in and dragged him over here."

"I don't pay much attention to that window." Donovan said. "Fact is, I don't come back here much. He could have laid there till I smelled him, but I happened to bust a lamp chimney, and the only extra one I had was in here."

Jim pushed past Gramp into the saloon. "Who bought your drinks this morning?"

"I . . . I bought 'em myself."

"You couldn't have got that drunk on the dollar I gave you," Jim said patiently.

"I couldn't shoot straight enough to kill him," Gramp quavered.

"You could at that distance," Jim said. "Boone was shot close up, judging by the powder burns. Now, who paid for your whisky?"

Gramp began to tremble. "I . . . I disremember."

Jim glanced at Donovan, but the bartender shook his

head. "Nobody gave him anything that I saw after he came in. He had a fistful of silver dollars, and he was showing that gun around and swearing he was gonna get Latigo and Boone."

"All right," Jim said. "You're going to jail, Gramp. You're going to stay locked up till you remember who bought your whisky. Lucky, go tell Doc Horton he's got another carcass."

But Gramp wouldn't say anything after the cell door had closed on him, except to repeat: "I didn't do it. Don't you believe me, Jim?"

"I'll believe you when you tell me who bought your whisky. You're a blabber, Gramp. You duck around and look in windows and listen at keyholes. Then you sell what you've learned."

"I don't neither," Gramp howled.

"Then how come you told Boone me and Kitsie were at Nell Craft's place?"

Gramp gripped the bars with his gnarled hands, bearded face pressed against them. "Aw, Jim, I had to have a drink. I got a dollar out of Boone. Bowing and scraping just like everybody's done for years. I didn't know I was gonna get twenty dollars from. . . ." He stopped and began to tremble. "I'm just a born liar. You can't believe anything I say."

"I told you they hang old men for murder."

"He won't let me hang. He's got money. I didn't plug Boone no-how." Gramp rattled the bars. "Let me out."

Jim walked away and went back to the dining room. He ate the steak he had ordered, thinking about Boone Wyatt's murder. Kitsie had called the turn when she had said they had no reason to kill Latigo without killing Boone.

It had been set up skillfully with much thought and careful planning. Jim was supposed to think that Boone had killed his father, and that Gramp Tatum had shot Boone. Gramp was a safe victim for everybody. He was a washed-up whisky bum. If Jim didn't see it that way, a dry-gulcher's slug could take care of him, and Buck Deeter, as county commissioner, could wangle the appointment of a new sheriff who would call the case settled.

It was dusk when Jim stepped out of the dining room to the hotel porch. He shaped a smoke and lighted it, the match flame throwing a quick red light across his face. Another thought had come to him, a thought that jabbed him with a sharp edge of fear. If Stub and Kitsie were dead, the Wyatts would be finished, and Jim knew there were no other heirs.

A brief crimson glory painted the western sky. Then the sun was gone, and the color faded. A dry wind, strong with the smell of sage, touched Jim and rattled the hotel sign above his head. Then he heard the sound of a horse, and he stepped into the street, hand on gun belt, and watched horse and rider take shape. It was, he saw with surprise, the Yellowby boy, and he was hanging to the horn as if he were wounded.

"Doc," Jim cried, "come here!"

"I'm all right." Yellowby reined up. His head and chest dropped lower against the horn, and Jim, stepping to him, steadied him in the saddle. It was then that he saw the dark stain on the boy's shirt.

"Who done it, Bud?"

"Deeter. He's bad with a gun, Jim. Been acting damned pious, thinking you wouldn't catch on, and wanting to fool Latigo, but he's twice as bad as Vinton. They're gonna hit Ernie Craft's place tonight and salivate him. They want you to think Wagon Wheel done it."

Yellowby fainted then, sliding off the saddle into Jim's

arms. Doc Horton was there, saying: "Bring him to my office. I'll go light a lamp."

Another man who had come into the street at Jim's call gave him a hand, and they carried Yellowby to the medico's office.

"He'll be all right," Horton said after a quick look. "Slug caught him a little high to finish him. Lost a lot of blood, though."

Yellowby's eyes came open. "Jim."

"Here." Jim came close to the cot.

"I ain't plumb yellow," the boy breathed. "I saw you was calling it right today in the Bonanza. I blabbed, and Deeter would have got me. I got boogered, and I had to make a run for it." He swallowed, fists clenched. "After I got out of town, I thought how it left you. I came back, aiming to give you a hand, but I ran into Deeter. My horse is faster'n his, or I wouldn't have got here."

"What happened when Latigo was shot?"

"I don't know for sure. We was having this poker game when all of a sudden Vinton jumped up and said he had business outside, but I was supposed to tell you he didn't leave the room. Deeter said he had business, too. He said to open the door into the saloon and watch for you. They pulled out, and I stayed there, watching. Then I heard the shooting. Purty soon they came back, and we started playing again."

"Where was the shooting?"

"One of the guns sounded like it was upstairs, maybe in one of them rooms facing the street. Other one was in the alley."

"Thanks, Bud."

Jim stepped into the street, knowing that he had to get to Ernie Craft's place, but at the same time realizing how long the odds were against him. Stub Wyatt was entirely unpredictable. He had shouted in what had been a mere show of bravado that Wagon Wheel would move Ernie Craft off his place. Kitsie had said they would leave him alone, but whether she could handle Stub after she got home was a question.

The bulk of the Wagon Wheel hands were in the high country with the cattle. Some would come to town to let their collective wolf loose, but there were a few older men, largely pensioners, who stayed around the ranch. Stub could use them against Craft if they'd follow him, but the real danger, as Jim saw it, came from Deeter and Vinton and the Poverty Flat boys. There was no telling what would happen if Deeter elected to move against Wagon Wheel after they had attacked Ernie Craft.

Jim saddled his horse, thinking of this and finding only one possible chance to stop Deeter. Lippy Ord and most of the Poverty Flat cowmen were good men, misled by Deeter but fundamentally sound. If he could break Ord and the rest from Deeter—it was only a wild hope. Deeter had fooled Latigo, and he had fooled Jim. There was little chance, then, that Ord and the rest could be kept from going all the way with Deeter. Then Jim thought of Gramp Tatum. Smiling grimly, Jim saddled another horse and went back to the jail.

Gramp was sleeping when Jim came along the corridor with a lighted lamp. He stirred uneasily and sat up. "What's biting you?" he asked truculently. "I tell you and I'll keep telling you . . . I didn't kill Boone."

"I know." Jim unlocked the door. "I'm letting you out, a sort of parole, you might call it."

Gramp followed Jim back to the office, staring at him suspiciously. Jim picked up the old cap and ball pistol he had taken from Gramp, shook his head, and laid it down.

"You know, Gramp, they tell me you used to be a pretty

good man. That was before I got here. Since I been in the valley, you've just been a no-good bum, a barfly mooching drinks off anybody you could. You'd crawl, belly down, like a whipped pup."

"Now you lookee here," Gramp began, "you ain't got no call. . . ."

"Gramp, how'd you like to be a man again?"

Some of the truculence went out of the oldster's face. He bowed his head, gnarled hands gripping the edge of Jim's desk. "Too late, son. I'm a crawling thing that ought to git under a rock and stay there."

Jim took down a gun belt from the wall and handed it to Gramp. "Try it on. That's a good iron in the holster. A Thirty-Eight. Be about right for you. Beats the old relic you've been toting."

Gramp extended a trembling hand. "What's this about?" He buckled the belt around him, pulled the gun and hefted it and slid it back.

"You know Ernie Craft?"

"A damned good man," Gramp said, as if, by some miracle, he had suddenly become Jim's equal in toughness.

Jim turned to the door to hide his grin. He had gambled that far inside Gramp Tatum there was a spark of his old pride. He said—"Let's ride, Gramp."—and stepped into the saddle.

IX

They rode directly south from town, following the road to Wagon Wheel until they climbed a ridge. This long finger of rock that extended nearly across the valley was, according

162

to the law Latigo had laid down years ago, the deadline. The Poverty Flat cowmen could use the grass to the north, that to the south was Wagon Wheel's. Actually it was as Lippy Ord had said in the Bonanza that morning: nothing was said if Wyatt cattle drifted north, but the heavens were pulled down on the man whose stock was found south of the deadline.

Swinging west, they followed the ridge for a mile. It was fully dark now, the lights of the town lost behind a swell in the sage flat. A wafer moon showed above the eastern hills; stars freckled a black sky, beacons to troubled men filled with hungers and dreams and sorrows. The lights of Wagon Wheel glittered to the south, and Jim's mind turned to Kitsie as it did much of the time. Hers was a sorrow drowning the dreams, but because she was a Wyatt, she would hug her sorrow to herself and no one could comfort her.

The ridge broke off sharply, and they angled down the steep slope to the bowl-like valley where Ernie Craft had settled beside a small spring. A light showed in the tarpaper shack, and Jim breathed a long, relieved sigh. He said: "Ernie's all right."

"What'd you figure was wrong?" Gramp asked. "Think the Wyatts would beef him?"

"Or Buck Deeter." Jim slapped the words at him. "He wants the Wyatts wiped out, so it'd be fine to get Ernie's killing laid on 'em. The hell of it is you're helping him. He got you worked up by telling you what a bunch of skunks the Wyatts are. Then he gives you a fistful of silver. . . ."

"It wasn't Deeter," Gramp cried. "It was. . . ." He caught himself and swore bitterly. "You're purty cute, Jim, but it didn't work."

"You're a damned fool," Jim flung out. "I need your say-so to bust 'em, and you're too scared to talk."

"I know which side of my bread the butter's on," Gramp mumbled.

They had reached the bottom of Craft's valley when the thunder of hoofs from the south came to them.

"Wagon Wheel!" Jim yelled. "Damn that crazy Stub. Come on, Gramp." He cracked steel to his horse, heading directly toward Craft's shack. He called: "Blow out your light, Ernie!"

The light went out. Jim reined up and, swinging down, gave the animal a slap on the rump. "It's Jim Hallet, Ernie."

Gramp pulled up and dismounted stiffly, cursing his sore muscles. He grumbled: "What'n hell did you bring me on this joy ride for? I won't be able to sit for a month."

"It ain't a joy ride," Jim said. "Get your horse out of here. Ernie, got your cutter?"

"I've got my Thirty-Thirty," the nester said. "Who's coming?"

"You guess."

They stood in front of the shack for a moment, listening, until Gramp came back. Then Craft said: "I reckon Boone's making his promise good."

"It'd be Stub," Jim said, and told him quickly what had happened. "I figured Deeter and the Poverty Flat boys would be paying you a visit, but they wouldn't come from that direction."

The horses were close now, ten or more, Jim guessed from the sound. They were racing across the valley floor in a hard run toward the shack.

"Inside," Jim said.

The thin walls of the shack gave poor shelter, but there was no time to find anything better. Jim lunged through the door and, turning to the window, smashed the glass out with his gun barrel and eared back the hammer. Craft had dropped on his belly in the doorway, and Gramp Tatum had disappeared.

The attackers were almost to the shack before the first gun sounded. Then they all cut loose at once. Lead rapped into the wall beside the window. Other bullets snapped through the open door to splinter against the opposite wall. Some tore through the boards and screamed across the room. Craft's Winchester was blazing now, but Jim held his fire until they were close.

He thought they would pull up in front of the cabin and rush, for they would expect no one but Craft, and he was a notoriously poor shot, but instead they split around the shack and kept on. Jim pulled trigger twice. Then they were gone, and the sudden silence squeezed against Jim, strange and stifling after the shooting.

"They've gone," Craft breathed. "How do you figure it, Jim? Ain't like no Wyatt outfit to quit that easy."

"No," Jim agreed. "Where's Gramp?"

"Lit a shuck, I guess," Craft said sourly. "What'd you bring that old barfly along for?"

"To see if he'd whisky-drowned all the man that was in him." Jim stepped past Craft and went outside. The beat of hoofs could be heard to the north. Then they died, and the night stillness pressed in around them again.

"Jim." It was Gramp Tatum, hiding in the sagebrush past the house. "You there?"

"I'm here," Jim growled. "Thanks for your help, Gramp."

"You don't need to be sore 'cause I was too smart to get penned up in a shack that wouldn't do no good against a kid with a bean shooter. I figured they'd get down and fog. Then a gun outside might do some good."

"All right," Jim said testily. "Come in."

Gramp lurched toward the shack. "That wasn't no Wagon Wheel bunch, I'm thinking. The light was sure thin, but that front *hombre* rode plumb tall in the saddle. Just like Buck Deeter."

It could have been Deeter and his neighbors, circling the house and riding north to make Craft think it was a band of Wagon Wheel men. If Craft had brought the story to Jim in town, it would have set the law against Wagon Wheel. That was exactly what the Poverty Flat cowmen would want. Deeter had said: "We aim to get good graze." This was one way to do it, and all of them, Jim and Biddle and the Poverty Flat bunch, had heard Stub, brash and rebellious and trying to hold the tag end of Wyatt glory, call out: "We started to move Ernie Craft, and we will move him!"

Gramp asked: "You reckon that was Deeter, Jim?"

"Might have been," Jim grunted.

Craft had gone into the shack and lighted the lamp. He appeared in the doorway, a stooped, gentle man who showed in his weather-stained face and knob-jointed fingers the result of his long struggle against a reluctant nature. He said: "Come in, and I'll warm up the coffee." He stopped, eyes fixed on a motionless bulk in the fringe of light that washed past him from the lamp on the table. "Jim, we got one of 'em."

Jim had already seen it. He strode past Gramp and, kneeling beside the body, turned it over. Stub Wyatt! Gramp and Craft had followed him, and Craft, knowing how Jim felt toward Kitsie, said: "It was me that got him. Reckon it'd be justifiable homicide, wouldn't it?"

Jim had picked up the boy's wrist. He dropped it and, rising, faced Craft. "No, it's murder, Ernie. Stub must have died several hours ago. He wasn't shot by either one of us."

166

"But how in hell . . . ?" Gramp began.

"We'll find out. Ernie, harness up and take the body into town. Come on, Gramp. We've got riding to do."

Kitsie was the only Wyatt left, and Zane Biddle had said he'd go out to Wagon Wheel that night. Honey Nolan was there, and, if she could make her claim of marriage stick, she would become the sole heir, once Kitsie was out of the way. Jim, thinking of this in one terrible moment of insight, shouted: "Damn you, Gramp, you'll give me the evidence I want or I'll cut it out of you!"

Gramp, shocked by the violence that was in Jim Hallet, laid a hand on his gun butt and muttered in a voice too low for Jim to hear: "You'd better not try, bucko. You'd better not try."

At midnight, Jim and Gramp Tatum rode into the Wagon Wheel ranch yard. The only light was in the long front room that, except for a small corner walled off for Latigo's office, ran the full width of the house. It was a rambling two-story building made on pine lumber hauled from the Blue Mountains to the north. Latigo had allowed it was the finest house in the valley, and it undoubtedly was, although Zane Biddle had bragged he was going to build a stone house that would make a bigger shine than Latigo's.

Dismounting, Jim racked his horse at the pole in front of the tall, close-growing poplars and said—"Come on."—as he strode across the trodden, packed earth of the yard. Gramp followed, slowly and cautiously, eyes probing the shadows.

X

The front door was open, for the night still held evidence of the day's heat. Jim, looking in, saw Kitsie sitting on the divan, Zane Biddle beside her, leaning forward and talking in a soft, persuasive voice. Honey Nolan sat facing them, head back as if she were asleep, high breasts lifting and dropping with her breathing.

A tension that had been gathering in Jim from the time he'd left Craft's place broke in relief when he saw Kitsie. He stepped up on the porch and crossed it, spurs jangling. Kitsie jumped up and started toward the door when Jim appeared in it, a square-shouldered, lanky man, gaze sweeping the room, hand held close to gun butt.

Kitsie stopped, wide-eyed. She said: "Jim." Just the one word, and he couldn't tell by the way she said it what was in her mind.

Biddle stood beside the divan, irritated and trying not to show it. He said pointedly: "I thought your duties would keep you in town, Hallet."

"My duties take me wherever I think there's going to be trouble," Jim murmured. "Anybody else here, Kitsie?"

"No. Nobody but Ling. The boys went to town, and Stub got angry at me and rode off."

"Stub's dead," Jim said.

Kitsie flinched as if she'd been struck, but she didn't move and she didn't cry. Honey Nolan reared up and shook her head. "What kind of a wild country is this?" she demanded.

"Wild enough," Jim said. "You'll get used to it if you live."

"I won't live long if I stay here!" she cried. "I never saw anything like it."

"Didn't your friend who brought you here tell you what you were in for?" Jim asked.

"What friend?"

Biddle coughed. "Latigo would not tell her, Hallet. You should know that."

"It's been a right peaceful country," Jim murmured. "Till today. You accept Biddle's proposal, Kitsie?"

"Did you have to come here tonight, Jim?" she asked.

"I know. You had your own ideas about how to handle her." He jabbed a finger at Honey Nolan. "It would have worked, I reckon, except you didn't count on him." He motioned to Biddle. "Everybody gone. Stub shot. You're the only Wyatt left, Kitsie. If he marries you, he wins. If you won't have him, you'll die. In that case, he still wins because he's got little Honey all trained for the job."

Kitsie kept her feet long enough to reach the divan. She dropped, her control giving way all at once. She leaned back, her face ivory white. Jim saw that she was close to fainting, but he had to keep pushing. Deeter and Vinton and their bunch might come, and this job had to be done first.

"You don't make yourself plain, Hallet," Biddle said tonelessly, "but if I understand your inference, I shall see Deeter in the morning. We will not have your kind as sheriff in this county."

Jim half turned toward the door, still watching Biddle. He said: "Gramp, get in here."

Gramp Tatum came reluctantly into the room and sidled along the wall. "He made me come, Mister Biddle, but I didn't tell him nothing. No, sir."

"Shut up, you drunken fool!" Biddle shrilled. "You don't know anything to tell him."

169

"He knows plenty, Biddle. Let's get our cards out where we can see 'em. We'll start with you. You're a soft-bellied little gent who wants to be big but don't know how. You had money enough to start your bank, but you needed Latigo's business. Latigo being what he was, you did your share of the kowtowing, but all the time it was festering up inside of you until you were damned near loco."

"Shut up!" Biddle cried. "Shut up and get out. You can't talk to me. . . ."

"I am talking, Fatty. You didn't kill Latigo or Boone, but you'll go to jail for attempted fraud. Might be, when Gramp gets done, you'll hang along with Deeter and Vinton."

"Nobody would believe a broken-down old sot like Tatum," Biddle squealed. "Not against me."

"You see what he thinks of you, Gramp?" Jim swung to face the old man. "A broken-down old sot. That's why he handed you them twenty silver dollars. He knew you had that gun. So did Deeter. They knew Latigo would come across the street from the bank. They knew mighty close to when because I'd left the Bonanza to fetch him. They wanted Boone, too, so one of 'em got into the alley. Caught him in the hotel, I reckon, when he left Kitsie's room."

"Theory," Biddle howled. "All theory. You don't hang men on theories, Hallet. You're talking big now, but it'll be different when Deeter shows up."

"You're wrong on that, too, Biddle. I'll arrest Deeter for Latigo's murder, or I'll kill him. Right now, I'm after something else. That woman." He threw a hand out toward Honey Nolan. "She was your idea, wasn't she? You knew what Deeter aimed to do, didn't you? At first, you thought you'd play it safe, since Boone wanted Kitsie to marry you. Then Deeter came to you with his idea. You saw that was better, so you fetched in this floozie."

170

"Deeter will be along . . . ," Biddle began.

"You reckon you'll be alive to know about it?" Jim motioned to Gramp. "You never thought about it, but you done the same to Gramp that Latigo done to you, stomping on him like he was a rag to wipe your feet on. Only you didn't know Gramp had a little man left in him. Enough to fill you full of lead. That's why I gave him that iron. Look at him, Biddle! He knows why you done it. Twenty dollars to get drunk on so he'd go to sleep in the alley and Vinton could get his gun and shoot Boone. Then he'd hang. You thought he was just a broken-down old sot, but you're wrong. When he testifies in court who gave him. . . ."

Jim had to keep talking, keep pressing. He had to work Gramp into admitting it was Biddle who had given him the twenty dollars. Now he got what he wanted, but not in the way he expected, for it was Biddle who broke. He grabbed for his gun, shouting: "He won't testify against me!"

Gramp tried to pull his gun, but it stuck in the holster. If Jim had not drawn and fired, shooting Biddle's gun out of his hand, Gramp Tatum would have died.

When the last echo of the shot had faded, Jim asked: "Now you see, Gramp?"

The old man stood backed against the wall, knowledge of what Biddle had aimed to do breaking into his whisky-fogged mind. "Sure, and damned if I know why I should save his hide when he aimed to drill me. He gave me the twenty dollars, but I didn't know. . . ."

"All right, Gramp." Jim motioned with his gun at Biddle. "Now, Mister Banker, there's just one chance to save your neck."

Biddle, left hand clasping his bullet-grazed right, said in a trembling voice: "Your guesses are good, Hallet. Deeter was the one. He killed Latigo. Shot from one of the Bonanza rooms. Vinton caught Boone in the hotel lobby, told him Latigo was in the alley and wanted to see him. After he got him behind the hotel, he shoved Tatum's gun against him and held him until he heard Deeter shoot. Then he let him have it."

"What was Deeter after?"

"Wagon Wheel cattle. It was the biggest rustling job I ever heard of. When I married Kitsie, or got hold of Wagon Wheel through Honey, I was to pull off the Wagon Wheel riders. Deeter and Vinton aimed to push the herd south to the railroad."

"Two couldn't handle that big a job."

"Deeter knew a bunch that was hiding out over on Snake River. They were going to help him."

"Who is Deeter?"

"Wiley Coe."

Jim had heard of Wiley Coe, bank robber, con man, and gunman who was wanted in the Colorado mining camps for a dozen crimes. "Biddle, I can't make any promises, but I'll do what I can to keep you out of the pen. When this is over. . . ."

"They're coming, Jim," Gramp Tatum called.

Jim listened. Horses were close. Deeter and the Poverty Flat men, or Wagon Wheel buckaroos returning from town. Kitsie rose and came toward Jim. He turned his eyes to her and tried to smile. This was the test against Buck Deeter. If Jim Hallet died before the outlaw's gun, everything he had done would be lost.

"I'm all right, Jim," Kitsie said. "I'll see that neither Biddle nor the woman bother you."

She was all Wyatt now, tempered steel, but lovely in a way that only Latigo of the Wyatt men had had eyes to appreciate, and with an honest sense of justice sharing her pride that none of the men had had.

"I'll count on that," Jim said.

He stepped quickly through the door and into the shadows. There he waited, gun riding loosely in its holster, thinking he was a fool to give two killers an even break on the draw when they had murdered Latigo and Boone Wyatt. Still, it was the way he would play it because he was that kind of man.

He had heard of Wiley Coe, the same as he had heard of Soapy Smith or Butch Cassidy. Coe was a combination of the two, perhaps with a streak of Billy the Kid, for neither Smith nor Cassidy was a killer, and Coe was.

They were there then, riding boldly into the streak of light washing out through the open door, none suspecting that anything was wrong.

"Biddle?" Deeter called. "You get your answer?"

Jim stepped into the light. "Yes, he got his answer, Buck, and I got mine. I'm arresting you for the murder of Latigo Wyatt. Get down and put your hands up."

"What the hell, Jim?" Lippy Ord said. "You can't do that after the way the Wyatts have treated us."

"I've got nothing against you boys," Jim said flatly. "Stay out of it. You know who killed Latigo and Boone, and, if I've got you pegged right, you're ashamed of it. The part I can't understand is Stub. . . ."

"That was a fair fight," Ord said quickly. "He pulled first. Vinton had to shoot him. We was this side of Craft's place when we met up with him. He was on the prod. . . ."

"All right, Lippy. You can forget Stub, but you can't forget how Latigo was killed."

Neither Deeter nor Vinton had moved in his saddle. Both were staring at Jim. Vinton, pressed by the smoldering bitterness that was always in him, was ready to make his try, but Deeter, smarter than Vinton, was playing for time and feeling Jim out. He was smiling, white teeth bright in the light, swarthy face masking the pressure of the emotions in him.

He said: "I thought it was understood that Boone shot Latigo."

"It was the way you wanted it understood," Jim said. "Lippy, get this straight. I ain't defending the Wyatts for what they've done. Like I said in the Bonanza, you boys had plenty of cause to holler. From now on it's a different deal. I'll guarantee that because I know Kitsie ain't like her dad and granddad. You won't get pushed around. Wagon Wheel beef will stay on this side of the deadline, and the bank won't get tough on you because Biddle won't be in the bank."

Kitsie, standing in the doorway with a gun lined on Biddle, said: "That's right, Mister Ord."

Deeter had straightened, dark eyes probing Jim. He asked: "What's that about Biddle, Sheriff?"

"He won't be in the bank. He's played your game, and it didn't work."

"Jim, I don't like it," Lippy Ord broke in. "You can't arrest Deeter until you've got more than words to use on him. He's county commissioner. His Staircase is the biggest spread on the Flat. . . ."

"I know all that," Jim cut in, "but what you don't know is that he bought Staircase so he'd have a place to hide out. Then he sent for Vinton and began cooking up this game, taking advantage of how you boys felt about Wagon Wheel. If we don't hang him, Colorado will. His real name is Wiley Coe."

It came with suddenness that did not entirely surprise Jim, for when he showed Deeter that he knew who he was, the man had no choice. Deeter was as fast as the Yellowby boy had said, and Jim, making his choice, threw his first shot at him. The hard and bitter years that lay behind Jim had forced gun speed upon him. It had saved his life before, and it saved it now. His shot came before Deeter's by an immeasurable part of a second. The outlaw folded, dropping his gun and grabbing the horn. Then his grip gave way, and he slid out of leather, dead before he hit the ground.

Jim turned his gun to Vinton, but time had run out for him. The gunman got in one shot, the slug clubbing Jim in the chest and knocking the breath from him and taking him off his feet. He heard other shooting before he lost consciousness, tried to 'tilt his gun upward again, but he couldn't see. Then the guns were silent, and voices came softly from across a vast distance, and Jim Hallet was drifting out into that great unknown. The last words that came to him were Kitsie's: "Ride for the doctor, Lippy. We have so little time."

Lamp light hurting his eyes. Voices held low. The medico's cool orders: "More bandages . . . more hot water. Move that lamp a little. Get out of here, Lippy. . . . Pull that blind, Kitsie. . . . He'll be all right. Let him sleep. . . ."

Kitsie was sitting beside his bed when he was fully aware of things again, gaunt face dark against the pillow, stubble a rough fringe on his face. When his eyes locked with hers, she smiled, and something came alive in him that had been dead.

"You did a miracle on Gramp Tatum," she said. "He was the one who got Vinton. He's a new man. He wants a job to get the whisky worked out of him. I've put him on."

"That's fine," he murmured, knowing it was more than

that. The Wyatt men would have done nothing of the kind. It was a portent of the future.

Suddenly she reached forward and took his hand. "I was wrong in leaving you that day in Nell's place. I thought I'd save your life by breaking it up between us, but I didn't know how strong you were."

"Lucky, maybe," he said.

She shook her head. "No, it was strength and courage. It took that to tell me what you did that day. I've thought about it so much since. You said the ranch had become a god to the Wyatt men. I had never realized it, but that was exactly what it was."

He closed his eyes, for he was thinking of what he had called the fence between them. She was rich, and he was a poorly paid lawman. Stub had called it right when he'd said: "She ain't used to starving, tin star."

His fists clenched. Jaw muscles corded. "I can't stay here. Loving you like I do, and you owning Wagon Wheel. . . ."

"Why must a man be such a fool?" she cried. "Jim, Jim, I need your love. I need your strength and your courage if I'm to run Wagon Wheel. I need you. There is no fence between us. I've pulled it down."

"Don't pull it down," he breathed. "I'll step over it."

"Nell has made the wedding dress, Jim. She'll bake the cake whenever you say."

That was it, the last wire on the fence. He looked into her face, the blue eyes, the red lips with the smile that told him so much, the red-gold hair vibrant with life under the bright morning sun that laid its glory upon her.

He put a hand on the back of her head and pulled her down to him. "The first day I can stand on my feet," he said, and kissed her.

176

Rainbow Rider

The early 1950s were a prolific time for Wayne D. Overholser. He was writing books under his own name published by The Macmillan Company. He was publishing a series of hardcover novels as Joseph Wayne in E. P. Dutton and Company's Diamond D Westerns, hardcover novels as John S. Daniels in J. B. Lippincott's Western series, and in 1953 Ballantine Books published LAW MAN by Lee Leighton, a novel that earned Overholser the first of his Spur Awards from the Western Writers of America. "Rainbow Rider" by Wayne D. Overholser first appeared in *Ranch Romances* (3rd September Number: 9/28/51).

I

It was a warm June morning with a bank of clouds hanging over Long's Peak, the kind of morning that started the meadowlarks singing and made a man feel good right down to his bootheels. But to Mark Prentice, marshal of Tumello, it was more than that. It was *the* morning! Carla Baggot was going to say yes, or she was going to say no, and there would be no more dilly-dallying.

Mark cooked breakfast in his one-room shack behind the jail. He shaved and changed to a clean shirt, knowing it was still too early to see Carla. For a moment he stood in the doorway, a hard-muscled shoulder against the jamb, and looked distastefully at Tumello.

Not much of a town. Just one short business block surrounded by a collection of dwellings, many of them shacks. The only house in town that indicated any real prosperity belonged to Judge Baggot, Carla's father, and that was the rub.

Too nervous to remain still, Mark started walking, aimlessly at first. Five minutes later he found himself on Main Street for the simple reason that there was nowhere else to go. He paused in front of Baggot's bank, took the diamond ring out of his pocket, and watched it catch fire from the sun, then dropped it back, thinking ruefully that it had taken almost every cent he had.

Under other circumstances a girl would be glad to put the ring on her finger if she loved a man, Mark thought, and he could not consider the possibility that Carla didn't love him. A woman could lie to a man with words, but not with every nerve and fiber of her being.

Still she had refused to take his ring. The trouble, Mark knew, lay with her father and her aunt Delphine, and

Carla's misplaced sense of loyalty to them.

Mark moved on down the street, reached the corner and almost ran into Judge Baggot. He said: " 'Morning, Judge. Ain't you out a little early?"

Baggot was usually an easygoing man, slender and blue-eyed and a little gray at the temples. Actually he wasn't a judge at all, and Mark had never heard how the man had come by the title. He was Tumello's banker, and for that reason the most important man on the St. Vrain. But his importance did not weigh heavily upon him, and the greed that was so often a part of small-town bankers was entirely absent from his make-up.

"Howdy, Marshal," Baggot said, worried eyes on Mark. "I didn't sleep much last night. Indigestion, I guess."

Mark smiled at that, and wondered how Carla and Aunt Delphine had slept. Well, he hadn't slept much, either. Perhaps he had been wrong last night when he had insisted on an answer, but it had gone on this way for weeks, Carla hedging when he had tried to pin her down.

Last night he'd made it plain. If she loved him, she'd marry him. If she didn't, he'd be on his way. And finally Carla, unable to say no, had told him to come back in the morning. Now, looking at the dark pouches under Baggot's eyes, Mark guessed the three of them had sat up most of the night.

"I was headed for your place," Mark said, "but I didn't know whether Carla was up yet or not."

"She's up." Baggot looked down the street, refusing to meet Mark's eyes. "She didn't sleep very well, either."

"Then I'll get it over with," Mark said.

Baggot brought his eyes to Mark then, a hand coming up to grip his arm. "It would be easier on both of you if you didn't see her. She's taking it pretty hard, you know."

"She shouldn't," Mark said bitterly. "If she loves me, she'll marry me. If she doesn't love me, it shouldn't be hard to say so. I'd never bother her again if she gave me my walking papers."

Baggot's grip tightened on Mark's arm. "It isn't that simple, boy. Come on down to the bank and we'll talk. There's a lot more to it than she's ever told you."

"You mean you and Aunt Delphine don't like me. That's it, isn't it?"

Baggot dropped his hand. "No, Mark. You've done a good job here. The law means something in Tumello now, and it didn't six months ago. For that reason I respect you. It's . . . well, you're just not the man for Carla."

"Is that you and Aunt Delphine talking?" Mark asked bitterly. "Or Carla?"

"All right," Baggot said heavily. "Go ahead and get your answer. But before you leave town, I'd like for you to stop in at the bank. Will you do that?"

"Sure, I'll see you," Mark said, and moved past Baggot toward the big house a block to the east. He had his answer. They'd stayed up all night to beat her down, and they'd won. As the judge had said, it would be easier to pack his war bag and ride out of town. Forget the lot of them, forget the months he'd lingered here wearing a town marshal's badge and drawing a meager salary when he could have earned three times as much in any mining camp in the Rockies. He'd been a lawman since he had been twenty-one. He had established a reputation. But he had stayed in Tumello because of Carla.

Sure, it would be easier to go on, but he couldn't. Probably Carla would cry and Aunt Delphine would fly at him like a mother hen defending a chick. Delphine had no children of her own, so she mothered Carla. Actually she wasn't much older than Carla, and Mark had the feeling that it was a simple matter of her wanting to have her own way regardless of Carla's happiness. She was that kind of person. Well, he was going to hear his answer from Carla's own lips, not her father's or Delphine's.

He reached the Baggot place and went up the walk, head tipped back to look at the house. It was a two-story pile of brick with a mansard roof and a great lawn in front surrounded by a carefully trimmed hedge.

Delphine had built it for her brother, or so Mark had heard. He had heard, too, that she had loaned the judge enough money to start the bank, and he'd be broke without her backing. It was probably true, he thought. At least it explained some things that otherwise made little sense to him.

He stepped up on the porch and yanked the bell pull.

The door swung open, and Delphine stood there, very tall, her head high, a dark-eyed woman who was always conscious of her beauty. Colored light from the small stained-glass windows beside the door fell on her fine-featured face, giving the effect of a rainbow.

The thought made him remember something with piercing impact. She had a name for him. She called him a rainbow rider and meant it for an insult. She had said he was always looking for something—the rainbow over the next hill, maybe—and never settling down to anything. If she had been a man, he would have broken her with his two hands months ago, but he had no way to fight a woman.

"You're early, Marshal," Delphine said in her cool way. "Usually no one is up and dressed at this hour."

"This is not a usual morning," he said, and pushed past her into the hall.

She shut the door, dark eyes measuring him as if trying to gauge his temper. She said: "I'll tell Carla you called,

Mister Prentice. I don't think she feels like seeing you today."

"Tell her I'm here."

She threw out a slim hand. "Take my word for it. It would be a mistake for you to see her. She can't marry you. We talked it over last night, Carla and her father and me. We have big plans for her, you know."

"Every plan but for her happiness," Mark said. "I reckon you never thought about that."

"You're wrong. Her happiness is the thing we think of most." Delphine's lips tightened. "I wonder if you actually think that you are the only man who can make her happy."

"If she loves me, that's exactly what I think. If she doesn't, I'll never bother her again."

"Listen to me, Prentice. Look at yourself. You don't have any money. You've admitted that. All you know is packing a star. You could get a better job than you have here in some tough mining camp, and what would happen? Every day Carla would worry about you. Is that any kind of life for a woman?"

She was smart, this Delphine Travis, smart and ruthless and beautiful. He said: "Why don't you marry Rolly Benson and have someone to run? Why don't you get out of Carla's life and quit telling her how to live?"

She was angry then. She said in a low voice: "If I were a man, I'd kill you."

"I've often wished you were a man," he said. "And there are things I can do besides pack a star. I know cattle. I'll get a job on a ranch."

"At thirty a month and beans," she said scornfully. "I have a ranch, you know. I don't have one married man on the T-in-a-Heart. They don't make enough to support a woman."

"Then you ought to pay them more."

"Delphine." It was Carla, standing on the stair landing. "Is it Mark?" She couldn't see him from where she stood.

He called: "It's me, Carla!"

She came running down the carpeted stairs, her skirt billowing out so that he could see her trim ankles. She reached the hall and came quickly to him, smiling. "I'm so glad you're here, Mark." She turned to Delphine. "You promised to call me when he came."

"I was trying to talk some sense into this mule head," Delphine said stiffly.

Carla took Mark's hand. "Come into the library," she said, and led him through a door.

For a moment Mark stood looking at her, thinking this would be the last time he'd see her. Maybe Delphine and the judge were right. It would have been easier if he hadn't insisted on hearing his answer from her. He was breaking her heart by dragging it out this way.

"Come here, Mark," she said.

He crossed the room and sat down beside her, a blocky, brown-haired man who was suddenly conscious of his stubbornness. There was a lot of truth in what Delphine had said, more truth than he liked to admit. A lawman's wife would not be a happy fate, and a cowboy couldn't afford a wife.

He had insisted on his answer, and now he'd have it. He took the ring from his pocket and held it up in the sunlight. "Take it or leave it," he said huskily. "Last chance, you know."

"I know." She took it and stared at it, blinking back her tears. "It's a beautiful ring, Mark, but I can't take it. I can't marry you. We . . . we decided last night."

She handed the ring back to him, and he dropped it into

184

his pocket. "Well, that's it, I guess. I wanted to hear you say you didn't love me. That's the only reason for turning me down."

"No, it isn't the reason at all, Mark," she whispered. "I love you. I think you know that. You must have, or you would have left Tumello a long time ago."

"Why, then?" he asked bitterly. "Just tell me why."

She was silent a moment, her eyes on the great walnut secretary across the room. Then she said: "I don't think I can tell you so you would understand, Mark, but I'll try. It's not because Aunt Delphine tells me what to do. It's Daddy. I'm all he has, and he wants me to marry better. You know what he means, somebody who can give me a nice home and all that."

"Like Ed Runyan," Mark said bitterly.

She was silent again. Mark could not look at her. He sat with his hands knotted on his knees, thinking of Ed Runyan who owned the store and who had tea in his veins instead of good red blood, a wealthy man who was twice Carla's age and had the smell of the store about him when he stepped into the sunlight which he seldom did.

Sure, Runyan could build a fine house like this, but it would be a barren life, and he was sure Carla knew that.

"I guess somebody like Ed," she said finally. "It's more than that, Mark. It's just that I owe so much to Daddy. Mother died when I was a girl. It's been me and him for so long. I think maybe I'll never marry as long as he's alive."

The judge wasn't over forty-five and he had good health. "No, Carla. You were meant to be a wife and have children. You were meant to be happy and . . . and build something that will last."

"If I had my life to live the way I wanted to, I'd like that. But I don't, Mark. That's the thing you can't understand."

He rose and looked down at her, finding it hard to say what was in his heart. Perhaps it wasn't right to try, he thought. If he talked her into marrying him and her life was filled with poverty, she might hold it against him. Then he knew that was wrong. Carla wasn't made that way.

"Money hasn't hurt you like it would most women," he said. "If we had nothing but a cabin and it was full of kids, you'd work, and I think you'd like it."

"Yes, Mark, but I still can't marry you."

"Listen to me," he said with sudden passion. "I've thrown away a lot of chances because I was young and footloose same as a lot of men. Now I've got something to live for. They're opening up the Ute Reservation on the Uncompahgre this summer. I'll go over there and get land. When I get a start, I'll send for you."

"No, Mark. Let's break it clean. The nicest thing that ever happened to me was knowing you and loving you and having you ask me to marry you. But I can't." She looked up then, trying to smile, as if wanting him to have that last memory of her. She said again: "Let's break it clean."

"All right." He laid the ring down on the massive oak table in the middle of the room. "I won't need this. There'll never be another woman for me."

He crossed to the door and opened it. He looked back at her and wished he hadn't, for she was crying now, and she had not wanted him to see her that way. When he went into the hall, he saw that Delphine had gone.

Let's break it clean. He went out, closing the heavy front door, her words droning through his mind like a dismal refrain. If that was the way she wanted it, that was the way it would be. He'd never forget her, and she'd never forget him.

He went down the path and turned toward the business

block, thinking that he wouldn't see the judge. He'd be out of town within the hour.

The town was awake now. Mark heard a rooster crow from somewhere to his left. He saw the swamper step out of the Red Front Saloon and slosh his bucket of dirty water into the street. Doc Frisbie, coming in from an early morning call, went into his office ahead of Mark, not seeing him.

Tumello! A dirty little town on the banks of the St. Vrain, a town of little people who looked to Judge Baggot for credit when times were bad, a trading town set here in an irrigated country where the farmers depended on the judge to see them through from one harvest to another. And the judge depended on his sister Delphine to keep the bank solvent.

There it was, Delphine Travis, and Mark could blame her for everything.

He thought of her ranch, T-in-a-Heart, that lay to the west where the North St. Vrain tumbled down through the foothill range. She'd inherited it from her husband who had been killed two years before, inherited it with a lot of his dreams, and she was failing. She needed a good foreman to pull the ranch back on the black ink side of the ledger, but that was the last thing she would ever admit.

II

When Mark passed the bank, he saw that the front door was locked, the blind pulled. It was still an hour before opening time. Mark went on down the street to the jail. There were a few things he had left there. He'd pick them up, saddle his buckskin, and be on his way. Then he thought about the judge and felt a faint prickle of conscience about leaving town without seeing him.

Mark stepped into the jail and stopped flat-footed in the doorway. A sleepy-eyed young man sat in his swivel chair back of the desk, skinny and long-nosed, with a face that had been burned red by the sun. It was the face of a man who had been indoors for a long time and then had suddenly overexposed himself. In time it would be bronze. Now it was scarlet.

This was Wally Kane, released from the Canon City pen less than a month ago.

Wally rose and, coming around the desk, held out his hand. "I thought you'd be around somewhere, Mark. You sure as hell ain't busy. Your cells're plumb empty."

Mark gripped his hand. "I'm glad to see you, Wally. I figured you'd be along a couple of weeks ago."

"I was the color of a potato sprout in a cellar when they let me out," Wally said. "Figured it'd look kind of funny, showing up here to visit with the marshal and still wearing the stony lonesome look I had."

"Sit down." Mark pulled a rawhide-bottom chair away from the far wall and dropped into it. "When did you get in?"

" 'Bout an hour ago. Left my horse in the stable. I didn't know where I'd find you, so I just sat and waited."

"Ride all night?"

Wally nodded. "Left Denver yesterday, 'bout sundown."

Mark rolled a cigarette, taking a moment to release his thoughts from his own troubles. He had sent a number of men to Canon City, most of them confirmed law-breakers who would never be anything else as long as they were free. Wally Kane was different. He was the only man Mark had sent up he could call a friend.

He remembered how it had been, because it was one of those things a man never forgets. That was one time he'd regretted what he had been forced to do. Wally, wild and fiercely hating organized society, held up a Trinidad bank and got away with five thousand dollars. At the time Mark had been a deputy in Las Animas County. He had chased Wally up the Picketwire, caught up with him somewhere in the Culebra Range west of Trinidad, and wounded him when he had resisted arrest.

It had been touch and go with Wally for a while, but Mark had nursed him until he had enough strength to ride back to Trinidad. Wally was grateful because he had known little kindness in his short, turbulent life, and he had talked to Mark about his boyhood on a ranch south of Raton. He'd told how his folks had lost their place to a grant company; his father had been killed in a fight with officers when they were evicted, and his mother had died later from a broken heart.

Mark had done all he could for him at the trial, and the boy was given a shorter sentence than he would have had otherwise. Whenever Mark was near Canon City, he made a point to visit the kid in prison, and he'd written to him often. As soon as he heard the date Wally was to be freed, he had asked him to come to Tumello. Now, he wondered. . . .

As if sensing the question that was in Mark's mind, Wally said: "Don't worry about me none. I had a bellyful of stony lonesome. They'll never get me back." He reached for the makings, found none, and dropped his hand. "I never really thanked you for what you done for me, Mark. I'm trying to now."

Mark handed him tobacco and papers. "No need to.

189

Fact is, I was never very proud about fetching you in. Not that knocking over a bank is good business, but seemed like you had enough bad luck."

The ex-convict rolled a cigarette and handed the makings back. "I had had too much, but robbing the bank didn't set anything right. I was mad at everybody, and that's no good. A lot of the boys get out of the pen hating everybody and swearing they'll raise hell. They'll wind up right where they were." Wally shook his head. "I figure I'm smarter than that. If it hadn't been for you, I'd have had a longer stretch. Nobody else ever came to see me. Nobody wrote to me but you." He lowered his gaze. "Hell, I ain't much on words, but, damn it, I'm obliged."

"Forget it," Mark said. "What do you figure you'll do now?"

"Well, I reckon that's why I'm here." He scratched his nose, embarrassed. "It's kind of hard to say what I had in mind. Sounds crazy. Maybe it ain't, neither. After I got here, I started wondering why you were toting the star in a burg like this."

"It was tough enough when I took the job," Mark said. "We're close to the Greeley colony where the big guns figure whisky is a tool of the devil. Some of the boys get thirsty, so they ride over here on Saturday nights, get drunk, and raise hell. For a couple of months I had this jug crammed every Sunday morning. Now they behave."

"What do they pay you?"

"Fifty a month."

Wally snorted. "Don't they know who they've got?"

Mark shrugged. "Wouldn't make any difference if they did. I'm pulling out today. My job's done."

Wally took a long breath, the cigarette dangling from a corner of his mouth. "Where are you headed?"

Mark spread his hands. "No place in particular, but I know one thing. I'm done rodding a town for peanuts . . . if that's what you mean."

"Ever think of doing anything else? Like taking up land and raising cattle?"

"Sure, I've thought about it, but I'm broke. Didn't save anything when I had a chance. Now I've got to make a stake."

The other man leaned forward. "Mark, I've had time to think. Nothing but time. Well, I ain't going back to the pen. Likewise, I don't cotton to the notion of working for some moneybags and just making enough to eat on. I figure a man ought to have his own place, and I'm willing to work to have it."

"I wrote to you about the Ute Reservation they're opening up. Why don't you go over there?"

Wally squirmed uneasily. "That's just what I figured on doing. I ain't no prize package, but I thought maybe you'd . . . I mean. . . ." He stopped and stared at the ceiling. "Hell, forget it. I just wanted to see you."

Mark rose. "Kid, you just made yourself a deal. We'll throw in together."

Wally jumped up. "You mean that?"

"Sure I do." Mark held out his hand. "Shake, partner?"

Wally gripped his hand. He said eagerly: "I've thought about it ever since I got your letter, but I didn't figure you'd really do it. A man like you throwing in with an ex-con. . . ."

"None of that," Mark said sharply. "What's behind is one thing, and what's ahead is another. Trouble is, we need a little *dinero* to start on. We'd better light out for Gunnison and get a job in the mines. Or the railroad. Then we'll be on the Uncompahgre when they open the reservation, and

191

we'll grab ourselves the best land on the river. There's talk that the railroad will build on. . . ."

He paused. A buggy had rattled up the street and pulled to a stop in front of the jail. Turning, he glanced through the window. Delphine was stepping down, and he heard her say: "I'll be just a minute, Rolly."

"No hurry, Delphine," a man said.

It was Rolly Benson driving a livery rig, smiling genially as only Rolly Benson could smile. He was a big man, black-haired and handsome, with a sweeping mustache in which he took inordinate pride. He had a taste for expensive clothes like the white Stetson, silk shirt, and the black broadcloth suit he was wearing now.

Mark knew nothing about Benson except that he claimed to be a cattleman from New Mexico, but he didn't like him, a feeling that stemmed from the contemptuous insolence that was always a part of Benson when he talked to Mark. The fellow had seen a great deal of Delphine in the month he had been in Tumello.

Mark said softly: "Step outside, Wally."

The other man nodded and rose as Delphine came in. She glanced curiously at the ex-convict, as if puzzled by his presence here, then brought her gaze to Mark.

She said smugly: "Well, you got your answer, Marshal."

Mark waited until Wally had moved to the door. He said: "I guess you're happy."

He watched Wally reach the doorway, take one look at Benson, then wheel and stalk back through the office and into the cell area.

Delphine asked: "Who's that?"

"A friend of mine. You make big tracks, but not big enough to be nosy about my friends."

She shrugged. "I stopped to see if you were keeping your

word. You told Carla you'd break it off clean. You can't do that and stay in town."

"Don't push me," Mark said grimly, "or I might decide I like Tumello real well."

"I expect you to keep your word. You have three days till the end of the month. If you'll stop in at the bank, the judge will pay you for the whole month, and you can leave town."

She stood tall and arrow-straight, her dark hair pulled tightly back from her forehead and pinned in a bun at the base of her neck.

"Funny you don't have time to be a woman, Delphine," he said. "If you wore a dress with a few doodads on it and you fixed up your hair, you'd be kind of pretty."

Her lips tightened. "No soft soap, Marshal. It won't do you any good."

"You aiming to marry Benson?"

She usually held her temper, but this was too much. She stamped her foot, her cheeks scarlet. "You get out of town! We're sending Carla back East to school next year. When she returns here, she'll marry a man who can give her something. I won't let her throw herself away on you!"

He was past the point where she could make him angry. He said: "You're a little mixed up, Delphine. You ain't God."

She had her temper under control then. "You were talking to Carla about getting land on the western slope and sending for her. That's like you. I've said before you were just a rainbow rider. You'll never amount to anything. That's why we won't let Carla marry you. Now I'm going out to the ranch. I'll be back this evening. I expect you to be gone."

Suddenly he realized that he'd had his moment of weakness, and now he knew he wasn't going to leave. Not the

193

way things stood. Carla had said she loved him. That was enough. He said: "So you had to rub it in. Well, I've changed my mind. I'm going to see Carla again. I think she'll wait for me."

Delphine opened her mouth and closed it, swallowing, her body rigid. Then she said slowly: "I want you to understand how you stand. There will be a council meeting tonight, and I'll see that you lose your star."

"Did you ever make a mistake, Delphine?"

"No," she said, and, turning, walked out of the office.

Perhaps he should have let it drop there, but struck by a sudden streak of perverseness, he followed her to the buggy. Benson had stepped down and was giving her a hand up to the seat.

"Know who you're riding with today, Benson?" Mark said.

The big man turned, insolent eyes on Mark. "Yeah, I know, and I know who I'm talking to."

Benson walked around the buggy and stepped up. As he took the lines from the whip stock, Mark said: "Marry her, Benson. She needs gentling. You might be man enough to do it. Anyhow, she's got money."

Benson froze, eyes suddenly wicked. Delphine looked straight ahead. She said: "Let's get along, Rolly."

"I advise you not to be in town when I get back, Prentice," Benson said. The tail of his coat had fallen back, and now he laid a hand on the ivory butt of his gun. "I am not like the drunks you toss in jail."

Benson spoke to the team. He drove out of town, taking the west road that led to the T-in-a-Heart. Mark watched them as wheels and hoofs raised a dust bank that lay motionless in a gray haze. He was ashamed of himself. He had brought himself down to Delphine's level, and he had accomplished nothing. If she could be shown she wasn't infallible. . . .

"How long has he been here?"

Wally Kane had come out of the cell area. He stood before Mark, eyes on Benson's buggy. Mark made a slow turn to face the other. He said: "About a month. You looked like you'd seen a ghost when you spotted him."

"No ghost," Wally said. "And I wasn't scared, if that's what you're thinking. I don't want him to recognize me. Wouldn't do you no good, having it passed around that a fellow just out of Canon City was a friend of yours."

Curious now, Mark asked: "You know him?"

"You bet I do. He was in Raton when we had the trouble. Had a couple of tough hands with him like he always did. I was on the prod then and figured I wanted to throw in with him. Hell, he didn't want a younker like me. Good thing, too. I mean, for me."

"Who is he?"

"You don't know?" Wally asked.

"Calls himself Rolly Benson. That's all I know. Been shining up to that woman you saw."

"Right pretty filly," Wally murmured. "A widow, maybe? And rich?"

"How'd you know?"

The kid chuckled. "Funny what a man learns in stony lonesome. I met a fellow who used to ride with that *hombre*. Back in the Nations, it was. Talked a lot about him. Smart and ornery as all hell. This fellow said he worked on rich widows because it paid better than hiring his guns out like he done in New Mexico, and wasn't as dangerous." He scratched the back of his neck. "Calls himself Rolly Benson, does he?"

"Who is he?" Mark demanded.

"Nick Munger. Ever hear of him?"

Mark felt like a man who had been clubbed in the stomach. He'd heard of Nick Munger, all right. He asked: "You sure?"

"Of course, I'm sure. He's the kind you can't make a mistake on. Same big mustache. Same kind of duds. Showy like a prize stallion. But I don't reckon you can touch him. He's never operated in Colorado."

"Nick Munger," Mark breathed. "Well, I'll be damned."

This was his chance. Delphine was making a mistake, the biggest mistake a woman could make. When Delphine found out who Rolly Benson was, she'd be red in the face all the way down to her neck.

"I can't leave town just now, Wally," Mark said. "All of a sudden I've got some unfinished business."

He started toward the bank, thinking he would tell the judge about Benson. Then he heard Wally say: "Don't go off half-cocked, Mark. You've just got my word for it, and who in this burg would believe me?"

Mark turned back. That was true, so true that the good feeling in him died as suddenly as it had been born. "He's a wanted man, ain't he?"

"Not in Colorado, he ain't! I told you he was smart. Works in one state long enough to get his nest feathered, but he always pulls out ahead of trouble. By the time you got anyone in here from New Mexico, your bird would be in Wyoming."

Mark stood there, seeing the logic in this. Then he was filled with a burst of anger. "But damn it, he's up to something. I'll sit around and wait till he pulls it off."

"From the talk you had with that filly, you ain't real popular with her," Wally said. "She wouldn't believe you. Now just how are you going to get the deadwood on him?"

"I don't know," Mark said bitterly. "What sort of a game did he work on these widows you were talking about?"

Wally shrugged. "Anything. Sell 'em fake mining stock. Or maybe a new town site that was gonna make 'em a lot of *dinero*. Got 'em to trust him, and then they'd go for any deal he had rigged up for 'em."

Delphine wouldn't be fooled by mining stock, and she wouldn't be interested in a town site, Mark knew. Benson had something else on the fire, and it wasn't likely that Delphine would tell him what it was.

"Stay here," Mark said. "I'll be back by noon. My shack's behind the jail. Make yourself at home."

Turning, Mark strode toward the livery stable. Within five minutes he was riding out of town on his buckskin.

III

A mile from Tumello the road left the river to follow a ridge toward the mountains. There were a few small ranches on the upland, and to Mark's left there were some farms along the St. Vrain that were irrigated from the river.

Mark rode slowly, not wanting to catch up with Benson and Delphine before they reached the ranch. He had one hope. If he could surprise Benson with the knowledge that he knew the man's identity, he might be able to trap him into admitting who he was. Even that might accomplish nothing, for it was possible Delphine would say she had never heard of Nick Munger. Still, even a very small chance that Delphine's attitude toward him and Carla would be changed was worth taking.

It was mid-morning when he reached the side road that

turned toward T-in-a-Heart. Mark pulled up and sat his saddle for a time, the hot sun raising sweat from his body and soaking the back of his shirt. It was the finest location for a ranch that Mark had ever seen. There was a patch of alfalfa along the river below the ranch house, a field of oats upstream, and the grass on the uplands on both sides of the stream was good winter graze.

The crew had moved the cattle into the foothills to the west, and it was probable that no one was around except Delphine and Benson, and the handyman who was irrigating the oats above the house. Mark rode slowly down the slope, noting the signs of slackness that were so evident about the place. The frame ranch house needed paint; the corrals should have been repaired months ago. Even some of the doors of the outbuildings hung crazily from one hinge.

A foreman who would be careless about the headquarters ranch would be equally careless about cattle, and Mark knew that Delphine's winter loss had been tragically large. The T-in-a-Heart ramrod should have been fired months ago, but that would force Delphine to admit a mistake, the one thing she was not capable of doing.

Evidently Delphine and Benson planned to spend most of the day here, for the team had been unharnessed and put away. Mark dismounted in front of the house and tied, his eyes on the bare unfriendly ranch house.

For a moment he fought the temptation to get on his horse and ride back to town. Then, lips tightly pressed, he walked up the path to the house. He'd have his try, now that he was here.

He was halfway to the front door when he heard Benson call: "Delphine, you've got company!"

She stepped out on the porch, her hands clenched at her

sides. She said—"Get out!"—her voice high and shrewish. Her hair hung loosely about her face. Had she just redone it, taunted by Mark's words, or had Rolly tousled it? He never knew.

"Am I interrupting something?" Mark asked.

She raised a hand to clutch a post at the corner of the porch, fighting her temper for a moment. Then she said, her voice lower now: "If you think you can come out here and argue me into changing my mind, you're crazier than I thought you were."

He said solemnly: "No, I'm not that crazy, ma'am. Everybody knows Missus Travis never changes her mind. She never makes a mistake, either."

"Then what do you want?"

"Benson. Where is he?"

Benson had been watching from a living room window. He came out of the house, cool and very sure of himself. He said: "I will be back in town early this afternoon. If you're planning on taking up our. . . ."

"I ain't taking up anything that's behind us," Mark said. "This is something else. I just heard you were Nick Munger."

Mark let him have it that way, without warning, without preliminaries, and he had hoped that the surprise of it might even jolt the man into giving himself away. It was a futile hope. The shock that Mark's words must have given the other man was not apparent. There was nothing but the slight flicker in his eyes.

"You've been misinformed, friend," Benson said. "I never heard of this man Munger."

"You're lying even if you aren't Munger," Mark said. "He was in Raton a few years ago, and you claim to come from New Mexico."

Benson spread his hands. "I'm sorry, but I still say I never heard of him. Even if I was Munger and he's wanted by the law, which I suppose is what you're driving at, you're out of your bailiwick. You're a town marshal, Prentice, and we're a long ways from your town."

Ignoring that, Mark turned his gaze to Delphine. "Nick Munger may be just a name to you, but he's more than that to anyone who's been a lawman as long as I have. He's handy at several things, and he's wanted in more than one state, but there's one thing he does that should interest you. Munger is an expert con man who works on wealthy widows. What sort of a game has he cooked up for you?"

"I suppose I should have some pity for a man who is as desperately in love as you are," Delphine said. "That's the only way I can excuse you for what you are doing. It's no good, Prentice. Now will you go?"

No, it wasn't any good. He nodded and would have turned away, letting it stand there, if Benson had not said: "Wait, Prentice."

"Speak your piece," Mark said. "I've spoken mine. Looks like I wasted a morning riding out here."

"Not exactly." Benson took off his gun belt and handed it to Delphine. "I passed up an insult in town because I didn't want to start a brawl in front of a lady, but I can't pass this up. Delphine, go inside if you don't want to watch this."

"I'll enjoy seeing it," she said. "We would have been spared a great deal of trouble if he'd had a licking a long time ago."

Benson stepped down off the porch. "Take off your gun belt."

Mark hesitated, knowing this would buy him nothing. But there was no escaping unless he crawled, and that was something he could not do.

He tossed his gun belt behind him. "All right, Benson. We'll put on a show for the lady."

Mark glanced at Delphine and was shocked at the hate and joy in her face. All womanliness was gone.

Benson moved slowly toward him, his feet stirring the dust of the yard, ham-like fists cocked in front of him. Mark stood motionless until Benson was within a step of him, then he drove in, feinting with his right and bringing a sledging left through to Benson's chin.

Benson wheeled and rushed, cursing, and swung a right that caught Mark in the chest. For a time they stood close, exchanging blow for blow. They were hurting each other, and Mark began to give ground before Benson's greater strength and weight. He knew at once this wouldn't do.

He moved back, taunting: "You're better with women than men, Munger."

Benson took the bait and lunged at him, wasting no breath now with words, his face hard-set. Mark ducked a wildly swinging fist and, coming in close, caught Benson in the stomach—a hard punch that knocked wind out of him.

Benson stood motionless, bruised lips parted as he struggled for breath, and Mark was on him, battering his face with both fists.

He got Benson on the chin with a smashing blow. The man went down and rolled, and Delphine's voice, coming from a great distance, beat against Mark's ear: "Get up, Rolly. Get up!"

Mark wiped a hand across his face, sucking air into his lungs in great gulps.

Slowly Benson got to his feet, blood pouring down his face from a cut above an eye, and again Delphine's words came to Mark: "Get him, Rolly. Get him!"

Benson might have quit if it had not been for Delphine.

Her presence made it impossible for him to quit as long as he was on his feet.

He staggered forward. He got his hands on Mark and tried to pull him down. The big man's white Stetson was on the ground, trampled underfoot. His handsome face was a mass of blood and bruises.

Mark secured a fistful of Benson's hair and jerked the man's head back. He felt Benson's arms around him in a great squeeze. Benson's chin was pointed at him. Mark had his right free, and now he swung it. He felt the shock of the impact on his knuckles, felt it run up his arm, and for one horrible moment he was afraid he had broken his hand.

Benson's knees gave. His head rolled, and his grip on Mark relaxed. He slid like a half-filled sack of grain down the length of Mark's body and fell into the dust.

Mark stepped back, opening and closing his right hand. He stared at Benson for a moment, relieved by the knowledge that his hand had not been broken, then he raised his eyes to Delphine. As long as he lived, he would never forget the horror he saw in her face, the disbelief, as if she were seeing a thing that could not have happened.

"You're a fool, Delphine." Mark stepped back to the hitch pole and held himself upright. For a moment his knees threatened to give way, then the moment passed. "You're the biggest fool I ever saw. He'll take you for everything you've got, and you still won't have sense enough to thank me for warning you."

Suddenly Delphine seemed to realize that she had Benson's gun belt in her hands. She snatched the Colt from holster and threw the belt down. She pointed the gun at Mark, screaming: "I'll kill you, Prentice!"

There was nothing he could do. His own gun was ten feet from him in the dust. She got the hammer back, and then the gun barrel began to waver. For all of her willful pride and the hate she had for him, she was not capable of killing him. She sat down and put the gun on the porch and began to cry.

Mark picked up his gun belt, walked to the horse trough, and sloshed water over his bruised face. When he looked up, he saw that Delphine was kneeling beside Benson who was beginning to stir.

Mark went back to his horse. He lifted himself into the saddle and clutched the horn. His face and chest and sides hurt with a dozen throbbing aches.

No good, he thought as he reined away. No good at all. Benson had not given himself away, and Delphine had not believed anything Mark had said.

He put his horse up the ridge slope to the county road, his left eye swollen shut. He was now able to think clearly about all of it, about Carla who had said she loved him and couldn't marry him because of her father. That brought him to Judge Baggot.

If the judge really understood, he would not stand between Mark and Carla. But there was the problem of making him understand.

It was noon when Mark reached town. He put his buckskin in the shed back of his shack. He usually left him there when he knew he would need him soon. He went in and saw that Wally Kane had a fire going. The coffee pot was on the stove.

Mark dropped flat on the bed, murmuring: "I hope you make good coffee."

"What happened to you?" the other demanded.

"Had a tussle with your man Munger," Mark said, and told him about it.

"I wish I could have seen it," Wally said reverently.

"They used to say he could lick any man in Raton. That makes you pretty good."

"I don't feel good," Mark said.

"You'd better get a hunk of beefsteak on that eye."

"If I had a piece of beefsteak, I'd eat it. Want to rustle a meal? There's enough stuff on them shelves back of the stove."

"I was just looking it over," the kid said. "I'm kind of lank myself."

IV

Later, lingering over his third cup of coffee, Mark told Wally about Carla. He needed to talk, and he was not sure what his next move should be. He only knew one thing—he was not leaving town.

Mark rolled a smoke. Then, remembering that Wally was out of tobacco, tossed the half-filled sack of Durham and the package of papers on the table. He said: "If I had some notion about what Benson is up to, I'd go see the judge. Reckon I will anyhow."

"You ought to be able to figure it out," Wally said thoughtfully. "Everybody wants something. You can bet your bottom dollar Munger is smart enough to figure what this Delphine woman wants and work along that line."

"Then he's smarter than I am," Mark said somberly. "I'm going over to see the judge. You were up all night, Wally. Why don't you go to sleep?"

"Figured I would." He yawned. "Don't forget one thing about Munger. He usually don't work alone, and you're dangerous because you know who he is. If he's got this here widow ready to pluck, he ain't gonna scare easy."

"What you mean is that he'll put one of his men on my tail." Mark shrugged. "He's alone, kid. There hasn't been a stranger in town for a week or more."

"There will be," Wally said. "You can be damned sure of one thing. His men ain't far away."

"Munger's got no way to send word to 'em till he gets back to town and gets rid of Delphine." Mark moved to the door. "Get some sleep."

"Sure." Wally got up from the table. "Mark, I don't have a gun. If we're gonna be partners. . . ."

"Stay out of this ruckus," Mark said curtly. "It's my trouble."

"Either we're partners, or we ain't!" Wally cried. "What the hell kind of a hairpin do you think I am?"

Mark hesitated, putting a shoulder against the doorjamb, his one good eye on the kid. This was something else to worry about, and he had enough. When he had befriended Wally, he had no way of knowing it would work like this. But now that it had, he couldn't say the wrong thing, or he'd destroy all the work he had done in salvaging this boy from the Owlhoot.

"Thanks, kid," Mark said softly. "You'll find a gun belt and a Forty-Five in the top bureau drawer. It's a pretty fair iron, but don't get the notion it's up to you to go after Munger. He's my meat."

Wally hesitated, chewing his upper lip. Then he said: "He's right handy with his cutter, Mark. I'm surprised he didn't use it."

"I think he would have if it hadn't been for Delphine," Mark said, and left the cabin.

Clouds had worked up into a black, sullen mass above the mountains. The wind, cool now, held the damp promise of rain. There would be a thundershower before night, Mark thought absently as he walked to the bank.

It was a few minutes after one. When Mark stepped into the bank, he saw that the judge was out for dinner, and that Carla was working at a desk in the back of the room.

She rose when she heard Mark come in, saw who it was, and sat down again, a hand instinctively coming up to her blonde hair to push a pin back into place.

Carla's eyes were red, and her mouth, usually so quick to smile, made a tight, grave line across her face. "Mark," she said softly, "I thought you were gone. Do we have to go through this again?"

He shook his head and came around the end of the counter to the desk. "I didn't think I'd find you here. I want to see your dad."

"Oh, I forgot about your pay." She opened a drawer and dropped a sack of money on the desk. "I remember now. Daddy said you might be in. He expected you this morning."

Mark sat down, making no move to take the sack. "I didn't come after money. I want to talk to the judge."

Carla rose and moved to the window. "I made a mistake. If I'd said I never wanted to lay eyes on you again, you'd have ridden away, wouldn't you?"

"I reckon I would," he admitted.

She stood with her back to him, her eyes on the weed-covered alley behind the bank. "Then I'm saying it now. I hate you. Go away. Just let me alone."

"You're a poor liar, Carla." He rose and walked to her. "I told you there would never be another woman for me, and I don't think you'll forget me."

She still stood with her back to him, her head high. "I'll

forget you. Delphine's right. You're just a rainbow rider, Mark, talking about what you're going to do, but you haven't done anything yet."

"There's two ways of looking at that," he said softly. "My way and Delphine's."

He put a hand on her arm and turned her to face him. He kissed her, holding her stiff, reluctant body hard in his grip, and he forced her lips against his bruised ones. The stiffness went out of her, and her arms came up around his neck, and she let him feel the hunger she had for him.

Judge Baggot, coming in from the street, called angrily: "I didn't think you'd do this, Mark! I thought it was settled."

Carla stepped back, hands dropping to her sides. Mark made a slow turn to face the judge. He said: "I didn't hear you come in."

"Neither did Carla," Baggot said dryly. "You were both right busy." He looked at Mark's face, and asked: "What happened to you?"

"I rode out to the T-in-a-Heart and wound up having a fight with Rolly Benson."

"You didn't!" Carla cried. "I was afraid to ask you what had happened. Did Delphine see it?"

"She saw it all right, and she was hoping he'd knock my head off, but when I left 'em, she was holding his head in her lap."

"She'll never forgive you," Carla breathed. "Mark, you fool. If there was any hope for us, it's gone now."

Baggot sat down heavily at his desk. "You made a mistake, Mark, a bad mistake. Why did you leave town? Your money's here. All you had to do was to come in for it."

"I've got three days before my month's out," Mark said sharply, "and I don't aim to give up my star before then.

207

I've got a job to do before I leave town."

"Looks to me like it's done," Baggot said wearily. "You've cleaned up our town, and that's what we hired you for. Falling in love with Carla wasn't part of the deal."

Mark grinned wryly. "No, it just happened, and I'm not sorry. I almost made the mistake of leaving this morning, but Delphine changed my mind without aiming to. She stopped at the office to rawhide me."

"That's like her," Baggot muttered. "She never could leave well enough alone." He turned to Carla. "I'll be here the rest of the afternoon. You can go home."

Carla hesitated, eyes on Mark. Then she said impulsively: "I'm glad you didn't go, Mark. We've been cowards, Daddy and me. We've let her run us, and she's run the town. It's time somebody stood up to her."

"Carla!" Baggot shouted. "Go on home!"

She ran out of the room, slamming the bank door as she left. Baggot put a cigar into his mouth, giving Mark an appraising look. "She's right, but it's hard to break an old habit. Mark, I can loan you a little money. Enough to get a start. If you want to buy a small outfit and show us you can do something besides pack a star. . . ."

"No," Mark said. "I'll make out. I don't think Carla expects me to change my life."

Baggot fished a match out of his vest pocket and toyed with it, chewing on his cold cigar. He said: "I'm to blame for Delphine being like she is. There was just two of us children in the family, and she's fifteen years younger than I am. I spoiled her, me and our mother. We were poor, so poor we didn't know where our next meal was coming from. That's why Delphine is so set on Carla's marrying someone like Ed Runyan who can take care of her."

Mark nodded, saying nothing, for he sensed that Baggot

208

wanted to talk. He had not known about their background, and for the first time he had some understanding of Delphine's reasons for taking the stand she had.

"We lived in Denver," Baggot went on. "Dad died when Delphine was a baby, and I supported the family until Delphine married Harry Travis. She was sixteen then. Ma died. So did my wife, and Delphine took care of Carla. Harry was gone a lot, prospecting in the mountains, so I still had to support Delphine and grubstake Harry. It was mighty poor living for all of us, and Delphine got enough of living from hand to mouth. Well, Harry made a strike and came back with a fortune. We moved up here. Harry bought the T-in-a-Heart. Delphine set me up in the banking business and built our house. You see how it's been, Mark. Carla and me owe her a lot."

"That isn't exactly the point," Mark said. "She doesn't have the right to tell Carla who she can marry."

"There's something else. Somewhere along the line she developed a bossy streak. Sometimes she's downright mean, like stopping in at your office this morning just to rawhide you. She made Harry tow the mark, but he was so crazy in love with her he never bucked her on anything. She got so she thought she was always right and other people were wrong. I can't tell her anything. Like that ranch of hers. She's lost money on it ever since Harry died, but she's so stubborn she won't give it up."

Baggot rose and began pacing the floor, chewing fiercely on his cigar. "She's bent on marrying Carla off to Runyan. If you hadn't showed up, she'd have pulled it off. She thinks that, if you're out of the way, Carla will take Runyan."

"And be miserable all of her life," Mark said bitterly. "I won't let her do it."

"Try to see it my way," Baggot said. "A lot of folks depend on me to see 'em through when times are tough. Delphine lets me run the bank the way I see it, but she thinks I'm too easy. If Carla doesn't break off with you, Delphine will take the bank over. She won't be easy with folks like I am. She'll close 'em out." Baggot spread his hands. "Do you savvy that, Mark? I guess I'd shoot myself. These folks are my friends and neighbors. I just can't let it happen."

So that was it! Mark understood now, understood a great many things that had made no sense to him before. He said: "Sit down, Judge. I've got something to tell you."

Baggot dropped into his swivel chair. "You can't change anything, Mark. Delphine is what she is, and I reckon she'll always be that way. I'm ashamed of myself, but when a man reaches the place where he doesn't have any backbone left, I guess there's nothing anybody can do."

"It isn't exactly a case of backbone," Mark said, "and I'm not so sure she won't change. What is there between her and Benson?"

"I don't know. I think she'd marry him if he asked her. If she does, well, she may find out he's one man she can't run. Maybe she'll go back to New Mexico with him and let me run the bank. I'm hoping she'll turn the ranch over to me. I can think of several men I could put out there who would make it pay."

"Did Benson ever explain why he's here?"

"He came up here looking for a ranch to buy. Then for some reason he changed his mind. Seems like he started a herd north, planning to find a spread up here and sell out in New Mexico. Now he's decided to sell his herd and go back. Says his ranch was overstocked."

It struck Mark then. He leaned forward, asking: "Tell

me something, Judge. I know Delphine lost a lot of cattle last year. You reckon she's figuring on buying Benson's herd?"

Baggot scratched his head. "She hasn't said so, but I've been afraid that's what she aimed to do. She sent to Denver for thirty thousand dollars."

"Is it here now?"

Baggot nodded. "Came in on the stage this morning. More money than I ever had in my safe before. Makes me a little uneasy."

"And you want to get rid of me." Mark laughed softly. "Judge, get a good hold on yourself. Benson is a crook, a con man."

Baggot's mouth fell open, color leaving his face. For a moment he was shocked into silence, then shook his head. "You've got every reason to hate Delphine, and I reckon it's natural you'd want to hit back at her. . . ."

"My feelings have no part in this, Judge," Mark cut in sharply. "Personally I don't give a damn about Delphine. It might make things easier for me if she lost every nickel she had, but I've been a lawman too long to let Benson pull this off. Trouble is, I'll need your help."

Baggot rose and began pacing the floor, his face gray. "Mark, I always thought I was a pretty good judge of men. You have to be to run a bank. But I've made a mistake with you or Benson, and I don't know for sure which one it is."

Irritated, Mark said: "Judge, I've packed a star since I was twenty-one. I'm twenty-seven now. I could go into any mining camp or border town in the southwest and get a job. Do you think I've made my reputation on lies and petty revenge like you seem to think I'm trying to do now?"

"I don't know," Baggot whispered. "I just don't know. I've talked to Benson at least once a day since he's been in

Tumello. I've gone riding with him. Showed him some ranches he could buy. I've eaten with him, slept beside a campfire with him, drunk out of the same bottle. Damn it, I don't see how I could be wrong about him."

"You ever hear of Nick Munger?"

"Sure I've heard of him. Heard of Jesse James and Cole Younger, too. You want me to believe that Benson is Nick Munger?"

"That's exactly what I want you to believe."

Baggot was motionless now, shoulders slack. He put a hand up to his head as if to help him think. "It could be, I suppose," he muttered. "Nobody around here would know Munger, and I've heard he's tricky." Then a new thought struck Baggot. "If you knew all the time who Benson was, why didn't you tell me or Carla before this?"

"I didn't know till this morning. I'd never seen him."

"How did you know now?"

Here it was. Mark had known it would come to this. As Wally Kane had said, no one would believe him, an ex-con only a few weeks out of Canon City. Mark rose. "You'll have to take my word."

"If I'm going to do anything for Delphine, I've got to have proof."

"A friend of mine hit town this morning," Mark said. "He recognized Benson."

"Who is he, another lawman?"

"No."

"Fetch him over. Let me talk to him."

Mark hesitated, knowing that it would not do any good. Baggot would want to bring Wally and Benson face to face, Benson would recognize Wally, and tell Baggot and Delphine he was an ex-con. In the end it would be a matter of one man's word against another, and the kid's word would not carry any weight.

"He's asleep at my place," Mark said. "He rode all night. I don't want to wake him. Besides, if you won't believe me, you wouldn't believe him."

Baggot began pacing the floor again, his obligation to Delphine weighing heavily upon him. He said finally: "You couldn't arrest Benson, could you?"

Mark shook his head. "He's not wanted in this state. Until he breaks the law, I can't hold him. I could send to New Mexico for someone to identify him, but that would be too late."

"Hell, it doesn't make any difference whether he's wanted in this state or some other state. Throw him in jail and wire New Mexico. They'll send someone up here. If your friend knows. . . ."

"No," Mark said grimly. "It's up to you. And if you don't keep that money away from Delphine, she'll lose her thirty thousand as sure as you're a foot high."

He had done all he could. He turned and would have gone out then if a man had not come in from the street, a stocky, bow-legged man who looked as if he had just come in off the range. His face and clothes were dusty, and, as he came toward the teller's window, Mark saw that his lips were dry and cracked.

"Which one of you *hombres* is the banker?" the man asked.

"Me," Baggot said, and stepped to the window.

"Maybe you know where Rolly Benson is," the man said. "I'm Andy Akin, Rolly's ramrod. I was supposed to meet him in Tumello, but he ain't in the hotel or the saloon. I figured you might know."

"He's out of town," Baggot said, glancing back at Mark as if wondering what he should do.

Mark came to the end of the counter. Akin, he thought, fitted the part of a trail hand as perfectly as Benson fitted the part of a wealthy rancher. Mark said: "Benson will be in town in an hour or so."

Akin grinned. "Well, that's fine. I'll just go over and wet my whistle. If you see him, tell him I'll be in the saloon."

Akin turned toward the door and swung back when Mark asked: "What did you want to meet Benson for?"

Akin bristled. "That's Rolly's business. It sure as hell ain't yours."

"It might be mine," Mark said. "Benson lets on he's got a herd coming north from New Mexico."

"It's here," Akin said. "He came on ahead to buy a ranch. Our home range was overgrazed. We're holding the herd two, three miles east of town on the river, and we'll keep 'em there till I find out where he wants to take 'em."

"He hasn't bought a ranch," Baggot said. "Couldn't find anything he wanted."

Akin scowled. "Now ain't that a hell of a note."

"How big a herd is it?" Mark asked.

"Two thousand prime steers," Akin said. "We took it easy all the way up. They're in damned fine shape." He scratched a stubble-covered chin. "Well, it's Rolly's problem. I ain't gonna worry."

Akin wheeled and went out. Mark moved to the window. A sorrel gelding was hitched in front of the saloon.

Mark said: "Come here, Judge."

Baggot came to the window in time to see Akin cross the street and go into the saloon. He said: "Well?"

"Take a look at that sorrel. Akin might have been riding drag for all the dust he had on him, but that horse hasn't been ridden very far."

"Doesn't prove anything," Baggot muttered. "Might

214

have got a fresh animal. He wouldn't ride one horse all the way up the trail."

"All right, Judge," Mark murmured. "I've just got one piece of advice. You'd better be sure that herd's out there before Delphine takes her thirty thousand out of the bank."

Mark walked out the door, leaving Baggot staring worriedly at the sorrel gelding.

V

Mark stepped into Runyan's store and bought a sack of Durham and a package of papers. Runyan picked up the money Mark dropped on the counter, thin lips curled in a malicious smile. He said: "I hear you're leaving town, Prentice."

"Delphine tell you?"

Runyan nodded. "She thought you'd be gone before noon."

"I guess you'd like for me to get out, wouldn't you?"

Runyan shrugged his shoulders. He was forty or older, a pale-faced man who seldom stepped outside his store. Mark had heard him cursed long and fervently by the farmers when they gathered in the saloon on Saturday nights. Ed Runyan was a dollar worshipper who limited all credit to thirty days, and that was no credit at all to men who had cash only in the fall. If Judge Baggot had not been liberal with bank money, more than one family would have starved out and left the country years ago.

"Why, it ain't no skin off my nose," Runyan said plaintively. "I just heard you were leaving. Didn't aim to kick up no ruckus. We don't need you now. Besides, a fiddle-footed fellow like you wouldn't stay in a town like Tumello."

Mark picked up the tobacco and package of papers and left the store. Six months ago they had begged him to take the star. Baggot and Runyan and the other businessmen on Main Street. They were tired of the brawling, tired of having drunks shoot up the town every Saturday night. They'd wanted a marshal then, all right. There hadn't been a man in Tumello who had enough courage to poke his head out of doors on Saturday night. But it was different now. Runyan was right when he'd said they didn't need him.

He went into the jail, sat down, and cocked his feet on the desk. He rolled a smoke, thinking there wasn't any doubt about what would happen. Delphine would call a meeting of the town council. Runyan was the mayor. They'd fire him. He didn't have three days. Not if he was going to have a star to give him authority in whatever action he was forced to take against Benson.

He had finished his cigarette when he heard the clatter of a buggy in the street. He rose and went to the door. Benson wheeled past in the livery rig, Delphine beside him. Mark smiled when he saw the raw-meat look of Benson's face. It would be days before it healed.

Benson stopped in front of the bank and stepped down. Baggot came out of the bank and talked to him a moment. Benson nodded, said something to Delphine, and then Delphine and Baggot went into the bank. Benson got back into the buggy and drove on down the street to the stable. In a moment he appeared again, walking rapidly to the saloon.

Mark had never, in all the years he had packed a star, felt as helpless as he did now. He knew a crime was about to be committed, and still there seemed to be nothing he could do.

He glanced at his watch. It was almost time to close the bank. Baggot was probably telling Delphine what Mark had said about Benson. He'd be wasting his breath. She'd take her money out of the bank, and she'd ride out of town with Benson because he would want a cash deal.

If Delphine decided to buy the cattle, she could pay for them, and Benson's crew would drive them onto her range. Then Benson and his men would head back for New Mexico. That's the way Benson would tell it. By the time she found out there wasn't any herd, it would be too late. They'd be out toward Wyoming. Probably they'd take Delphine along. Or they'd kill her. Before the sheriff could be notified and a posse organized, Benson and his men would be miles away.

He made up his mind then. Whatever he did, he had to do before they left town. If it meant dragging Wally Kane into it, that's what he would do. If it meant fighting it out with Benson and Andy Akin on the street, he would do that. He could not dismiss from his conscience the duty that years of carrying a star had imposed upon him.

When Mark left the jail, he saw that there were two more horses beside the one Andy Akin had ridden into town. As he moved along the boardwalk in front of the saloon, he noticed that the brands were unfamiliar to him.

He swung across the street to the bank, a new worry nagging him. If Benson had three men to back him, instead of one, the job of stopping him became an impossibility.

Mark was on the walk in front of the bank, one hand reaching for the door to open it, when a man called: "Prentice!"

Mark swung around. He'd had a brief glance of Judge Baggot and Delphine watching him through the window, Baggot's face taut with worry, Delphine's as smug as when she'd taken Benson's gun belt that morning, expecting to see Benson whip him.

A faint warning stirred in the back of Mark's mind as he stepped off the boardwalk into the street and moved to one side so the solid wall of the bank was behind him. Delphine, he thought, knew what was coming. Hating him as she did, there was nothing she wanted more than to see him dead.

Mark asked: "You want something, friend?"

The fellow was in the street, a small, knobby-faced man with two guns tied low on his thighs, long-fingered hands hanging loosely at his sides. A gunman and a stranger, Mark saw.

"I want you," the man said. "I've trailed you for a long time. I'm gonna kill you, Prentice. Solo McKay always squares his debts."

There were plenty of men who had debts to square with Mark. No man could carry a star through six turbulent years as he had without making enemies. But this Solo McKay was not one of them. He was Benson's man. Yet no matter how the fight turned out, Benson would claim he had never seen McKay before.

"You've got the wrong man, mister," Mark said.

McKay came down off the walk and took two steps into the street. He shouted: "The hell I have! You sent me to Canon City on a frame just to collect a bounty. Well, I'm out now, and I'll do the collecting."

McKay stood there motionless for a few seconds, letting the tension build, and Mark knew how it was with men like this. Coldly confident, McKay was gambling that Mark's nerves would tie him up and slow his draw.

But it was not McKay who worried Mark. He knew what he could do with a gun. He had faced the best, and he'd won, but no man was fast enough to beat a cold deck. In the saloon behind McKay, Rolly Benson was waiting with Akin and probably a second man, and Benson was the kind who liked a sure thing.

Then McKay made his draw, right hand gripping gun butt and sweeping the Colt from leather. It was a fast, smooth draw, but not fast enough. Mark's gun sounded first. He felt the buck of it against his palm, felt it run up his arm, and McKay was down in the dust, his gun falling from lax fingers.

The report of Mark's .44 seemed very loud in the late afternoon silence. The echoes were thrown back by the false fronts that lined the street. Mark waited for a moment, expecting to feel the smashing impact of a slug from the saloon. McKay was not dead. He pulled himself up to his hands and knees and reached for his gun.

"Don't try it!" Mark called.

He heard running steps on the boardwalk; he heard Carla call: "Mark, Mark, are you all right?"

Without turning his head, he shouted: "Stay back!"

Blood made a scarlet froth on McKay's lips. He was dying, but he had the strength to pick up the gun and prong back the hammer. That was all. He fell back into the dust, a paroxysm of death jerking his finger and pulling the trigger.

The bullet kicked up dust in the middle of the street. McKay's hand was flung out. His hat fell from his head and lay beside him.

Carla was there then, gripping Mark's arm, crying: "Are you all right, Mark? Are you?"

He wheeled on her, furious. "Get into the bank! You want to get killed?"

He gave her a shove. She went back a step and stood there, her face very pale. "Who is he? Why did he try it?"

"Damn it," Mark shouted. "Get into the bank. Benson's waiting in the saloon. This isn't over yet."

Instinctively her eyes swung to the saloon. Benson's gun was still silent. Mark could not understand that, unless Carla's appearance had made Benson hold his fire. It would come, the instant Carla was off the street, and he'd be in the open, a target too big for Benson to miss.

"Mark!" the girl cried. "Look, Mark!"

He swung toward the saloon. He stood motionless, shocked by surprise. Benson, Akin, and a third man were coming through the batwings, their hands high. Wally Kane was behind them, a cocked gun in his hand.

"Here's your meat, Mark!" the kid called. "How do you want it cooked?"

"You can't do this," Benson bawled. "Who do you think you are, Prentice? You have no charge against me."

"I was watching from the back door," Wally said, "figuring that it would blow up this afternoon, and the most likely place they'd be was the saloon. They was there, all right. Had their guns out waiting to smoke you down just when McKay drew. I changed their minds for 'em."

Suddenly Delphine was beside Mark, appearing out of nowhere, clutching his arm. "Let them go, Prentice. I'm telling you to let them go if you want to stay out of trouble."

"Hold 'em, Wally," Mark said. "I reckon we can call this attempted murder till I wire New Mexico." He turned to Delphine. "For once in your life, try to get something through your skull. If you'd ridden out of town with Benson and your thirty thousand, you'd never have come back. I've saved your life and your money. Can you savvy that?"

Delphine struck at him, her face alive with fury. She

screamed: "You're just trying to be a hero! Why can't you stay out of my business?"

Mark threw up his left arm, warding off her blow. Carla stepped between them, trying to force Delphine back, and Baggot, coming out of the bank, gripped his sister's arms and held them behind her.

She quit struggling and gained control of herself. She said: "All right, Prentice. They won't stay locked up long. You're finished in Tumello."

Runyan and Doc Frisbie and other townsmen had appeared in the street, approaching slowly as if they were puzzled by what had happened. Mark called: "Doc, pick this carrion up off the street." He nodded at Benson. "Start walking."

Benson swung toward the jail, his white Stetson, smeared with dirt, pulled low over his eyes. Akin and the other man fell into step beside him.

"I pulled their teeth," Wally said with evident pride. "Their guns are in the saloon."

Mark said nothing until Benson and the other two were in a cell. He felt of them for hide-out guns, Wally standing in the doorway, keeping them covered. Mark stepped back and locked the cell door.

"You gonna let them 'em get away with this, Rolly?" Akin shouted.

Still Benson held his silence. Mark hesitated, staring at the third man. He asked Wally: "Know that *hombre?*"

"Bill Nix," Wally said. "He was in Raton with them. I didn't know the fellow you drilled."

"Nix, we might make a deal if you want to talk," Mark said.

Nix was a tall, yellow-eyed man with a strawberry splotch on his right cheek. He glanced at the smoldering

Benson, hesitating as if this had happened too fast for his mind to catch up with events. Then he brought his gaze to Mark. He said: "Go to hell."

Mark swung away from the cell and walked into his office. He asked, his voice loud enough for the men in the cell to hear: "What's the charge in New Mexico, kid?"

"Murder. It was during the trouble there. They got out just ahead of the sheriff's posse."

"I've got enough to hold 'em on," Mark said. "I'll get a wire off to Raton. You stay here. Somebody might get the notion to bust 'em out."

Wally nodded. "I was thinking that."

Mark moved to the door and paused there, searching for the right thing to say. Wally grinned at him, filled with pride over what he had done. Mark said: "You saved my hide, kid. I'm obliged."

VI

It took several minutes for Mark to write his message and get it on the wire. When he returned to Main Street, Carla was standing in front of the bank doorway, motioning to him. He frowned, not wanting to talk to Delphine, but there was a taut urgency about Carla he could not ignore.

When he came up, Carla said: "Dad wants to see you."

Mark nodded and followed her into the bank. Delphine was sitting at the desk, several sacks of money in front of her. She glared at Mark, her lips tightly pressed, her face barren of expression.

Baggot took a long breath. "Mark, she's bound to take her money and go out and look at Benson's herd. She says she got a good price, and he'll be out of jail soon to make the deal."

"Let her go," Carla said. "Mark, I made a mistake this morning. I'm going to run my own life. If you want me. . . ."

He shook his head at her, frowning. "You know I want you, but I found out something about myself today. When a man has been on the side of the law as long as I have, he sort of gets into a rut. I mean, I couldn't stand around and let Benson pull this off. I guess I'll always be that way."

"I wouldn't want you to be any other way," Carla said softly.

"But if you marry me," Mark said, "you'll have that to worry about all of your life."

Impatiently Baggot cut in: "Mark, we've got a bull by the tail. Throwing Benson into the jug isn't the whole answer. You said a while ago you didn't have anything to hold him on."

"He aimed to kill me while McKay and I were shooting it out," Mark said. "That'll do to hold him. I'll get an answer to the wire I sent to Raton, and I'll have a description then of Benson and his men that even Delphine can recognize."

"Delphine has sent a man to the county seat for the sheriff," Baggot said. "You know what he'll do when he gets here?"

Mark nodded, knowing exactly what the sheriff would do. The man was anxious to stay in office. He was a hack politician who looked to Delphine for the Tumello votes she could deliver to him. He had been jealous of Mark from the first. He would listen to Delphine and do what she asked.

"Maybe the light's beginning to dawn, Prentice,"

Delphine breathed. "The sheriff will be here before evening, and you'll be in jail for false arrest. You can't do this to a man like Rolly Benson, and you can't do it to me."

Carla gripped his arm. "Do what you have to do, Mark."

He looked at her, realizing more than he ever had before how much he loved her and how empty his life would be without her. She would never again bow to Delphine's will, but her father had made no such decision.

Mark dropped into a chair, suddenly tired and plagued by bitterness. A man could fight for his principles, and still destroy the thing he loved. He said: "Judge, you're still thinking about how Delphine would run the bank, aren't you?"

"That's right," Baggot said.

Delphine laughed, sure of herself again. "You're a town marshal, Prentice. Nothing more. Your fight with the man you killed was one thing. Arresting Rolly and his trail hands is another matter. You went over your authority."

Mark rolled and fired a smoke, thinking again that if Delphine could be shown she was making a mistake, she might be humbled to the point where she would let Baggot run the bank the way he wanted to. That would be the only thing that could release the judge from her control.

"I'm wondering about something, Judge," Mark said finally. "Would it make any difference to you if Delphine lost her thirty thousand?"

Baggot shook his head. "It's all up to her now."

"It wouldn't affect the bank?"

"No."

"Would it make any difference if Benson killed her?"

Baggot's face was gray, his mouth a grim line. Looking at him now, it seemed to Mark that he had aged ten years in these last few hours. "Of course, it would," Baggot whispered. "I would blame myself."

"You believe what I said about Benson?"

"I don't know," Baggot said. "But it seems to me that he's unreasonable in wanting her to take the money with her when they look at his herd. He might not keep his promise about delivering the cattle to the T-in-a-Heart."

Delphine rose. "That's my worry," she said curtly. "This palaver is just wasting time. If you don't release Rolly and his men, Prentice, you're in trouble."

"This man who says Benson is Munger," Baggot said. "Is he the fellow who brought them out of the saloon?" When Mark nodded, he asked: "Who is he?"

So they were back to that again! "A friend of mine," Mark said. He sat slumped in his chair, cigarette hanging from the corner of his mouth. He knew that, when Baggot found out who Wally Kane was, there would be no chance of convincing him that Rolly Benson was Nick Munger.

Someone came in, and Mark turned his head. It was Ed Runyan, standing hesitantly on the other side of the counter.

"The council has met, Missus Travis," Runyan said. "We voted to remove Prentice from office."

"Then we don't have a marshal," Baggot shouted. "What kind of a fool business is that?"

"We don't need one," Runyan said. "Or if we do, we'll hire a man who obeys orders."

Mark removed his star and tossed it on the desk. "I guess that does it, Judge." He turned to Carla. "Did you mean what you said a while ago?"

"I never meant anything more in my life." She held up her left hand, and he saw his ring on her second finger, the diamond flaming in a ray of sunlight. "I'll go with you, Mark, anywhere."

"You can't . . . !" Runyan shouted.

"Get back to your counter jumping," Mark said angrily, and Runyan backed out of the door and disappeared.

Mark turned back to Carla, the quick flash of anger dying in him. "I'm a rainbow rider, you know. I guess Delphine was right about that."

"Then I'll ride the rainbow with you," she said.

"Carla, I don't think . . . ," Baggot began.

"I'm standing on my feet!" the girl cried. "Someday you'll get up off your knees, too, Dad."

"How soon can you leave town?" Mark asked.

"In half an hour," she said eagerly. "I'll saddle my horse. Stop by at the house for me."

"Prentice, are you going to let Rolly out of that stinking jail?" Delphine demanded.

"I'm not the marshal now," Mark said. "I reckon you'd like to tote that star yourself."

He wheeled and walked out. As he strode toward the jail, he looked back once and saw Carla run out of the bank and go down the walk toward her house. She would come with him, and that was what he wanted. He should, he thought, feel better than he did.

He was done, his string wound up. It was Delphine's deal from here on out, and she deserved all she'd get. But the bitterness of failure was in him.

He paused in the jail doorway. Wally Kane was sitting at the desk, his feet cocked on it, and, when he saw Mark, he said: "Sure feels good, sitting here like I was a big gun." Then he saw that the star was not on Mark's vest, and he jumped up. "What happened?"

Mark jerked his head toward the street. "Come on. We're sloping out of town."

Benson shouted: "Prentice, if you don't . . . !"

Mark stepped into the street. Wally followed slowly, puzzled.

When they were far enough from the door so that the men in the jail could not hear them, Mark said: "The town council fired me. Nothing I can do now. We're pulling our freight. Carla's going with us."

Wally threw up his hands. "You've got that ornery son-of-a-bitch locked up for the first time in his life. They'll let him go."

"That's just what they'll do," Mark said. "Get your horse."

Mark strode around the jail toward his shack. Half an hour, Carla had said. That would be long enough. He remembered that he was broke. He didn't have enough money in his pocket to pay a preacher and get a hotel room and buy meals for the three of them for a week. Well, he'd get his money from Baggot. He had fifty dollars coming. It would help.

It took a few minutes to pack his war bag. He left the shack and tied the war bag behind the saddle. It was then that he heard the shots from Main Street, several of them rolling out together. He stepped up and cracked steel to his gelding.

When he reached Main Street, he saw Benson and one of his men leave town in a cloud of dust. Then he saw Wally hanging to a hitch rail and Judge Baggot lying on the boardwalk in front of the bank. Farther down the street another man lay face down in the dust.

Mark swung down in front of the bank and knelt beside Baggot. He had been hit in the left shoulder.

The banker looked up at Mark, whispering: "Delphine got them out of jail, and Benson came after the money. Delphine had gone for her horse. All of a sudden I knew you were right about Benson. It was in his face when he saw the money on my desk. I tried to keep him from taking it. He knocked me down and took the money. I got a gun and followed them into the street. Then he plugged me."

"I got Nix," Wally called. "Go after 'em, Mark."

Men were running toward them, Doc Frisbie in the lead. Wally lost his hold on the hitch pole and sprawled flat in the street dust.

Mark ran to him, but the kid pulled himself upright. "I ain't hit bad. Damn it, I should have got all three of 'em, but Munger was too fast for me."

Runyan and several others were there, standing awkwardly in the street as if not knowing what to do. Mark said: "Get him into the doc's office and take care of the judge." He ran toward his horse and mounted.

Carla and Delphine were running up the walk. Mark rode toward them, and, when he reached them, he reined up. "You never made a mistake, Delphine, but Benson did. Take a look at your brother."

Only one thing was important now, to bring Benson and Akin back to Tumello. Other problems could be settled later. With Judge Baggot wounded, Carla could not leave town with Mark. And there was Wally Kane. Mark would not ride without him, so he would have to wait, perhaps for weeks.

VII

The sun was well down toward the Rockies now. Mark was cutting down the distance between him and his quarry. Apparently Benson had taken the horse Solo McKay had ridden into town. It was not a fast animal, and Benson was a heavy man.

Akin was forging ahead of Benson, but he would not go on unless he had the money, and that was not likely. They would have fresh horses waiting somewhere along the river, perhaps other relay stations between here and the Wyoming line. This was an old game to Benson, and he was a careful man.

There were always a few ranchers out here on the thinly settled plains who were willing to pick up a few extra dollars by furnishing horses to outlaws who needed them in a hurry. While Benson was making his play with Delphine, Akin and the others had probably arranged for horses and a hide-out somewhere across the state line. Thirty thousand dollars was enough of a stake to warrant the planning they had put into this.

If it hadn't been for Wally Kane, Benson would have pulled it off. But when the scheme had turned sour, Benson had lost his head. He could have played it out.

Mark held his buckskin at a hard run, knowing he would never be sure what had been in Benson's mind except that Delphine had not been important to him. It was a question now whether Benson and Akin could reach fresh horses in time to outrun Mark. If they did, he would never catch them. If they didn't, they would stand and fight.

Benson's horse was almost finished. Mark was within gun range, but he held his fire. He was too old a hand at this game to waste lead when there was still a chance of closing in. Akin, well in the lead now, had reined up and was motioning to Benson. Benson waved him on, but Akin sat his saddle, holding his horse motionless until Benson caught up. Then they wheeled off the road toward the river.

Fresh horses were probably waiting behind the willows,

Mark judged. He angled toward the river, realizing that he would be at a disadvantage. They'd reach the willows ahead of him, and he'd be in the open, an easy target.

But it didn't work that way. Benson's horse, so weary it was stumbling, fell and threw Benson when he was still twenty yards from the river.

Akin went on, but Benson lay still for a moment, the wind knocked out of him. Akin, in the willows then, called: "Come on, Nick! Make a run for it. I'll cover you."

Benson came to his feet and pulled his gun. He might have been panicky, or perhaps he was overconfident of his own gun skill. In either case, he held his ground and brought his gun up. Mark, riding low in the saddle, pulled his Colt. Benson fired, the bullet slapping through the crown of Mark's hat.

With the echoes of that shot still hammering out across the grass, Mark fired. He missed, but he was cutting the distance between them with every stride of his buckskin.

Benson shot, the slug going wide this time, and Mark, quite close now, cut loose with his second shot. Benson went back a step, gun slipping out of his fingers, bending forward as a hand came up to stem the flow of blood from his stomach.

Mark felt heady with exuberance. "I got Nick Munger!"

Akin was in the fight now, emptying his gun at Mark. One bullet hit him, smashing club-like into his left side. He kept his seat and swept on past Benson who was flat on his stomach.

Akin had hurried his shots. Now, with his gun empty, there was no time to reload. He jerked his Winchester from the scabbard and brought it up as Mark came plunging through the close-growing willows. It was touch and go for an instant, Mark holding the one advantage of being on the move. Akin fired and missed, and Mark got him in the left arm.

Akin's horse, spooked by the firing, began to plunge. Akin, the wounded arm useless, lost his seat and was thrown into the shallow water at the edge of the river. Mark pulled his buckskin up as Akin scrambled to the bank and, grabbing his rifle from where it had fallen in the grass, whipped it up and lined the barrel on Mark.

It took a second, a precious second that made the difference between life and death for him. Mark fired downward at him, and Akin toppled forward and lay motionless, his feet in the water.

Mark reined up and dismounted. For a moment the world seemed to tip crazily and whirl. He stumbled and fell.

He was hit harder than he had realized. He started crawling toward his horse, wondering if Benson was still alive. There was only one bullet left in his gun. He stopped, fighting the nausea that swept over him, fumbled at his cartridge belt.

It was then that he heard the rustle of dry leaves in the willows. He looked up. Benson was crawling toward him, white Stetson gone from his head, face smeared with blood and dirt.

Mark lifted his gun. He heard as if from a great distance the roar of Benson's gun, saw the ribbon of fire leap from the muzzle of the Colt. The bullet kicked up sand to Mark's right. He gripped the butt of his gun with both hands. Benson seemed to be weaving back and forth in front of him.

One bullet left! This moment seemed to run on through eternity. Mark's gun steadied, and he pulled the trigger. Then he toppled forward into the sand.

He heard the rush of the water and the soft sound of wind in the willows. Then blackness blotted out all sight and sound.

It was dark when Mark came to. He was in bed. His side hurt, and he found it hard to breathe. He called out, steps sounded, and Carla came in carrying a lighted lamp. She put it on a stand beside his bed and, drawing up a chair, sat down beside him.

She took his hand, saying softly: "It's all right, Mark. It's all right."

"Where am I?"

"In our house, Mark. You've got some broken ribs and you lost some meat and a lot of blood, but you'll be all right."

He remembered now, Benson crawling through the willows toward him, his trouble in getting off that last shot. He asked: "Benson?"

"Dead. So is Akin. They found the money in the grass beside Benson's horse where he'd dropped it. It's in the safe."

He shut his eyes against the lamplight. He remembered the rest of it. And he remembered Carla's father who ran a bank he didn't really control. Now he'd lose it, and the men he had called his friends and neighbors would be at Delphine's mercy.

Well, Mark had done all he could. It just hadn't been good enough. He asked: "How'd I get here?"

"Delphine brought you."

He opened his eyes to look at Carla, shocked by what she had said. "Why didn't she leave me to the buzzards?"

232

"Something happened to her when she saw Daddy lying there in front of the bank. She almost went out of her head. She got a bunch of men together, and they went after you."

"Are your dad and Wally all right?"

"They're fine. I mean, they will be. I'm head nurse, and I guess I've got the biggest hospital in the county." She leaned toward him. "Mark, none of us understood Delphine. Maybe she didn't understand herself. But tonight I saw her cry for the first time in her life. She talked to me. I don't think she had ever been honest with herself before." Carla cleared her throat. "Dad told you about her. I think she was sincere in not wanting me to marry someone who didn't have money. But tonight she admitted she was wrong. You see, she was in love with Benson. She wanted him to stay here and run her ranch and sell out in New Mexico. She trusted in him because she loved him, and that's why she wouldn't believe anything you said about him."

Mark lay motionless, thinking about that.

"She's gone," Carla went on. "She couldn't face you. Or any of us, I guess. She had to admit she was wrong, and you know what that would do to her."

"What about the bank?" Mark asked. "And her ranch?"

"She's left it to Daddy," Carla said. "She's going to Europe. I don't think she'll ever come back." Carla's hand tightened on his. "Mark, Daddy wants you to run the T-in-a-Heart, but if you'd rather not stay here, I'll go anywhere you want to."

He grinned at her, knowing that he had all of her love, and that made him the luckiest man in the world. "I'm more'n a rainbow rider," he said. "I kissed the rainbow. Sure, I'll try my hand at running a ranch, but. . . ."

"I know, Mark," she said gravely. "You've worn a star for so long that it's part of your life. I've been thinking about that. This county needs a good sheriff. We'd never find a better one than you."

"We'll see," he breathed. "We'll see when the time comes." He held her hand toward the light, watched the diamond come to life with a dozen flashing colors. Then he said: "We'll give Wally Kane a job. Someday I'll tell you about him."

"He's already told me," Carla said. "He thinks you're the most wonderful man that ever walked." She smiled. "So do I." Bending down, she kissed him, and his arm came around her and held her hard against him.

About the Author

Wayne D. Overholser won three Spur Awards from the Western Writers of America and has a long list of fine Western titles to his credit. He was born in Pomeroy, Washington, and attended the University of Montana, University of Oregon, and the University of Southern California before becoming a public schoolteacher and principal in various Oregon communities. He began writing for Western pulp magazines in 1936 and within a couple of years was a regular contributor to Street & Smith's *Western Story Magazine* and Fiction House's *Lariat Story Magazine*. BUCKAROO'S CODE (1947) was his first Western novel and remains one of his best. In the 1950s and 1960s, having retired from academic work to concentrate on writing, he would publish as many as four books a year under his own name or a pseudonym, most prominently as Joseph Wayne. THE VIOLENT LAND (1954), THE LONE DEPUTY (1957), THE BITTER NIGHT (1961), and RIDERS OF THE SUNDOWNS (1997) are among the finest of the Overholser titles. THE SWEET AND BITTER LAND (1950), BUNCH GRASS (1955), and LAND OF PROMISES (1962) are among the best Joseph Wayne titles, and LAW MAN (1953) is a most rewarding novel under the pseudonym Lee Leighton. Overholser's Western novels, whatever the byline, are based on a solid knowledge of the history and customs of the 19th-Century West, particularly when set in his two favorite Western states, Oregon and Colorado. Many of his novels are first-person narratives, a technique that tends to bring an added dimension of vividness to the frontier experiences of his narrators and frequently, as in CAST A LONG SHADOW (1957), the female characters one encounters are among the most memorable. He wrote his numerous novels with a consistent skill and an uncommon sensitivity to the depths of human character. Almost invariably, his stories weave a spell of their own with their scenes and images of social and economic forces often in conflict and the diverse ways of life and personalities that made the American Western frontier so unique a time and place in human history. WHEELS ROLL WEST will be his next **Five Star Western**.